The Publishing Lab
Volume 2, Spring 2025

Photo: Kate Nahvi

The Publishing Lab
An Anthology of Student Creative Work
Volume 2, Spring 2025

Pace University
MS in Publishing Program

Published by Pace University Press
41 Park Row
New York, NY 10038

ISSN: 2996-5993
ISBN: 978-1-965246-00-9

Cover Photo by Shea Dunlop
Back Cover Photo by Kate Nahvi

Printed in the United States of America

CONTENTS

Welcome to *The Publishing Lab*!

This anthology of student creative work was inspired and organized by students in the MS in Publishing program at Pace University, led by a small cohort who have acquired, edited, copyedited, proofread, and designed this volume.

This experiential and immersive project is a distinctive experience provided by the Publishing program. Our students are passionate about books and are avid readers and often, writers. Providing this outlet for their creativity has brought them together and facilitated an environment of collaboration, respect, and support.

Students in our program are interested in all areas of publishing—editorial, production, design, sales, marketing, and publicity. By being part of this publication, they have fostered their skillsets in those areas and put into practice what they are learning in our program. Both our in-person and online students contributed to the success of this anthology. There are twenty student authors who submitted their work—short stories, poetry, plays, essays, and photography.

The Publishing Lab is administered each year by voluntary board members and is managed and coordinated by an Editor-in-Chief. This year, Kayleigh Woltal was at the helm, and we thank her for her organization and commitment to this project. We are grateful to all the contributors and board members for their dedication and hard work in making this volume of *The Publishing Lab* a reality.

The Publishing Lab transforms our students into published authors and accomplished professionals who have applied their classroom learning in creating this volume. We hope you enjoy *The Publishing Lab* and celebrate our students' work.

Manuela Soares
Director, MS in Publishing Program
Director, Pace University Press

Eileen Bishop Kreit
Lecturer and Faculty Advisor, MS in Publishing Program
Associate Director, Pace University Press

Editor's Note

The second volume of *The Publishing Lab* is the result of tremendous effort by Pace MS in Publishing students. *The Publishing Lab* would not be here without the hard work from the students who contributed to the anthology and put their trust in our student editors and Volume 2 team members who edited, marketed, and produced this volume. It takes a strong team of dedicated students and countless talented writers to make an anthology like this a reality.

I would like to thank all of the contributors, whether you are a new or returning voice, for being an integral part of this journey. I also want to thank *The Publishing Lab* advisors, Professor Soares and Professor Kreit, for helping the team along the way. We appreciate your support.

Thank you to everyone at Pace University Press for helping with the logistics of putting this book together. To every member of *The Publishing Lab* thank you for working tirelessly to make this book and to promote it.

Thank you to Luiza Guimarães for bringing this project to life last year. Without you, our students would not have the opportunity to gain hands-on experience in a safe environment.

And to our next generation of students, thank you for allowing *The Publishing Lab* to live on with your literary contributions. Thank you for embracing it and allowing the next set of publishing students to have the same opportunity to learn from this anthology.

Kayleigh Woltal
Editor-in-Chief, *The Publishing Lab*

The Publishing Lab
Volume 2, Spring 2025

Pace University
MS in Publishing Program

Poultry in Motion

Jack Niemczyk

It is a simple fact of metropolitan life to crave the end of summer and await autumn's fall. Yet, at the end of this contemptuous season there is a slight beauty about it, when the sun begins to set and the air chills to the perfect temperature, even keeping Luke warm. These final days of summer are, I find, the most romantic, and are perhaps some of my favorites—when the chill of the air is broken by bodies touching, by adolescence leaving and a more solid energy entering the city's air, leaving all to embrace the childish goodbye of summer. Upon reflecting on this unique season, my memory is flooded with images of former trysts where we sat on the roof of my East Village apartment and absorbed this wondrous energy, flitted about the city with gusto and adoration for the life that we get to live, and thought of how lucky we were to enjoy summer with one another. Yet in this moment, in this year of 2024, I am alone.

I embrace this feeling of solitude, and take myself on the adventure. I point my feet in the direction of Union Square, for on this beautiful Wednesday evening, I am craving duck. My mother always taught me that the way to someone's heart is through their stomach. Whether it be friends, confidants, enemies, or lovers, the simple delicacy of food—especially good food—can change a relationship in the best of ways. I have always approached my life with this mantra that food can change our lives for the better and distract us from the woes and worries that we may be facing. I keep this in mind as I head, alone, I reiterate, to the greenmarket.

The end of summer air engulfs me and I breathe in this slight crispness and picture the dish that I know so well: duck salad with blood orange slivers and toasted walnuts. Simple and fatty, yet bursting citrus juice. Easy and impressive, a perfect dish for a date. It seems every year my culinary arm would reach for the delicious fatty nature of a duck breast, and just as quickly, I would indulge in the beauty of a blood orange or ruby grapefruit to perfectly garnish the poultry in question. Whenever asked for my go-to meal to cook for someone, this dish always is the answer. There is something so wonderful about duck as meat—as poultry—so delicious and sensual and loved by most. I find even the pickiest eaters enjoy its beautiful fattiness once talked over the ledge that duck presents. Perhaps this is why I introduce it to my gentlemen friends. The dish is snobby enough while still being rather provincial, just like me.

At the farmers market, the summer sun still beams down as the time gets later and later. The market is beginning to close and I know I must sweep through the stalls with the speed and accuracy of a Midwest housewife in a Piggly Wiggly. My first stop is the duck stand. I make my usual entendre saying I love the duck pic they have posted which is greeted with the standard giggle that comes along with the natural flirtation that is present in my voice. I make my way through the market, grabbing all the necessary ingredients and haggling the price down when I can. With my haul in hand, I trek my way down 3rd Avenue, passing by couples hand in hand as I caress the cold duck breast, happy to have that company.

I return to the sanctuary of my tiny apartment. With little counter space, I score the skin of the duck, wedge the citrus, and toast the walnuts all while playing a Barbra Streisand vinyl on my record player. The sear of the duck perfectly underscores her bewitching voice and I realize, I am making this dish for one for the first time. At the moment, I am perfectly neutral, like the weather outside—not happy, not sad, but just neutral. As I slice the duck, cooked to perfection I may add, I think about making a meal for one, how much I love cooking for others, how so many have enjoyed and praised me for my cooking ability and yet, I don't need it. I am happy enough for things to just be Barbra, the duck, and I.

I pour myself a glass of orange wine and plate my dish, preparing for the six-flight journey up to the roof of my pre-war apartment. When greeted with this skyline, I know I am not alone—not in feeling or in thought or in experience—and I am somehow content with that. I sit on my roof, greeted with the memories of former boys I brought up here, the perfect weather, and the wonderful sensation of enough. A quick sip of wine cools my palette as the sweat from my forehead settles into a perfect warmth. I sit back and enjoy my usual meal for two as one, and when the fatty duck pops into my mouth with fireworks of citrus and the sweetness of walnuts, I think that perhaps the closing of summer is not a goodbye to adolescence but a see-you-later. An ode to summer is within every bit of joy, of love, and of being alone. And here on this roof, I eat my dinner in the amazing middle, the delicious neutral that is perfect, poultry in motion.

End-of-Summer Duck Salad

Makes two pretty hearty salads, but the recipe is easily enjoyed by one!

Ingredients

2 duck breasts about 3 ounces each

Citrus of your choice (I believe blood orange, grapefruit, and navel oranges work the best)

Arugula

Walnuts

Sliced baguette

Olive oil

Salt

Pepper

Instructions

1. Begin by scoring the skin of the duck breasts. Season both sides with salt and pepper.

2. Slice the citrus into wedges, keeping all the juice.

3. Dress the arugula with juice from citrus and a little bit of olive oil and salt. Add citrus wedges and toss again.

4. Heat a pan to high heat and place the duck skin-side down. Cook for about 4 minutes on each side. You want an internal temp of about 130–135°F for a medium-rare duck breast.

5. Chop walnuts.

6. Remove the duck when fully cooked and let it rest on the cutting board. Leave the duck fat in the pan and add the walnuts.

7. When the walnuts are fragrant and toasted, remove them from the pan and toast slices of bread with the remaining fat.

8. Slice the duck breasts and place a sliver on a piece of toasted bread.

9. Assemble: Add arugula and citrus, top with walnuts, and add toast points and the duck.

Game Over

Hailey Hovey

I open my eyes, but all I see is darkness. Are my eyes open? I press them shut to feel the difference. Yep. Definitely open. I lift my hands in front of my face, but they feel strangely disconnected from me. Because I can't see them? I don't really want to know. My whole body prickles like the blood is having difficulty getting everywhere it needs to go.

Where am I? is the first thought that whispers in my mind, but then a slightly louder, more anxious voice asks, *Where was I before this?*

Feeling around my brain for something, anything—I realize with a physical start: *Who am I?* Spinning around myself, squinting into the empty distance, I feel strangely calm for someone whose entire past has been erased and then dumped into an endless void.

Out of nowhere I hear soft, mumbling voices from behind, like a crowd anxiously waiting for bad news. As ominous as the sound is, what other choice do I have? I follow the noise blindly.

One step in front of the other, and eventually, I get used to the strange tingling in my feet. How long have I been walking? Fifteen minutes or hours—it's impossible to tell. But the dark fog eventually dissipates, and I can faintly see a single-file line, a soft glow emanating from the desk at the front.

What do you do when you see a line and have no recollection of where or who you are? You stand in it.

I clear my throat before reaching out to tap the person in front of me. "Excuse me?" My voice is quieter than I intended; it feels as if I haven't spoken in a century.

Instead of reaching their shoulder, my finger passes right through them, the solid form of the shoulder bursting into vapor before stitching itself back together. I gasp and take a step back.

"Yes?" The vaporous person turns around slowly, and it takes more than all my strength to dig my heels into the ground and put on a pleasant face. The person—if they could even be classified as one—has a soft smile, but that's the only feature that stays the same. Every half

5

second, their face dissipates, as their shoulder did, and shifts. First, they're child-like, then model-gorgeous, then haggard and wrinkled. I could swear I even saw bug eyes one second and a snout the next.

It takes me a second to remember that I had a question. "Erm, where are we?"

"In line, silly." The soft smile remains. "And I'm no longer last. How exciting." While their words are enthusiastic, their voice is sleepy.

"How long have you been waiting here, last in line?"

They shrug. "At least an infinity. Or an hour? Who am I to tell?"

Helpful. I decide to try my luck with one more attempt for information before I accept my fate of waiting in line indefinitely. "And who are you? Where are you from?"

They squint their ever-changing eyes. "Hm. I don't know." As if they never thought to ask that question themself.

When I just blink, they swivel back around, the smile never leaving their face.

"Okayyyy, well, as nice as this has been, I think I'm going to go ask the people at the front desk up there what's going on." I take their lack of response as agreement and step around them, but in the blink of an eye, their hand materializes on my shoulder and pulls me back in line.

"No one is allowed to cut," they hiss, and—I kid you not—a snake's tongue rattles in front of my face.

I lift my hands in surrender. "Not trying to cut, don't worry. What if I just go ask my question then come right back here afterwards?"

"*No one is allowed to cut.*" Their long tongue slowly curls and reaches towards my throat, barely touching me, and I swallow my response. Instead I just nod my head, and the tongue retracts. Their soft smile now makes me shudder. "Everyone must wait their turn."

I take a deep breath to calm my stuttering heart climbing up my throat. *Okay, I can wait. It's not like I have anywhere else to be.*

So I wait.

And wait.

And wait.

And wait.

Wait.

I wait until I can't stop myself from screaming. I scream until my throat is raw. Yet no one looks in my direction. Did I scream, or did I imagine that? It's been so long since I've seen the person's face in front of me that I wonder if I imagined ther shape-shifting as well.

I clench my fists beside me to calm myself, take a deep breath, and tap on the stranger's nonexistent shoulder again. Just as I remember, their shoulder disappears and their face is many of a million.

"Yes?" they ask, and it's almost as if all that waiting didn't happen because I'm right back to where I started.

"We've been waiting for a really long time, and I don't think we've even moved forward one inch. How about we both go up to the front and ask what's going on?"

They squint as if they don't understand what I'm saying. "But when there's a line, you wait in line. And it's not right to cut in line."

"I'm not cutting!" I scream, and their smile disappears. I suddenly feel bad, so I lower my voice. "I'm just trying to find an alternate solution." I open my palms to convey all the innocence I possess.

They pause before dipping their head definitively. "There is no alternate solution. We all must wait."

But I can't wait any longer. Frustration builds in me until I just want to lie down and cry. Am I impulsive? Potentially. I consider bursting into a sprint so no one can reach me in time. But the thought of the tongue around my throat freezes me in place.

So I wait.

And wait.

And wait.

And wait.

This is your story. Do you wait?

Yes — 1

No — 2

1.

I wait.

And wait.

And wait.

Have I accepted my fate? The calmness I felt in the beginning has returned. We still haven't moved, but my urge to kick and scream has faded into quiet frustration.

Until a hand taps me on the shoulder. I feel the hand glide through my body just like mine did to the stranger before me. Excitement floods my senses at the touch, and the numbness fades away.

I turn around slowly, a smile forming, but it doesn't feel natural. I'm excited that someone might be on my side, ecstatic even, but my smile is soft, sleepy. "Yes?"

They have the same ever-changing face as the one in front of me, and by the look on their face, I do, too. "Where are we?" A soft whimper.

I mean to scream, to warn, to scheme. To my horror, very different words leave my mouth. "In line, silly. And I'm no longer last. How exciting."

2.

I can't wait anymore. Damn the consequences.

Without looking back, I sprint in a wide arc around the line. For a moment, the mumble of those in line goes silent—then, a screech from my front neighbor awakens the figures into action.

Ghostly hands that a second ago had no physical shape stretch towards me, farther than arms should reach. I dodge the first few but feel the next grab a strand of my hair, then my arm and my leg and I plummet to the ground.

Why am I vaporous until I really need to be?

I kick my leg free and crawl forward until I'm overwhelmed with gaseous limbs creating a wall around me.

"You think you're so special, you can cut while the rest of us wait?" Voices mix into one hideous melody.

Pounding my fist on the ground, I yell back, "You're all content waiting here forever, but I can't live like this! Please," my voice crumbles now to a soft whisper. "Let me see what's going on up there. I'll ask for you, too!"

The soft light from the front shines brighter, and I can almost make out the figures sitting at the long desk. The voices hiss around me and I can no longer make out what they're saying, only that they're pissed, and I don't want to wait to see what else their shape-shifting bodies can do.

In a vicious outburst, I bite and kick and tear my way free, run, get trapped again, then repeat with the next group of line ghosts. My breath comes in ragged huffs, but I've started and now I can't stop, the fear of what awaits me if I fail is more powerful than my exhaustion.

I barely notice that I've torn free of the first in line until I realize that no more arms are reaching for me. The light from the desk blinds me until my eyes adjust, and I see people—regular people, not shapeshifting ghosts—smiling kindly from behind their table.

"Congratulations! You passed," the one on the right says.

The left continues, arms outstretched behind them, "You may now move to the next level."

The table separates in the middle, the fog parting to reveal a walkway to an elevator.

Honestly, I don't even take a moment to be suspicious, as happy as I am just happy to rid myself of the ghosts. Stepping into the elevator, I breathe a sigh of relief.

The elevator ding echoes as the doors open, and I enter the darkness.

Are my eyes open? I press them shut to feel the difference. Yep. Definitely open.

Where am I? is the first thought that whispers in my mind. But then a slightly louder, more anxious voice asks, Where was I before this?

The Blue Room

Mia Ilie

Sometimes it felt like she was born in this room.

Born in a room with sky blue walls that were never evenly painted, but painted with love, so the walls had a texture.

Some of her earliest memories were of her walking around the room with her hands grazing the wall, up, down, up, down, up. It would feel rough in her palm when she reached the window but smooth by the time she got to her dresser. She would walk all the way around until she reached the painting.

If she was born in this room, then this painting was as well.

The artist who created this off-color painting must have dipped their paintbrush into a dull brown and dragged it onto the canvas in vertical lines to create the trunk of a tree, then dipped their next brush in a yellow to create the lemons that are dangling from the tree. They must have sat on the very stool that the girl sat in every morning to paint makeup on her face. The only difference was their canvas. She imagined them buying a giant can of orange paint and lugging it up the stairs of her family home, then using it all on the woman in the painting's dress. The orange dress was the only real color within the painting, even brighter than the yellow lemons.

Yes, this painting had to have been born in this room.

It would not have been blue at the time. Her mother chose sky blue when she found out she was pregnant. She always dreamed of flying, so she hoped her child would too.

But to the girl, the person who had created this painting seemed like the type of person to never want to lift a foot off the ground, so they would have found excitement in their art instead. They would have created dull scenarios and a splash of color in random parts of the painting: the woman's dress, a small patch of grass, one very specific lemon. So when she imagined the artist expressing their emotions of the world, she thought they must have done it in a similar type of room.

Perhaps beige walls but with a vibrant green duvet. The complete opposite of her outdoorsy walls and plain white duvet. Her bed looked like a cloud and the gray carpet looked like the sky before it released rain.

She suspected the artist wouldn't have had carpet in this room, not unless they wanted to risk washing paint stains every day. She could agree with the artist on that. She used to love the carpet, used to love to lay on the ground and melt into the soft yet itchy ground and close her eyes. She wouldn't sleep, but she would dream. She would dream of birds, trees, lemons, and of women in bright orange dresses. And then she would open her eyes again, sit up, and look at the bees flying around her window.

But then when she was eighteen she snuck a bottle of wine up to her room with a friend. The two girls talked and laughed, and at one point, they began to chase each other like they were ten again. It was fun until she spilled the bottle of wine. The stain never came out and her mother found out.

She wasn't in any real trouble, but she wished she could have been sneakier. She thought of the painter and if they ever spilled paint, then decided they must have never had carpet and that when she moves out, she will live in a home with no carpet at all. Then she could be as sneaky as she would like, move like a vigilante.

She did like the stain though. Despite her anger towards her clumsiness, the bright red stain reminded her of the painting. Gray carpet with one splash of color, like the woman and her bright-orange dress.

Some days she wondered where the painting took place and where the woman in the dress was running off to. She thinks that if she were the woman, she would have taken some lemons off the tree herself and brought them home to make the most deliciously tart lemonade. But the woman in the painting seemed to be running past the tree.

Was she a real woman? Did the painter feel inspired by someone in their life and paint her? Was it a gift to her that they never got to give? Was the woman in the painting running away from a man and running to another love instead? Perhaps to a woman? Or maybe she was running just to run.

She liked to do that. She loved running in the woods behind her house. She would take off and go until she could no longer feel her legs. And then she would keep going because by then it felt like she was flying; and yes, her mother succeeded, because she wished to fly too.

And maybe the woman in the painting did as well. Maybe she also longed for the feeling of numbness below her waist and a cold breeze on her face. She longed to be floating and weightless, being in the sky, grazing her hands on the clouds, up, down, up, down, up.

And perhaps the woman had a blue room with poorly painted walls filled with love. Perhaps she grazed her hands on the wall as well, up, down, up, down, up.

Leer es Resistir

Oriana Galvis Marín

*"Seguiremos leyendo porque las páginas que amamos,
en medio del infierno que vivimos día a día,
son nuestra única redención posible."*[1]
—Mario Mendoza

To read
is to escape from the limitless
and unstoppable reality
that torments our monotony.

To read
is to survive the burning and intense inferno
that is always alive, consuming us.
A nightmare that never ends,
where the limits between the worlds
of reality and fiction
are blurry, almost nonexistent.

To read
is to escape from these terrors,
bringing them to an end.
But is also to find traces of these unwanted moments
captured in someone else's ink, and
pictured in someone else's prose.

---

1 *We will continue reading, because the pages we love, in the middle of the hell that we live day by day, they are our only possible redemption*

Reading is resisting.
Is to devour the pages of a story,
so foreign but so familiar,
and to escape from a reality painted in gray,
in the midst of cruel words,
that narrates oddly familiar worlds.

Reading is resisting
is finding a refuge,
a lair made out of narratives,
surrounded by fragile sheets of paper.
A bunker in the middle of a bookstore,
a safe space in the middle of the war field.

Reading is resisting,
is building a capsule
where every nuance of our reality
lives in the words of a book,
ready for future readers to pick it up
and travel through our vicissitudes.

The Compound

Brittney Terrian

I stand in formation alongside my fellow community members, listening to the daily recitation of rules. The guardian attentively observes each of us, pacing along the line.

This has been our routine for the past three years. The schedule remains unchanged except for the monthly assembly.

"Remember: no pets, consume all provided food, avoid eye contact with guardians, stay within designated walking lines, and speak only when prompted," the lady concludes, her gaze scanning the lineup.

"Speak," she commands.

"Our adherence to these rules fosters unity, which brings peace to our community," we respond in unison. The words have been deeply ingrained in our minds since our arrival.

"Proceed."

She turns and leads us to our individual rooms identified by the numbers on our shirts. I'm assigned number 492351-L likely based on some form of age order. Though my age remains unknown, I estimate myself to be between fourteen and sixteen.

I gaze ahead, taking in the stark surroundings. The walls lack adornment, and the floors are marked by a continuous white line. I have been taught to never stray from this line, although I have never witnessed anyone do so. There must be severe consequences for such deviations. Our rules are designed to safeguard us, and any deviations must be corrected.

Guiding words are inscribed on the floor, directing our path throughout the entire building. After completing our daily walk within the community's premises to stimulate our minds, we head to our sleeping quarters. Physical activity is deemed vital for optimal brain function, or so we have been informed. Prior to our lessons, we always take a stroll around the community's foundation.

As my group, assigned to corridor L, follows the designated line, we each stop in front of our respective rooms, marked by a dash across the line.

I wait for the buzzer before turning toward my room. Once the second buzzer sounds, indicating it is time to enter, I swiftly move toward my desk and examine the subject we will be studying today. The desk is always prepared with a textbook, paper, and a pencil, aligned for the day's lesson. A glass of water is placed at the top left corner of the desk, emphasizing the importance of hydration for optimal cognitive function.

I take a seat and glance at the textbook before me.

ENGLISH.

The bold letters announce today's subject. I hold no particular affinity or distaste for English; it is simply another part of my day. This room serves as my classroom, bedroom, dining room, and any space that does not require face-to-face interaction. That privilege is reserved for older individuals.

The screen in front of me flickers to life, presenting the woman who delivers all our lessons.

"Good morning, class. Please turn to page 394. We will commence our lesson," she announces with a warm smile.

I skim through the pages until my gaze lands on page 296. A crumpled note is wedged within the book's folds. I hesitate, wondering how it got there.

I scrunch my face up, about to grab the note, when I hear the woman speak.

"492351-L is there something you'd like to share with the class?" she states, looking straight at me.

My brow furrows as I reach for the note, concealing it from the camera's view by discreetly slipping it between my thighs. "No, ma'am. I was momentarily confused about the new topic after glancing at the book. My apologies for interrupting the class," I respond, ensuring my voice remains composed.

"We accept your apology," the class says in unison.

The teacher gazes at me a moment longer before commencing the lesson. I exhale the breath I had been holding.

As the lesson delves into the principles of grammar, I sit upright, keeping the note safely concealed. It becomes challenging to concentrate as I work hard to appear unaffected. I haven't done anything wrong, but the thought of being caught with the note unnerves me.

Eventually, the class concludes, and we respectfully bid our goodbyes, waiting for the screen to turn off. As soon as it does, I have precisely four seconds to retrieve the note and find a discreet hiding place before the guides open our doors. I quickly survey the surroundings, but everything seems out of reach. I must keep the note on my person until the lights are out.

When the screen fades to black, I discreetly tuck the note into my waistband, the only available hiding spot without pockets.

On cue, the buzzer rings, and the door slides open.

The speakers above issue instructions, "Stand up and await guidance to the hallway."

I remain still, avoiding any sudden movements. The weight of the note nestled against my waistband feels significant.

The guide approaches me, signaling for me to step forward. Ever since the E-massacre, they have begun standing behind us.

I leave my room and join the line, patiently waiting to be directed to the assembly hall. It is the only occasion when all community members, regardless of group, are gathered together. It strikes me as peculiar that our groups solely consist of children of similar ages. I sit attentively, my back straight, ensuring the note remains secure against my waistband. Even a momentary lapse could cause it to slip.

"Good afternoon, esteemed children of the future," the leader, Julian Dender, greets us with a smile. He is the only person in the facility with a name. "As we approach the coming-of-age ceremonies, we draw nearer to selecting the future leaders for the next age group," he pauses, scanning the room. "This year, we are fortunate to have a remarkable cohort of young men and women. You possess the minds that will guide us, but first, you must learn to be guided."

The sensation of the note pressing against my waist grows uncomfortable. I resist the urge to adjust it and glance toward the aisle on my left. I spot only one guardian patrolling, yet it feels as though they can perceive my every move. My hand twitches, tempting me to readjust the note's position.

"That concludes today's assembly. Wait for your guardians to arrange you properly, and then we shall commence silent reading time through The Rulebook."

We align ourselves in our designated lines and begin our march toward the metal door, the sole exit from this place.

In a single file, we proceed through the doorway. Just as I am about to step outside, a hand halts me. I raise my eyes and find the guardian assigned to my group peering down at me. "The leader requests a conversation with you. Come with me." She gestures, and I cautiously step out of line. My breathing quickens; we were never instructed to deviate from the line. No lines guide us to the leader's office because no child is ever taken there. Tentatively, I raise my hand as I position myself before the guardian.

"Speak," she instructs.

"I— I don't know... There is no line, ma'am. I am uncertain where to go," I stutter.

"Walk forward until directed," she replies.

My leg feels as heavy as a mountain when I take my first step. Uncertain of my path from this point onward, I follow her guidance, slowly advancing. Every step feels like slow motion, the signs flashing by to my left. The rush of water-like sounds fill my ears, making it increasingly challenging to focus.

"Turn right."

My steps falter, and dizziness washes over me, but at that moment, I become acutely aware of the crumpled note concealed within my waistband. I freeze. I cannot afford to be discovered. I must regain composure before giving them a reason to reprimand me. Suddenly, my senses flood back, allowing me to hear everything around me and feel my legs once more.

"Proceed forward, 492351-L," I hear from behind. I resume walking, this time at a steady pace, following the instructions until I stand before a grand metal door.

"You may enter; they are expecting you," the guardian informs me.

I push open the doors. This marks my first entry into this room, having only encountered a handful of rooms thus far. It appears entirely unlike anything I have seen before. The high ceiling, wooden walls with a glossy finish, and bookshelves brimming with hundreds of books lining the walls all make for a stark contrast to the concrete environment. We are only permitted to read the assigned materials. Some of these book titles remain illegible, forcing me to squint in an attempt to decipher them.

"You may take a seat, 492351-L," a voice calls my attention to the right. The leader stands behind a broad desk, gesturing towards a plush chair opposite him. Complying with his instruction, I move forward, striving to appear composed. I must not arouse suspicion.

"You must be wondering why I have summoned you today," he states, walking around the desk. I nod slowly, my leg twitching nervously.

"You may speak. This is a serious discussion we are about to have," he encourages.

"Yes, sir," I whisper, determined to steady my trembling voice. I clamp my jaw shut to suppress any chattering teeth.

"As you may have heard during the assembly, the selection of the next class leaders is approaching. Your group falls within a significant time frame. The chosen leader must possess the qualities necessary to guide life," he declares, meeting my gaze.

The leader has always intimidated me, and at this moment, his presence feels more imposing than ever. He is a tall man, whom I have never been this close to before. His eyes are a deep brown, almost black. With his age and furrowed brow, his features exude a hardened resolve.

"It is a substantial responsibility, sir," I reply, my voice trembling.

A wide smile spreads across his face. Precisely. That is why the candidate must be carefully selected. We have assessed your group and concluded that you would be a suitable candidate."

I freeze. Me, a leader? Responsible for guiding life while concealing something from the very individuals who lead our entire community?

"You may speak," he prompts, his smile directed at me.

I gaze at him, contemplating my next words. "Am I the only candidate?"

He hesitates. "No, there is another we have in mind—492364-L. She is also a member of your group."

I recognize her; she stands behind me, visible only on rare occasions when we are outside.

He rises from his chair and circles the desk. "You will meet and be formally introduced to each other. Soon after, we will commence tests to accurately assess your abilities," he explains, pressing a button on his desk. The door opens, and the guardian steps inside. "That is all, 492351-L. You may now resume your designated schedule."

He motions towards the door. I rise calmly, though internally I am in disarray. I clench my jaw, preventing my anxious state from being visible to the guardian.

Following the designated lines that lead to my section, I hear the footsteps of the guardian trailing behind me. My mind is in turmoil. I have no knowledge of leadership.

I lift my gaze and blink at the door, the numbers 492351-L staring back at me. I had blanked out during the journey, my feet moving on autopilot.

As the buzzer sounds, my door slides open. I step inside, avoiding eye contact and concealing my anxiety from the guardian. I take a deep breath and decide this is a worry for tomorrow.

Dior Sauvage

Misha Puello Brasil

Last night, I could smell you in the air and on my sheets.
Lingering smoky citrus and vanilla, I inhaled deeply,
vivid vermillion visions of you left me intoxicated.

Your absence consumed me, turned my cotton concrete.
There's a sore, dull ache without you.
My body feels tense without your caress.

I paced around images of you.
I sat too still, my bluebird sang for you
perched on my windowsill, waiting to see you.

Your face filled the bottom of the bottle.
The bitter taste of your perfume
could not satiate the taste buds that yearn for you.
But it worked just the same for a desperate tongue.

Golden Mirrors

Chardonnae Simpson

Maybe it was your life's mission to sprinkle cinnamon
sugar on the pinnacle of my nose and fly away

To drop gems on the hall floor for me to retrieve

To address love letters to the deepest parts of me

So that I walk with my chest out and head held to the
gods

To never confuse someone else's inconsistency for my
own deficiency

To make the world my stage

Where I call the shots

I cast the actors

To bring my life to action

But who better than me?

Who better than me to bring the intensity of not only
acting the part but being the part?

I built this from the ground up

I'll be damned if I let you take the confidence she gave
me as I exchanged my tears for motivation

When she comes around, everyone is an understudy

No questions about it

Know the lines and know them well before she reminds
you that you're just getting started

Chapter from *Neither Heaven Nor Hell*
Mia Ilie

Chapter One

Screaming filled Cassie's head so loud she could feel blood trickling out of her ears, but all she could see was black. Dark, damning black and nothing, nothing, nothing, nothing. The blood-inducing screeches dug claws into her body, forcing her to come to a reality she did not want. When the screaming began to fade into the familiar buzzing of her family's old alarm clock, she almost missed and longed for the piercing noise that dampened her ears and the black nothing that chilled her to the bones.

Cassie opened her eyes, stuck her head out from the sleeping bag, and squinted at the alarm clock showing her the same time as every day.

6:01 a.m.

Her hands reached for her ears to feel for the blood she had felt, but they were dry. When she looked back at her fingers, there wasn't the deep burgundy she had become familiar with. Just her pale clean fingers with her white scars on her knuckles looking back at her almost in spite.

Cassie let the alarm go off for a bit longer as she took in her surroundings. Everything was as she left it last night: the alarm across from her so that it would be the first thing she saw every morning and the boxes of cardboard blocking all of the windows of the lighthouse so that the sun never disturbed her but also so that no one could watch her—even being as high up as she was, you could never be too careful. She was grateful for the new lighthouse a few miles down. This one was no longer in use and just acted as a historical monument and a home for her.

It was once a home to her and her family, and a museum with ghost tours to get money from tourists. But Cassie didn't do that anymore. Not since it happened.

She stood up from her makeshift bed, a sleeping bag with couch cushions from downstairs underneath and a cheap pillow. It wasn't all that comfortable, but it was safe and it worked. She walked over to the alarm, shut it off, and set it for the next morning at the same time. Always a minute past six. That's when it was safe.

She began to walk around the circular room, taking down the cardboard boxes one by one and letting the sun fill in the room. The golden sun almost made the place feel safe. Almost.

As Cassie pulled down the last of the boxes, she looked out the window and found a woman staring up at her. Cassie looked around the room to see if there was something behind her that the woman was looking at, but there was nothing, and as Cassie looked back, she had no doubt that the woman was staring directly at *her*.

She quickly ducked down, foolishly thinking the woman wouldn't see her from this far up. The woman looked familiar, though she had never seen her before. Her hair was around the same color as Cassie's, she thought, but that seemed to be it. Yet somehow, Cassie felt a familiar twinge at the woman, and that alone terrified her. Cassie crawled around the room to put the boxes back up on the windows. Let the room be dark so long as this woman could not see her.

Once she was done, she made the trek down the long spiral stairs to walk to her home.

§

At the bottom of the stairs, there was a door that led to the house where Cassie and her family used to live together. Cassie's mother and father taught her and her sister how to properly block the door without all the fancy locks they couldn't yet afford.

As Cassie took each handmade lock apart, memories of her parents' words filled her head.

She started with moving the chair under the doorknob like every day.

"Cass, it's important to not only lock the door but to understand how each trick works," her mother told her, tying her hair back to prepare for

this lesson. Cassie could feel her sister's presence, she hid behind Cassie because their mom didn't want her to know this just yet. She was too young.

Her mom pulled a broken fork out of her pocket and showed it to Cassie. "This is a small trick, but it comes in handy."

"But Mom, it's broken," Cassie points out, feeling pretty smart for noticing. The handle was cut off, and the end of the fork itself had prongs bent upwards.

"It's only broken if you're eating with it." Her mom winked at her, then opened the door slightly to put the bent prongs in the door latch. "The pointy part of the fork is bent at a 90-degree angle, so it grips the door. Once you close the door on the fork, we're going to place the handle through the points horizontally, half across the door and half on the door frame. This is like a tiny barricade for the door."

Cassie watches in amazement as her mom slightly pulls on the door to prove how it works. Then she grabs the chair next to her.

"Next, the chair, but before we put it in its proper place, we put it just close enough to the door to stand up on."

Her mother, despite being tall, was not quite tall enough to reach the door hinge at the top. So, she pulled up a chair, stood atop it, and pulled the belt out of her belt loops.

She looked down at Cassie. "You're going to want to move the end of the belt through the part of the hinge that is bolted to the door frame. Then you tightly wrap the belt around the rest of the hinge and weave the belt through the center. Make sure it's tight so it stays in place. The belt prevents the door from swinging open, but this alone won't be enough."

Cassie looked behind her to make sure her sister was listening from wherever she was hiding. A hand on her shoulder made her turn back around.

"Cass, you must pay attention to all of this. Now is not the time to be distracted," her mother told her, back on the floor from the chair. "The next step is easier. Just wedge the back of the chair under the doorknob at a forty-five-degree angle, and it jams the knob from the other side making it difficult to move the knob and push the door open from the other side.

"Are you following, Cassie?"

She nodded eagerly and pointed her finger at the belt on the door hinge. "Broken fork, horizontal, belt on the hinge, wrap it as tight as possible. Then hop down and put the chair under the knob at um..."

"A forty-five-degree angle." Her mom smiled at her.

Cassie grinned. "Forty-five-degree angle!"

Her mother's gaze was filled with pride and Cassie could feel her stomach doing summersaults of excitement. She loved it when she made her mom proud.

"Only two more steps. They're easier," her mom promised, then pointed to the metal beam that was leaning on the wall in the corner. "Your father inserted these two metal anchors on each side of the door so we can use a beam of metal as a barricade. All you have to do is slide the bar between the anchors, and you're done." Her mother did so, and Cassie again looked back to see if her sister was paying attention. She was hiding well, and Cassie couldn't see her, but she still felt her sister's presence.

Her mother then moves in front of Cassie and kneels in front of her, placing her hands on each shoulder. "Now this is the most important part. Despite all of these locks, they still may not be enough to keep what we're hiding from away."

Cassie knew. She knew that for the six months they had lived here, they were never truly safe, not until they were all at the top of the lighthouse, far away from whatever roamed the house below.

Her mother removed one hand from her shoulder and took out a small blue box. "Salt, all around the bottom of the door. Remember to pour this, and we will be safe."

Her mother poured a line then closed the box and put it back on the ground. Cassie heard shuffling and knew it was her sister running upstairs before her mom found her listening.

Her mom stood up and brushed her hands on her jeans. "Alright, now we're done. Let's head up to bed."

Cassie swiped away the salt with her foot and then walked through the door, shoving the memory aside and letting herself forget as she started the new day. Then, she opened the door on the other side of the room—the one that led to the old museum.

She took in her surroundings, taking note of what the Whispers had done to the house that night. That's what they called them, Cassie and her family, back when they were all here to call them anything.

Cassie's parents had always been interested in the paranormal; her mom had been a medium and used to take in clients to read for. Her latest client, a strange woman with way-too-curly hair and a hot pink trench coat from Rhode Island, had told her about the lighthouse that had been haunted for years on a small island near her home. Her mom had visited the place for a weekend, and the next thing Cassie knew, they were moving and opening a haunted museum tour in the building attached to the other side of the lighthouse, opposite where the house is.

The woman in the hot pink trench coat visited often and told them about the Whispers and how to never disturb them. She informed the family that they came out the second the sun came down and roamed the house, eager to cause chaos and lure anyone out, but lure them where, she was unsure of. The only thing she was sure of was that it was best to hide at the top of the lighthouse and just let them roam the house until exactly six in the morning. That was when they left. Cassie was terrified but remained brave for her family. They were getting a good income for once, and the house, though only one floor and quite small, was bigger than the one-bedroom apartment they used to live in.

Cassie walked to the kitchen counter, just across from the door, and grabbed a glass to fill with water. Glass in hand, she walked around the wooden house that felt more like one big room and took note of everything that had been touched.

A few pillows on the small couch had been tossed onto the rug underneath, and the rug itself had a few folded corners. A few paintings on the wall were crooked, and the television had been left on with just static playing. Cassie turned off the television and fixed everything else.

Overall, it wasn't too terrible. Some days were worse, with glasses broken, windows shattered, or once, all of the furniture in the rooms had been switched. The round wooden kitchen table stood in the middle of the living room, and the couch and television were where the table was supposed to be, by a window at the corner of the kitchen. That was not a fun day, but it at least gave Cassie and her sister something to do while her parents gave their tours.

Cassie put her glass of water down and took a deep breath before walking to the bathroom.

She flicked the light on and quickly shut her eyes. She hated this part. Hated checking the mirrors.

Deep breath. "One…" Breathe. "Two…" Breathe. "Three…"

She opened her eyes and was relieved to see the sheet still covering the mirror. Mirror number one was safe.

Slowly, she made her way to her parents' old bedroom, twisted the doorknob open, flicked the light, and looked everywhere except where the vanity with the mirror stood. She first took note of the thrown pillows and tossed blankets, but that wasn't the Whispers. That was how her parents had last left the bed, and that was how Cassie left it, unable to bring herself to fix it.

She and her family may have never spent the nights in their bedrooms, but they would often nap in them sometimes from a long day at the museum, and other days when the Whispers were particularly loud and it was difficult to sleep all the way upstairs in the lighthouse.

The day before everything happened, her parents had been asleep here and left it like this. Cassie felt like the Whispers didn't touch their bed to mock her.

Very slowly, she turned around and braced herself for the mirror. It was mostly covered, but the top left corner sheet looked like it was tugged slightly, and Cassie quickly ran to the front of the room and tucked the corner in tightly. Once done, she quickly ran out of the room and closed the door.

Mirror number two was safe.

Despite knowing it was pointless, Cassie walked a few feet to the next door. The door that led to her and her sister's room. She twisted the doorknob, but just like every day, the door was locked.

Ever since the incident, the door had been locked. She didn't know who locked it or why, but she knew it must have been for a good reason. Something was probably in the room.

Something was probably playing with her and her sister's old dolls. Something was probably jumping up and down on the beds just like she used to do. Something was probably drawing in her old notebooks with the purple crayon she used to love. And something was probably looking at the uncovered mirror and smiling a disgusting, too-wide smile.

Mirror number three was not safe.

Never One Place

Brittney Terrian

There was no reason to get attached to any one place. Saying this makes me sound cold, but it's what I learned growing up. My memories began in New Mexico; at the time I was three years old, and I understood very little of the world. It was a cloudy day, as if the clouds were deciding whether to grace us with a sprinkle or keep moving onto the piece of earth. I was playing in the fenced-in yard. The metal looked dry, as if it hurt to exist. I was tossing a ball across the lawn by myself. My siblings were too young to play. It was just a ball and the earth; those were my friends at the time.

I was in the midst of my imagination when I heard the sound of machinery. I hadn't noticed the hole in the earth outside the fence until then. I saw men surrounding it with huge shovels. It engulfed them entirely, and at that moment, I could hear the soil crying. It was hurt. *They* were hurting the soil. People were hurting my friend.

I ran to the fence, my little arms pumping, ready to take on anyone who would hurt my friend. My fingers wrapped around the fence. I felt the dryness from the fence fall to the ground as it gave way to the hands of man.

"Stop! You're hurting it! You're hurting it," I yelled. I had to let them know. How could they not hear the screaming? I began banging on the fence, trying desperately to be heard. Someone had to say something.

Why weren't they stopping? I thought to myself.

"Stop! Please! You're hurting the earth. You're being bad!" Finally, one looked over. He began to walk over to the fence and I quickly backed up. I knew I was in trouble. Speaking up always led to trouble. I tripped backward on the ball I had left behind. My friend wanted me to stay, but I was scared. I got up and ran into the house, ready to grab my mamma and tell her about the bad man. I didn't even notice the scrapes on my palms. The earth felt my pain and knew I was fighting for it.

My mom looked at my hands and scolded me for causing trouble. Then there was a knock on the door. I stayed in the back of the house, knowing that the man who was hurting my friend wanted to scold me too. I waited in the kitchen anxiously for the verdict.

I heard them talking and knew I was about to be in trouble. The scolding came shortly after. My father told me I always caused trouble and that I would never learn. I sat there and listened like I always did as my mom put ointment on my hands and tried to make the pain go away. Toward the end, I looked out the window. The rain finally came, and my friend, too, was trying to take the pain away.

Soon after, we moved on to the next place.

§

The next stop was Nevada. We stayed there for a while and I thought that it was the final stop for our family. I was a lot freer while living in Nevada. There was no real parental figure to watch over my siblings and me. My mom worked two to three jobs and my father was absent. The one who looked over us was my older brother. He was the protector of the family and always made sure I was okay, even when I put myself in compromising situations.

Every day, my brother and I walked to school together. It was a long walk, and my brother was never far from my side. On this particular day, we were walking through the apartments. They stood tall. The green paint chipped with the tinge of rust at the end. We were heading to the broken cedar block fence. We would pass from one complex to the other. I was looking around, taking in everything, even though I walked the same path every day.

An open door caught my eye on the second floor. There was yelling, maybe the couple was arguing about their daughter. And then all of a sudden something flew out of the window. My brother and I froze and watched as a half-eaten fish landed at our feet. I remember staring at the dead fish. I remember thinking it was upsetting that I could see all of its bones, yet it had a full head. I don't remember what we did with it. Maybe we walked past it and the image was forever seared into my brain. Or maybe he picked it up and threw it at his younger sister to hear her squeal.

That fish head wasn't important, it was the world around me. It was the fact that this core memory never left me. The way my breath felt walking that cool Vegas morning. The way my brother laughed, big and burly, yet still so tiny as he was growing.

§

I was still in Nevada when the next core memory came to mind years later. I was coming home from playing at the nearby playground with my sister. I was close to the house when I noticed a man's silhouette. The ember of his cigarette stood out. I looked at my sister, confused. Just then, my mom opened the door. "Get in here, girls." My confusion was offset by the happiness of seeing my mom. She worked three jobs, and we only saw her as she stumbled in, tired, and lay on the couch with us to get a few hours of shut-eye.

We were ushered into the room when I heard the man laugh behind me. I looked at my mom and asked "Mamma, who is that man?"

My mom hesitated and started to answer, "He's y—" but was cut off by my grandma's "Bobbie, can you come here?" My mom got up from the couch and walked into the soft glow that came from the room.

All of my siblings were sitting on our bed, not knowing what was going on. We heard our mom's voice getting louder. They were arguing. I went and grabbed my teddy bear off the shelf. I looked at my older brother, he was the next oldest, so I was hoping he would take control like he always did.

My mom came out of the room looking disheveled. "I would like you to meet someone." Just then the man came in. He was tall, eyes wide and blue... Like mine.

"This is your dad, and he is here to take us home." I sat there, still with my siblings. "We're going to Florida," she continued. Then I got excited. *Florida? That sounds fun! Beaches, trees, grass, and Disney World!*

The man, my dad, then spoke, "Yup, and we have a flight to catch tonight, so we have to pack!" It became a whirlwind. My mom rushed around grabbing our bags. I was grabbing the few toys I had. I looked over and saw my grandma in the frame of her door. Frowning. Wasn't she happy? We were going home.

My mom quickly grabbed my arm, and then we were gone.

The airport itself was a blur, but I do strangely remember asking the flight attendant for a cheeseburger. It was my first time on a plane, and I was giddy.

Then, of course, we were on to the next place.

New York Lessons: A Collection of Shorts
Jack Niemczyk

Nature Walk in New York
three cars almost hit me

Upside Down
Manhattan looks different after five manhattans

Writing School Broke My Sole
I could never figure out homonyms

There's a Wet Spot on the Subway
let it only be piss

Have You Ever?
probably

Bear Crossing
the intersection 47th and 9th ave

Finally, My Poetic Opus
—thank you

My Eyes
Kayleigh Woltal

I often wish I had a different pair of eyes,
Ones that do not betray me when I wish to keep things inside.

My body is a devious vessel.
It swallows the words that fight to spill through my lips,
And when I believe my secrets are sealed,
My eyes always allow them to leak.

I often wish I had a different pair of eyes,
Because mine never lie.

Becoming a Butterfly

Alena Williams

Who are you? *Mutable energy.*
Who are you? *Creating synergy.*
Who are you? *Taking the world by storm.*
Who are you? What's your form?
What's a flower to a thorn? A beetle to a butterfly?
Not far, but I want to fly! Fly so high I touch the sky!

Why? *Because I am mutable energy, creating synastry.*
A flower to a thorn, a beetle to a butterfly.
Not far, but I want to fly. Leave the clouds behind!
Be free, be fly, be elevated, and try.
Take the world by storm.

Who are you?
Who am I?
What's a beetle to a butterfly?

31 Willow Lake Avenue
Zetta Whiting

The house Yaritza Jacobs sold Mr. Greene killed him on a crisp October evening.

In truth, she wasn't even an official real estate agent. She was the *assistant* to an official real estate agent. It was her first job out of college. All she had to do was email paperwork to the new homeowner for a digital signature and file it away in the appropriate folder of the office's shared drive.

Yaritza shifted in her sweat-soaked seat across from her boss, her tan slacks doing nothing to wick up the moisture as she re-read the highlighted lines.

"Failure to provide clear information about a house's past residents and/or active passed residents and collect the homeowner's signature under Title 11:02 will result in immediate termination."

Dr. Dyer's office suddenly felt claustrophobic. The rain swept in a heady mustiness through the open window, making the space entirely too humid.

"You do realize you'll have to make an appearance in court. You and Ryan, since he also failed to double check your work," her boss said, giving her a pointed look.

Yaritza fiddled with the ends of her straightened brown hair as she racked her brain, trying to remember what she had done with the document after Mr. Greene had signed it.

Had I not saved it properly?

The clicks from Dr. Dyer's mouse were deafening, echoing around Yaritza's skull as if someone had popped bubblegum directly into her ear.

"The document is in here." Dr. Dyer squinted, his black glasses sliding down his nose. "But, yes, the signature line is indeed blank," he verified with a sigh.

Yaritza felt her face pale. *How could I have made such a careless mistake?*

"Now the listing won't be for sale again until a proper cleansing is done, that is, if the company survives this." Dr. Dyer leaned back in his chair. "And the ghost is what made it so valuable…" He said the last part more to himself than to Yaritza, regret dripping from his voice.

Half of the population of the small town of Sunken Valley, Maine, was able to see ghosts, Yaritza being one of them. Dr. Dyer could, too. He was always one of the first people from the agency to visit a new listing and determine if any spirits resided there. "More spirits, more spending" was his motto. Spending for the customer, that is. The value of the house, no matter how big or small, always rose when ghosts were involved. Yaritza had gotten that question right on her written exam to get her real estate license.

Ghosts were often blamed for unsolved deaths in town. They were an easy scapegoat when the police wanted to close an investigation, especially when there weren't any obvious leads. It also did wonders for Halloween tourism.

So, when the cops found William Greene lying at the foot of his very haunted spiral staircase with his neck snapped, they ruled out homicide. The poor old man had probably been frightened to death by the unruly ghost and tripped down the stairs even though his health records stated he was unable to see spirits.

"Doesn't matter, because the ghost could've slammed a door that spooked him, turned the kitchen sink faucet on, cut the power… The possibilities are endless," the cops had probably said after an hour of investigating, ready to settle the matter over a round of powdered donuts.

There didn't have to be a trial if a ghost scared someone to death, especially not in Sunken Valley. How could you punish someone who is already dead?

However, a trial *is* warranted if a real estate company *enabled* a ghost to scare someone to their death by not providing the homeowner with the proper documents that explicitly stated an entity's presence.

Yaritza remembered how Mr. Greene had greeted the spirit during the house tour. She had told him a ghost lingered there, and he hadn't minded, despite the fact that he couldn't see it. The ghost herself had seemed nice, a little standoffish, but Yaritza didn't think she was the type to bother with active disturbances.

"Ms. Jacobs," her boss's voice snapped her out of her thoughts. "You need to go to 31 Willow Lake Avenue and see what really went down over there."

The rain outside sounded like static as it thudded against his office windowsill.

"Isn't it a crime scene?"

"Yes, that's why you should go there and look for evidence that the police might have missed."

Yaritza couldn't tell if he was joking or not. What did this man get his PhD in? Scheming?

"And while you're there…" he rummaged through his desk drawer, shuffling through a disorganized cluster of paperclips, pens, sticky notes, and index cards. He sighed in relief as he pulled out a bag of what seemed to be strands of fine hair. Human hair.

"Put this on the windowsill of his bedroom."

Yaritza blinked.

"You want me to put a bag of someone's hair in that house?"

"Oh no, not the bag, just the hair."

She looked around the room, desperately wishing for anyone she could make eye contact with that wasn't Dr. Dyer. Unfortunately, no lonely ghosts had wandered into the office to keep her misery company.

"Tampering with evidence is illegal," she breathed, pulling on the cuff of her knit sweater.

"You're not tampering with evidence. You're *adding* evidence."

Yaritza bit her lip to keep from hysterically laughing at her boss' words. She bit hard enough that she tasted a pinprick of her own metallic blood.

Dr. Dyer leaned in upon seeing the look on Yaritza's face. "Do you know how much legal trouble the company will be in if we sold a haunted house to someone without having them sign the acknowledgment of said haunting? To someone over fifty, no less? And then he *died* because of it? Sure, Mr. Greene could have simply slipped and fallen down the stairs, but the fact that an active haunting was taking place there puts us in hot water."

Her face paled. The room was too warm. She needed to remove her sweater.

"We'll be ruined. Our jobs are all at risk. How's Tabitha going to afford childcare for her baby on the way? How's Ryan going to pay his rent next month?"

A hot flush of shame rushed across her cheeks. Ryan was hired alongside her as an assistant. They were both fresh out of college and grateful they had passed their real estate license exams, desperate to find any place to work. She knew he barely made his rent.

"And since *you* failed to have the homeowner sign the document, you will be the one to go to jail," Dr. Dyer said.

The periphery of Dr. Dyer's office darkened, and Yaritza knew she needed to steady her breathing if she was to keep from passing out.

"I'll send Ryan with you so you're not alone. Not to jail, but to the house." He smiled a close-mouthed, crooked grin. "You're dismissed."

§

Orange leaves shifted under Yartiza's boots as she trudged down Willow Lake Avenue's rain-slickened streets. The gray cloud coverage sped up the sunset. Soon, the only light would come from the street's lamp posts, which already emitted a hazy yellow glow. A family passed Yaritza, walking their dog and laughing as they enjoyed the fresh air after the storm, completely clueless about her task.

The feather-light plastic bag of human hair felt like it weighed a hundred pounds in her slack pocket. Yaritza debated flinging the bag into the wind and just letting the jury decide her fate, but that would be littering.

She hated people who littered.

"I can't believe we're actually doing this." Ryan's voice startled her. She had forgotten he was even there.

"Neither can I," she sighed, her breath clouding before her.

Yaritza spotted the first of ten lamp posts that should have been out—the first five before and the first five after 31 Willow Lake. Residents and locals assumed it was due to the storm. Yaritza knew Dr. Dyer sweet-talked a ghost associate of his to use their "telekinetic assets" and cut the power. If there were street cameras, they'd be off until morning.

"Where did Dyer even get Mr. Greene's ex-wife's hair anyway?" he asked.

"Dyer knows how to network, I guess. He's also crazy enough to have found the hair salon she goes to and collected her hair from off the floor," she said.

Ryan laughed at her response, albeit nervously.

Yaritza glared.

"I'm being serious. I wouldn't put it past him," she said.

"You didn't ask?"

"I was too stressed to think of rational questions in the moment."

They passed the third dark street lamp, then the fourth, and finally stopped at the fifth.

31 Willow Lake Avenue was a Victorian home built entirely of white wooden panels. The house had a steep, gabled slate roof complete with a turret. The mahogany front door with one large, circular knocker was anachronistically tattooed with bright yellow crime scene tape. Yaritza had the feeling the wooden steps leading up to the porch would creak in warning.

Or perhaps in disappointment.

As Dyer had instructed, they avoided the front door altogether and walked along the stone pathway that led around the back. Ryan reached over the white backyard gate and unlatched it. The bushes did nothing to muffle the grating sound it made as it reluctantly opened.

Yaritza followed closely behind Ryan into the backyard, trying to steady her beating heart. She instead decided she would focus on the moon, which had started to peek through the cloud coverage. A yellow, overgrown witch hazel shrub snagged Yaritza's sweater in protest, and she remembered that she had lost the privilege of having her head in the clouds. Not after what she and Ryan were about to do.

Yartiza stopped at the sound of the gate slowly creaking shut behind them, unprovoked. She felt the hair on the back of her neck stand on end and a pair of hollow eyes on her. When she looked up, she wasn't surprised to see 31 Willow Lake's ghost gazing down at her from the second-floor bedroom window. Like all ghosts, this one emitted a transparent glow with a murky blue tint. The figure wore a long, tattered dress with puff sleeves and a watchful face that would have sent a child running.

Yaritza had never been frightened of ghosts, not even after she had seen her first one at age five, but this one glowered at her even more unpleasantly than most ghosts did.

She would much rather the ghost howl in the wind or repeatedly slam the creaky backyard gate shut again than watch her with such disdain. Even the moon seemed to take the ghost's side, now aglow so brightly despite the clouds, it felt as if it was burning a hole through Yaritza's skin.

Maybe this ghost *had* spooked Mr. Greene to death. Maybe not. Or *could* it have been a homicide? Or had Mr. Greene merely slipped down the stairs by nothing but his own clumsiness? Yaritza couldn't quell her growing curiosity. There were so many ways that man could have fallen down the stairs and snapped his neck.

Could Mr. Green's spirit be in the house now, too?

Ryan snapped his fingers in front of Yaritza's face.

"You were zoning out," he sighed, ruffling the dark hair that hung over his forehead, "Don't tell me the ghost is staring at you."

"Yep."

"Well, don't let that freak you out." He slid the glass backdoor open that led directly to the living room, which had been left unlocked thanks to another one of Dr. Dyer's ghost friends telekinetically interfering with a crime scene. "We gotta drop this hair off," Ryan said.

Sometimes, Yaritza wished she was like Ryan, blissfully unaware of the dead... And consequences, apparently.

43

She removed the plastic bag from her pocket.

What the hell were they doing?

Maybe she could survive this. She'd probably get fired. She might even go to jail, but maybe Dr. Dyer was exaggerating to scare a young, new assistant into tampering with evidence. She would be in even more legal trouble if anyone found out about *this*. Not to mention emotional turmoil. Maybe she could find a new job. Her parents would understand; she could always go back to live with them.

Yaritza had made up her mind. Screw Dr. Dyer and his real estate company.

"This is literally crazy," Yaritza said, "I'm not doing this." She was going to flush the bag of hair down the toilet in her apartment.

Ryan looked flabbergasted. "What do you mean you're not doing this? We, the assistants who didn't do their jobs right, are gonna be blamed for Mr. Greene's death. We're gonna get fired and go to jail!"

"The *company* will be blamed for Greene's death. And when I'm thrown into the mix, I'll just tell the truth. I made a mistake," she said.

Ryan stared at her.

"I'm not sticking my neck out for a company that doesn't care if I live or die," she continued.

She was wrong. They probably would care if she died so they could somehow find a way to deposit her lifeless spirit form into one of their listings to up the price.

At that moment, Mr. Greene decided to materialize in the living room just beyond the threshold of the sliding door. His translucent face remained neutral, and an idea formed in Yaritza's head.

"Maybe I can ask Mr. Greene what really happened the night he died. He's right there!" she pointed behind Ryan.

Ryan didn't even turn around. "And what? Tell the police that you infiltrated an active crime scene and asked a ghost for clarification on their death? Sometimes, ghosts don't even know how they died! They're also capable of *lying*," Ryan huffed.

"Great, so you also see how crazy this whole idea of planting false evidence at a crime scene is and have realized we should leave." Yartiza grabbed Ryan's arm. "Let's go."

He shrugged her grip off. "I'm not leaving," he said, his eyes unwavering.

"We can get a job somewhere else. I don't want to work for Dyer anymore anyway," Yaritza said.

Ryan swallowed. "That's not an option for everyone, Yari."

His words felt like a bucket of ice water, but she didn't have time to let them sink in.

He took the hair-filled plastic bag from her hand and went inside 31 Willow Lake Avenue.

When Yaritza looked up again, the ghost in the window had vanished, and so had Mr. Greene.

Yaritza decided she would vanish then, too.

Sylvia Plath and The Female Gothic Intersection

Misha Puello Brasil

Though Sylvia Plath is not traditionally considered a Gothic author or writer, there are many more intersections between Plath and the Gothic genre than people may think of. Imagery and themes of vampires, death, and the uncanny appear throughout her poetry and short fiction. Plath's life heavily affected the themes of her work such as her suicide attempts, the death of her father, and her ex-husband's infidelity. The societal and political conditions around Plath as a child and adult affected her work as well, with Plath having grown up in the 1940s and 1950s. Using inspiration from her life, Plath beautifully crafted poetry and prose using gothic ideas, themes, and elements. Plath fits into the Female Gothic subgenre, focusing on the horrors of domestic life as a woman in a patriarchal society and reflecting fears in her own life.

Sylvia Plath is seen as a figure of a young woman's adulthood. There are certain taboos associated with reading Sylvia Plath like how young girls with a copy of *Ariel* or *The Bell Jar* are seen as "sad girls." This is presumably in connection with the fact that Sylvia Plath committed suicide—a fact that overshadows her legacy—and that Plath often wrote about the death of her father and her grief, her divorce from Ted Hughes after he had an affair, and her trouble finding the balance between mother, woman, and writer. Plath is most well known for her confessional poetry; her name is one of the first to come up when the style is researched online. Ted overtook Plath's estate and became the owner of her work after her death, and while Plath and Hughes are both acknowledged as great poets and they helped each other in their craft, Plath wasn't regarded as highly during her lifetime. In pictures, she's seen sitting below or behind Ted, helping him with his work. She commented on being both wife and writer, while Hughes only spoke about his writing. This narrative was common for these times when women were expected to be wives and mothers and to let go of their careers. Once Plath had settled into domestic life, she struggled with her love for her family and her desire to be a great writer.

The Gothic genre is traditionally characterized by supernatural elements, ambiguous endings, eerie scenes and descriptions, death, romanticization of nature, and high emotions. There is usually a male protagonist and a damsel in distress, and women usually only serve as background figures if they're not in need of saving. Since the Gothic genre first emerged with Horace Walpole's *Castle of Otranto* in the eighteenth century, it has grown and branched out from its original elements. Settings were moved away from haunted houses, and different types of fears and monsters emerged. The Gothic genre was used to speak of the "unspeakable," like in Oscar Wilde's *The Picture of Dorian Gray*—which, during a time when homosexual relationships could land you in jail, hid homoerotic themes—and Toni Morrison's *Beloved,* which used the real-life horrors of racism and slavery to create the gruesome descriptions, scenes, and traumas within the narrative. When female authors started prominently entering the scene, the protagonists, heroes, and horrors of the stories changed as well.

The Female Gothic, a term coined by Ellen Moers, is a subgenre of Gothic literature written by women. The one thing all Gothic stories have in common is fear, but the fears of women are much different than those of men. Traditionally, stories from men will surround powerlessness in the face of a foreign enemy, the fear of oncoming death, or the balance of science and nature. The Female Gothic takes a different approach, focusing on the fears that accompany being a woman, the horrors that domestic life may bring, and the terrors that women experience but are pressured to keep quiet about due to societal conventions. Common settings are the home, often a bedroom or a kitchen, and themes usually surrounding confinement, control, unwanted or forbidden desires, and birth and motherhood. In *The Yellow Wallpaper* by Charlotte Perkins Gilman, a woman is confined to a room by her husband and brother for a "rest cure" as she slowly goes insane after suffering from postpartum depression, and even though she pleads for release, they believe they know better. Mary Shelley's *Frankenstein* can be seen as a metaphor for the trauma of birth and an infant's need for a caring figure. Both these stories are easily defined as Gothic, but more specifically, they fit within the Female Gothic genre because the fears are ones that women are usually subject to. In Gilman's story, the horrors are in not being believed to know what is best for your own self and being left in the care of a man who does not truly have your best interest at heart. The protagonist is left to her own devices and succumbs to her illness in her own home, the only place where she would otherwise have had power.

Sylvia Plath is not unfamiliar with writing about the unspoken nuances of being a woman. Though her poetry is not traditionally thought of as Gothic, when we adjust our lens to account for the themes of the Female Gothic, we can find many elements of it in Plath's work. In her *Literary Women* chapter titled "Female Gothic," Ellen Moers writes about Plath. "It was Plath herself, with her superb eye for the imagery of self-hatred, who renewed for poets—Anne Sexton, Adrienne Rich, Erica Jong, and many others—the grotesque tradition of Female Gothic. Her terror was not the monster, the goblin, or the freak, but the living corpse," she says, and then quotes Plath's poem "Lady Lazarus" (Moers 1976, 109–110).

Sylvia Plath wrote "Lady Lazarus" during an intense creative burst shortly before her death. The poem is regarded as one of her best and is one of her most famous confessional poems. The poem surrounds death and rebirth, and the narrator tells of her three past suicide attempts, each enacted every ten years like a ritual—all familiar to the Gothic. If connecting the poem to Plath's life, one can assume she's talking about her own past suicide attempts and continuation of life, but by separating the narrator from the author, we can see a different type of figure emerge. In lines eleven to fourteen of "Lady Lazarus," the speaker directly addresses her audience:

O my enemy

Do I terrify?—

The nose, the eye pits, the full set of teeth?

The sour breath (Plath, 11–14)

The speaker expects her audience to be unsettled and then follows with a description as to why: the decaying smell of death. Normal (decaying) human features are described, but the speaker is not exactly human, having been resurrected many times. Plath is intentional with her gore, as "Plath's Gothic ... walks the tightrope between extremes—spinster/whore, conformist domesticated mother/daring creative artist—and between life and death" (Wisker 2004, 104). She compares her skin to a "Nazi lampshade" (Plath, 5) and refers to her skin as a napkin that can be peeled off. The dramatic and gruesome comparisons add to the intensity of the poem. The tone is dramatic and almost theatrical, with phrases such as the opening line, "I have done it again" (Plath, 1). The narrator feels as if their resurrection is an obligatory performance and the pacing of the poem is slow and steady, each line having a heavy impact, leaving the readers with an eerie feeling. The poem finishes with our narrator being turned to ash:

Ash, ash—

You poke and stir.

Flesh, bone, there is nothing there— (Plath, 73–75)

Our narrator is then resurrected:

Herr God, Herr Lucifer

Beware

Beware.

Out of the ash

I rise with my red hair

And I eat men like air. (Plath, 79–84)

This supernatural resurrection falls into Gothic tropes, and the final line can be interpreted as the speaker getting revenge on those who had wronged her and asked her to perform. The repetition serves as a looming effect, where through the use of sound, readers can feel the chant that helps the speaker rise.

We can interpret that the obligatory resurrection is the performance that women put on in a patriarchal society. From the final line, we get the picture of a femme fatale. In Gothic literature, this is usually a mysterious and enchanting figure that will cause the destruction of men, but through further analysis, we can see that there's more to the femme fatale character than meets the eye. As Pagnoni Berns states, "If we undress her from the patriarchal-infused clothes of the fatidic 'bad girl,' what remains is a Gothic heroine desperate to take the reins of her own life ... alongside misogynistic fears, the 'bad girl' also embodies female desire for alternative models of subjectivity and physical agency" (Pagnoni Berns, 45). It's clear that the speaker of the poem is suffering all while performing for the audience, representing the role that women usually take on. One of the most memorable and impactful stanzas reads:

Dying

Is an art, like everything else.

I do it exceptionally well." (Plath, 43–45)

The sarcastic tone leans into the idea that the masquerade is second nature and something which needs to be crafted.

Sylvia Plath performed for much of her life, having to pull herself together to be a student, wife, daughter, and mother, even when she was suffering terribly. In her final days, when Sylvia was struggling the most, she still felt the need to perform, as seen in *Rough Magic: A Biography of Sylvia Plath*. "From her outburst, the source of Plath's anguish became obvious. She might have pretended not to be jealous of Assia—she had even borrowed a table from her, she told mother—yet Sylvia *was*, now as much as ever," the biography states (Alexander 1999, 324). Just like the women in the Female Gothic, Plath was conditioned to alter her composure, even when it came to "the other woman," Assia, for society and her children's sake. In *Sylvia Plath in the Female Gothic*, Brittany Clark writes, "Sylvia Plath's literary works might therefore be considered a seminal example of the Female Gothic tradition due to its confessional nature, which enables her to probe themes of confinement, patriarchal subjugation, and the endangerment of feminine sexuality with a profound and emotive force. Her poetry and prose are distinguished by a sense of immediacy and urgency that is uncommon in literature, enabling her to communicate the emotional fervor of her female characters' experiences in a raw and impactful manner" (Clark 2023, 43).

Plath does as many female Gothic writers do and writes fears that live among women, drawing from her own experience, bringing life to life, and transcribing those feelings.

Elements of the uncanny are also found within Plath's "Lady Lazarus." The uncanny is said to "arouse dread and horror" (Freud 1919, 219) because it "leads back to what is known of old and long familiar" (Freud 1919, 220). The idea is that fear is brought on by a sense of being familiar with say, a person or object, but never being able to precisely place it or relate to it. The uncanny figure is a recurring one in Gothic literature, especially in the Female Gothic like in Shirley Jackson's "The Beautiful Stranger." In Jackson's short story, a woman greets her husband as he gets home from a business trip and immediately takes him for an imposter—one more pleasant than her husband. They then go home to a house she barely recognizes as her own, and when she leaves to get him a gift, she gets lost on the way home and can't make out which home is hers. The speaker in Plath's poem "Lady Lazarus" has the elements of an uncanny figure. She refers to worms being picked out of her, her body decaying, and flesh rotting. Visuals of eye pits and full sets of teeth mimic that of a corpse, yet the narrator refers to herself as a smiling woman.

The uncanny is a great representation and vessel for the themes of the domestic Gothic. Domestic Gothic has to do with where the fears are rooted, either in the home or because of the effects of domesticity. "Cut" by Sylvia Plath describes a woman in what we can presume is her home as she cuts her finger and goes through altering sets of emotions. In the opening stanza of the poem, the narrator is exhilarated that her finger was cut. She then begins observing and analyzing her own thumb, describing it in vivid detail and like a foreign object:

A flap like a hat,

Dead white.

That red plush. (Plath, 6–8)

By the final line of the poem, the thumb is no longer claimed as "my" but referred to as "Thumb stump" (Plath, 39). The speaker no longer feels attached to her body, emotions, or thumb, and creates distance.

The speaker compares the features of her thumb to ordinary objects such as hinges or hats, and the short lines and direct language make the speaker seem alienated from the incident. It can be interpreted that the speaker had cut her own thumb in hopes of getting rid of some internal trouble:

I have taken a pill to kill

The thin

Papery feeling. (Plath, 24–26)

The speaker's detachment from her thumb arises from the uncanny feeling of being familiar but emotional. The speaker has suffered a separation from self when faced with internal struggles that are too ugly to face head-on. In *Gothic Studies*, Gina Wisker writes, "I would like to argue she utilizes the strategies, images and tropes of the literary Gothic and horror as metaphors to express hidden secrets, the undersides of our complacent everyday worlds. ... Plath develops the domestic Gothic, expressing the home-confined life of the housewife/mother. Imagery of split selves exposes the constructedness, the performativity of gendered roles, the oscillation between versions of self." (Wisker 2004, 104)

This pattern is repeated and amplified in "The Applicant," where the speaker is trying to sell his audience a wife. In this poem, we can see two things. First, in the narrative of this poem, women are not valued or thought of as equals to men. This is reminiscent of our own world and the world in which Plath grew up and was writing in. The article "a" is used instead of "the," signaling that the woman is replaceable and vast in quantity. Second, detachment from the woman is represented. No proper nouns are used to describe the woman, and the only other pronoun used to refer to her for the majority of the poem is "it," as in, "And do whatever you tell it" (Plath, 13). The woman is not seen as human, though she would have all the same features and abilities as one. Once again, the uncanny shows up in Plath's work.

When describing the "perks" of purchasing, the speaker says:

Empty? Empty. Here is a hand

To fill it and willing

To bring teacups and roll away headaches

And do whatever you tell it.

Will you marry it?

It is guaranteed. (Plath, 10–15)

These lines exemplify what is expected of a wife and what is promised to the speaker's audience if he goes through with the purchase. The wife is described as a tool to help fill a void and an object that will prove useful when in need of comfort or someone to boss around. The question of marriage, followed by a promise of customer satisfaction, alludes to how women, once married to men, are expected to care for the men without exception, doing everything the men ask. The salesman continues with his list of positives:

Will you marry it?

It is waterproof, shatterproof, proof

Against fire and bombs through the roof.

Believe me, they'll bury you in it. (Plath, 22–25)

The salesman is almost tempting the man to try to destroy the woman, finding some sort of sinister enjoyment in it. Especially in the 1960s, violence against women was more common in domestic situations since women were essentially powerless in their marriages. At the time, men were seen as the head of the household and they were the ones to be making decisions.

Finally, the salesman presents the woman to the buyer:

Come here, sweetie, out of the closet.

Well, what do you think of *that?*

Naked as paper to start (Plath, 28–30)

The speaker uses a term of endearment that is commonly said condescendingly by men. The salesman is directing the woman around and talking down to her. The first time that the woman is being acknowledged directly and is called by a name that isn't used for objects, the term "sweetie" is chosen. Usually a nickname for children, this infantilization serves to undermine any autonomy or sense of self the woman may have when being introduced. The italicization of "that" serves to represent an inflection of the salesman's voice when telling the audience to look at the woman. He is instructing the buyer to gawk at her, placing her value in her looks and using her for aesthetic purposes. The woman is referred to as naked and is compared to the inanimate object, paper. The sexualization of the woman further proves that the woman's position is a vulnerable one and she is being taken advantage of. The poem ends with the last two lines:

My boy, it's your last resort.

Will you marry it, marry it, marry it. (Plath, 39–40)

These lines bring attention to the fact that the man being offered this woman is not respected in the scenario either. In the beginning of the poem, the salesman infers that his usual clientele is desperate or missing something—whether it's metaphorical or physical—and at the end of the poem, he refers to the audience as "boy" and tells him that he has no other options. In the world that Plath created, neither the man or the woman is valued, and instead the salesman is the only one with the upper hand.

"The Applicant" centers around themes of objectification, gender roles, and domesticity. In this narrative, marriage is portrayed in a negative light, focusing on the confinement and the roles the spouses are then expected to complete. The salesman, who serves as a representative of societal institutions, expectations, and capitalism, condenses both the man and the woman into buyer and merchandise. The uncanny is brought up once again through the representation of the women. The woman is determined to be an object and nothing more, her only reason for existence being to be sold and to serve. The woman is compared to a "living doll" (Plath, 33), an intimate being that pretends to be human. Though, the woman is a human being who is positioned as an object due to the poem's circumstances. On Plath and using the Female Gothic to capture her experience, Brittany Clark writes, "Gothic elements in Plath's oeuvre, such as the recurrent imagery of death, decay, the uncanny, and the supernatural, accentuate the oppressive nature of the American patriarchal society and the struggle for autonomy and agency experienced by women … Plath creates a sense of unease and discomfort that is associated with Gothic literature. This serves to draw attention to the oppressive nature of patriarchal societies more generally as well as the struggles faced by women within these societies (Clark 2023, 42)."

During the time when Sylvia Plath had finished writing "The Applicant," she was also settling her separation from Ted Hughes. As seen in *Rough Magic*, "Plath chose to write such a poem on the 11th, the date that, essentially, marked the end of her marriage to Ted Hughes" (Alexander 2003, 299).

Plath drew from her real-life experiences and troubles to write one of her most famous and controversial poems, "Daddy." Plath's father died when she was eight years old, and from that time on, Plath struggled to come to terms with what that meant. Many of Plath's poems are aimed at or centered around her father, earning her the stereotype of having "daddy issues." In "Daddy," Plath fights to let go of the memory of her father and the weight that his death carries in her life, but in the end, she ends up marrying a man who she says resembles her father. The most obvious Gothic feature of "Daddy" is the mentioning of vampires, a classic Gothic monster. Repeating the themes of the uncanny, vampires resemble humans as that was once their form, but they undergo a transformation that turns them into something that needs to feed off of others and is inherently harmful. "Daddy" explores how unresolved traumas reemerge and discusses marriage and the oppression that can follow it.

"Daddy" falls under the Gothic genre by discussing death, the process of letting go of that trauma to move on with your life, and providing vivid and brutal images and metaphors. The death of her father haunts the narrator, and she struggles to feel connected to him. Plath makes references to Nazis and the Holocaust, not to compare the grief but to express the impact the event had on her life. Wisker writes "Writing from the recesses of our dark imaginings, Plath brings us haunted, terrible figures of our shared fears ... Plath slices open, exposes, dramatizes those terrors in order to face them and refuse their power. Knowing them, she and we feel we can master them and come to some arrangement. They will always be lurking, but perhaps, if you recognize them, you too will not be theirs, quite yet (Wisker 2004, 104).

Though Wisker was not speaking specifically on Plath's tendency to compare her troubles to the Holocaust, the quote speaks to Plath's intentions and the effects of the poem.

Though "Daddy" pulls from Plath's real life, the poem's Gothic elements allow it to be read as a general story of grief. Plath writes:

Daddy, I have had to kill you.

You died before I had time— (Plath, 6–7)

It later refers to the father as a vampire. The lines speak to Plath having to get rid of the memories of her father since she does not have many memories of him to work with. If we interpret the line more metaphorically, we can understand that the narrator was not able to save their father before he turned into a vampire, forcing her to kill him. This can be understood as a literal vampire or the vampire as a representation of the draining effect of not being able to properly mourn her father. The line "Ghastly statue with one gray toe" (Plath, 9) refers to Plath's father's diabetes—diabetes sometimes resulting in a lost toe—and her father's looming but untouchable presence. Even when he was in the home and alive, Plath was mostly kept separate from her father, and once he got sick, she was no longer able to connect with him. While she admired and loved her father, hence the statue, she was unable to truly experience his presence. The line can also be understood as the memory of the father being so distant and unstable that the representation of that memory—the statue—is no longer looking well and starting to break apart.

The speaker of the poem goes on to bring up her father's German heritage and brings in Nazis, the Holocaust, and imagery of a swastika:

Not God but a swastika

So black no sky could squeak through. Every woman adores a Fascist,

The boot in the face, the brute

Brute heart of a brute like you. (Plath, 46–50)

The first line of the quote details exactly what light the speaker views their father in. Unlike God, where worshipers follow His word and think of Him as an all-powerful entity that can do no harm, the speaker poses her father as a controlling and oppressive figure of terror and cruelty. She positions his memory as so macabre that there can be no positives associated with it. The following lines lead readers into the next section of the poem, where the speaker is seen repeating cycles and marrying a man that she says has the same effect on her as her father. The narrator has an obsession with her father and his death, whether it be suffering because of it or trying to get rid of it.

The image of the vampire is brought up again, and explicitly for the first time towards the endings of the poem:

If I've killed one man, I've killed two—

The vampire who said he was you

And drank my blood for a year,

Seven years, if you want to know,

Daddy, you can lie back down now. (Plath, 71–75)

Parallels between the husband and the father are once again drawn. The speaker tells her father that she let the man into her life under the guise that he would amount to the pleasant memory of the father, but as has been established, memory of the father cannot be retrieved with positive emotions, so it changes to a nasty, gruesome thing. The love, for seven years, drained the speaker. When the speaker commands the father to lie down, we can assume she is coming to terms with the death of her father and choosing to let it go, or alternatively, we can determine that she is giving up her battle and succumbing to forgetting his memory.

Suicide is another topic brought up and discussed in "Daddy" when Plath writes:

At twenty I tried to die

And get back, back, back to you.

I thought even the bones would do.

But they pulled me out the sack,

And they stuck me together with glue. (Plath, 58–62)

With this, Plath is discussing her suicide attempt in her twenties. Separating the speaker from Plath, we see Gothic themes of death and suicide come back up, and a vivid image of a human body being harshly glued back together is used. The speaker states that, at the time, they would have settled to be close to the bones of her father, but after a failed suicide attempt, she was broken and had to undergo unwelcome formed or reparation. The intense, macabre scenes described throughout "Daddy" and the powerful emotion of the piece make for a Gothic poem, or at least a poem with many Gothic elements.

Plath's use of Gothic elements not only appears in her poetry, but also in her short stories. While arguments can be made for her short stories such as "Sunday at the Mintons" and "The Fifty-Ninth Bear," mostly because of the deaths and focus on the repressed female struggle, "Johnny Panic and The Bible of Dreams" is her short story that fits the Gothic genre the most. The story includes supernatural elements, where the protagonist is a transcriber of people's dreams. It has an overall ambiguous feeling where we follow what could be presumed as an unreliable narrator, and there are scenes of terror when it comes to the dreams transcribed and the electroshock therapy the protagonist receives in the end. Dreams and nightmares are a common motif in Gothic literature, and Johnny Panic represents fear. Nature is described within the short story, too, with the narrator going up to the roof at 3 a.m., the witching hour, and saying there's "some witchy invisible push and here and there in the husks of stone and brick I see a light. Most of all, though, I feel the city sleeping" (Plath, 157). Nature in this scene is personified and under the influence of the unknown. Parallels between Plath's life and "Johnny Panic and The Bible of Dreams" can be found, as both Plath and the protagonist undergo terrifying electroshock treatment, Plath having been traumatized by hers.

Plath fits into the Gothic genre, and more specifically, the Female Gothic subgenre, by using her real-life experiences and troubles to create stories of fear stemming from her day-to-day realities. Sylvia Plath uses ideas of the uncanny figure, the femme fatale, and domestic horror to create narratives and scenes where women can feel seen and heard. Plath's work does not need to be analyzed through the Gothic lens to be understood or appreciated, but doing so adds a layer that often gets overlooked. Plath was often reduced, even if it was to something great like a marvelous poet. She had many happy moments in life and many tragic ones, and she was interested in both the beautiful and the ugly, having written about her experiences seeing live births, corpses, and fetuses in jars. Sylvia Plath is regarded as a confessional poet and feminist writer, but through these things, she also dabbles in the Female Gothic genre.

Works Cited

Alexander, Paul. *Rough Magic: A biography of Sylvia Plath*. Da Capo Press, 2003.

Clark, Brittany. "'Something Beautiful but Annihilating:' Sylvia Plath and the Female Gothic," MA Thesis. Texas Tech University, 2023.

Freud, Sigmund, and James Strachey. *The Uncanny*. Imago, 1919.

Moers, Ellen. *Literary Women*. Oxford University Press, 1976.

Pagnoni Berns, Fernando Gabriel. "Deconstructing the Femme Fatale." *A Critical Companion to Robert Zemeckis*, 47–58. Lexington Books, 2020.

Plath, Sylvia. *Everyman's Library pocket poets: Poems*. Alfred K. Knopf, 1998.

———. *Johnny Panic and The Bible of Dreams*. HarperCollins, 2000.

Wisker, Gina. "Viciousness in the Kitchen: Sylvia Plath's Gothic." *Gothic Studies* 6, no. 1 (May 2004): 103–17.

11:07 Thoughts
Chardonnae Simpson

I will always question the sweetness you taste in my caramel

Why you compare my laugh to celestial kisses

Why you kiss my forehead in my moments of insanity

Why your hand hugs mine perfectly like winter gloves in a Park Avenue winter

Why you meet my impulses with calmness

Why you never let me quit this game the two of us call love

I will always wonder why you love me for exactly who I am

Between the cracks and crevices

The real me

I will always wonder

THE ART OF LETTING GO

Madhuri Pawar

I scan myself as I see my reflection in the mirror,
I have difficulty finding a clear slate to lay eyes on.
It's hard to tell what's stained, the mirror, or me?

I try touching the stained marks. To my surprise,
I touch my bosom and pelvis. I try erasing them,
but end up scratching off my skin.

I see blood marks from my scratches,
completely unaware of how they would reach between
my legs.
I don't recall anything, except feeling lonely,
abandoned, or dented.

Who called me out?
Who led me out?
Who passed me out?
Who ripped me out?

I stand in front of the mirror gawking at my physique,
Tracing the cuts on my face that no longer allow it to be
pretty.
It's been hours. I've been trying to find out what went
wrong.

I see pitch darkness in my deep brown eyes.
Did he not have mercy hearing me wail for help?
Did he not have mercy using his man-strength on my
slender wrists?

And now I recall it all.

I begin to wash myself in front of the mirror without water,

to cover myself under the duvet.

Cut myself to end it all.

Slit my slender wrists so that they don't have to face man-strength ever.

I guess this is the art of letting go.

Letting yourself go, so that you don't have to face anything that breaks you.

Letting yourself go, so that you forever wash away the blood between your legs.

Letting yourself go, so that you don't stand in front of stained mirrors.

I finally take a deep breath and hear a shattering noise.

I break the stained mirror and myself together.

That is *the art of letting go!*

The Skyline That Built Me

Amber Grell

This place built around me
While I built within
The roots I planted
Are where this new me begins.

The curves of the shadows
Pulling at my spine
As I stand up straighter
And slip further from being kind.

There's wear and tear
From place to place
But I see the same
From the lines on my face.

The City is always changing
Yet never faster than me
The City is always running
Yet neither of us are free.

From my tears to the sea,
The salt simultaneously
Bands together
To forever raise me.

This will always be
The skyline that built me.

Biography of John Hersey

Jana Lewis

John Hersey was born to missionaries in Tientsin, China in 1914, but his ancestry reaches back to Colonial America.[1] Chinese was one of the first languages he learned, along with English. At the age of ten, Hersey moved to the United States with his family and attended school, eventually entering Yale and Cambridge.[2] After graduating, Hersey became a foreign correspondent for *Time* and *Life* magazines in 1936, covering events in Asia, Italy, and the Soviet Union for a decade. During this time, he also began writing novels. In 1944, he won the Pulitzer Prize for *A Bell for Adano,* a novel he wrote about the Allied occupation of Sicily during World War II (WWII).[3]

One of Hersey's best-known pieces is the article he wrote for *The New Yorker* in 1946, "Hiroshima," which filled the magazine. The magazine even announced that the issue would be entirely devoted to this article and added an introduction to warn readers of the level of human suffering they were about to encounter. "Hiroshima" was released on August 31, 1946 and describes the sites Hersey saw when he visited the city as well as the stories of six of the survivors of the atomic bomb. *The New Yorker* staff believed that the people needed to understand the devastation of the bomb. "Hersey's graphic and gut-wrenching description of the misery he encountered on Hiroshima offered what officials could not: the human cost of the bomb," said historian Stephanie Hinnerschitz.[4] Hersey had been to the war zone and wrote about what most other journalists did not. He also found a way to do it in a way that made his writing timeless.[5] Hersey wanted

1 Nicholas Lemann, "John Hersey and the Art of Fact," *The New Yorker*, April 22, 2019. https://www.newyorker.com/magazine/2019/04/29/john-hersey-and-the-art-of-fact.
2 John Hersey, "It Happened in History," *American Society of Authors and Writers.* Accessed January 15, 2025. https://amsaw.org/amsaw-ithappenedinhistory-061704-hersey.html.
3 Stephanie Hinnershitz, "The Legacy of John Hersey's 'Hiroshima': *The National WWII Museum: New Orleans,*" The National WWII Museum | New Orleans. August 20, 2021. https://www.nationalww2museum.org/war/articles/john-herseys-hiroshima-1946.
4 Ibid.
5 Lemann, "John Hersey and the Art of Fact."

the readers to know what these survivors saw, heard, smelled, and felt. He wanted readers to know what people endured from before the bomb dropped to a year later. Hersey's writing style gave depth to the story and is described as "unembellished language that makes his writing so haunting."[6] Survivors reported that they never heard the bomb at all, only a plane flying overhead followed by a bright flash of light which then sent people, buildings, and earth flying. A fisherman reported hearing a massive explosion from twenty miles away.[7] Hersey didn't alter any of the survivors' descriptions and went for the graphic detail that effectively made his point. Hersey was also able to comment on the lasting effects on the survivors like radiation sickness, as he wrote the article a year after the bomb was dropped.[8]

Hersey's endeavor to show the world the harsh realities of what it was like to drop an atomic bomb broke sales records for *The New Yorker*. All 300,000 copies printed sold out quickly, leading to the article being printed in a book form.[9] Not only was this a successful piece for Hersey, but it also reflected a turning point for *The New Yorker* which was transitioning out of its "founding era" and moving more toward mature content that was more morally engaging.[10]

Later in life, Hersey became a writing teacher at Yale from 1965 to 1984. In 1980, he wrote an article for *The Yale Review* called "The Legend on the License" where he argued that nonfiction writers were beginning to blur the lines between fact and fiction, something he considered to be a violation of the one sacred rule of journalism. However, he was later accused of plagiarizing some of this content and apologized for potentially leaving out attributions for some source material.[11] It is possible that Hersey may have created the concept of the nonfiction novel, even if the term wasn't yet established.[12]

---

6 Hinnershitz, "The Legacy of John Hersey's 'Hiroshima': The National WWII Museum: New Orleans,"
7 John Hersey, "Hiroshima," *The New Yorker*, August 23, 1946, https://www.newyorker.com/magazine/1946/08/31/hiroshima.
8 Hinnershitz, "The Legacy of John Hersey's 'Hiroshima': The National WWII Museum: New Orleans,
9 Ibid.
10 Lemann, "John Hersey and the Art of Fact."
11 Ibid.
12 Ibid.

Contribution to the Magazine Industry

John Hersey was instrumental to the magazine industry because he created a new way of reporting information, though it wasn't fully labeled at the time. Hersey was dedicated to his writing, focusing on details and getting the story right, but he also pushed the boundaries of what a magazine would be comfortable printing. Considering that Hersey spent the earliest years of his life growing up in a missionary capacity in China, then eventually took a job as a foreign correspondent, his world view was different from most journalists in America. He was able and willing to write about world problems rather than entertainment and superficial topics. His first magazine job was as a foreign correspondent in WWII in China and Japan. Because he was in Asia during the war, Hersey saw first-hand what war was really like and recognized that the public was not shown this side of the conflict. Hersey was even recognized for helping with the evacuation of wounded American soldiers from Guadalcanal,[13] so it is clear that he did not shy away from horror. When the atomic bomb was dropped, he knew that people needed to realize how destructive it was on a human level to ensure that it was never done again. All that the public would see from the government was censored material focusing on why it was dropped and how it achieved the goal of ending the war. The recognition of what it did to the civilians who were left behind was always left out. With Hersey's creation of nonfiction writing, it became possible for magazine journalists to write about serious situations and events. He proved that the public wanted this type of content and was willing to buy it.

Impact and Influence

I will admit, when starting out I had never heard of John Hersey. The name "Hiroshima" obviously caught my eye, but reading his story was eye-opening. The content he wrote about was unfiltered and real and painted a picture of America with all the dirt that the government wanted to hide. Journalism had a rule about staying

---

13 Nick Turse, "John Hersey, Hiroshima and the End of World," *Fair Observer.* October 5, 2020. https://www.fairobserver.com/region/north_america/nick-turse-hiroshima-atomic-bomb-world-war-ii-john-hersey-world-history-news-79173/#.

unbiased in reporting, but Hersey pushed that to another level. His writing encouraged journalists to not be intimidated by corporate or governmental power. Not everything America did during WWII was positive, and some could say that nothing justified the dropping of the atomic bomb on two cities in Japan. Through this type of reporting, journalists were given the freedom to find ways of examining the world around them without restriction and talk about the negatives of the US. That is a lasting trait today, with reporters everywhere releasing stories in print and on television talking about riots in the streets, issues with gun control, the negatives of war, and abortion bans. People have become numb to the devastation that always happens around the world, and the emotion behind the stories can not only sell a magazine but, more importantly, bring greater attention to issues that need to be addressed.

Works Cited

Hersey, John. "Hiroshima," *The New Yorker*, August 23, 1946, https://www.newyorker.com/magazine/1946/08/31/hiroshima.

———. "It Happened in History," *American Society of Authors and Writers*. Accessed January 15, 2025. https://amsaw.org/amsaw-ithappenedinhistory-061704-hersey.html.

Hinnershitz, Stephanie. "The Legacy of John Hersey's 'Hiroshima': *The National WWII Museum: New Orleans*," The National WWII Museum | New Orleans. August 20, 2021. https://www.national ww2museum.org/war/articles/john-herseys-hiroshima-1946.

Lemann, Nicholas. "John Hersey and the Art of Fact," *The New Yorker*, April 22, 2019. https://www.newyorker.com/magazine/2019/04/29/john-hersey-and-the-art-of-fact.

Turse, Nick. "John Hersey, Hiroshima and the End of World," *Fair Observer*. October 5, 2020. https://www.fairobserver.com/region/north_america/nick-turse-hiroshima-atomic-bomb-world-war-ii-john-hersey-world-history-news-79173/#.

Still Life with Ham

Jack Niemczyk

A bead of sweat drips down my face, as I am regretting the extra layer I threw on to brace the cold of Museum Drive, thinking the coat check would be open once again. I taste the eight-dollar iced chai that not only almost gave me hypothermia, but that I had to toss while half full, or half empty depending on your view. But no matter, I am at The Met! I put in my AirPods and slowly listened to the soft jazz being emitted from the minuscule speakers. As I stare into the abyss of the folks who call themselves artsy, I begin making my way through the crowd of trench coats, turtlenecks, and any other "museum outfit" that is presented by those who only go to these palaces of culture to say, "Hey look what I did today!" But hey, am I any different as I roleplay as the main character while wholly obtaining obscurity? Now, I am no museum snob. I love art and museums, but at times the cost of having to weave through these people is more striking than the art itself. The characters that often reek of pretension and the bored child all under one roof are tantalizing for my senses. I make my way up the grand stairs slowly, listening to any and all conversations. I stroll into the impressionist's gallery. I look at these paintings I have seen ad-nauseum, searching for a detail or a texture that I must have missed in Monet's *Bridge Over Waterlilies*. Making my way around, never spending too much time at any specific work, I suddenly stop—*The Swan* by Yehuda Hanani rings through my head. I stare, almost blankly at a painting I never seemed to notice. A Rousseau. An eighteenth century painting showing nothing but a messy yet seemingly perfect set table. A dark faded wallpaper hugs the backdrop as a wrinkly white tablecloth draws the eye into the center. A slab of meat, sitting right in the center of the table draws the eye with its fleshy color and green garnish springing out atop it. Surrounded by a bottle of olive oil, a nice chianti, a plate of buttered bread, a knife, and a letter. The inscription, almost too fine to read. A gold frame hugs this snapshot of life, standing out from the white walls, yet somehow blending in. This grey toned dining setup is so simple, so serene, and yet almost cynical in nature. I was drawn in, staring at this gorgeous painting so aptly, and almost wittingly, named *Still Life with Ham*. I am not sure why this certain piece drew me in, or why I had never taken time to gaze upon this porked painting. Perhaps it was that fact that food was depicted. After all, it was three in the afternoon and all I had was half of an iced chai. Perhaps it was because it was a slab of meat. There are plenty of jokes there. Or perhaps it was because I saw myself through Rousseau's work. Strangely enough, this gorgeous painting had a humor about it. It didn't take itself too seriously. In gallery 810, surrounded by portraits of beautiful women and towering mountain ranges, in one corner of the room sits a ham. Nothing too complex and yet beautiful in its own nature. The juxtaposition of the olive colors dripping through the backdrop as the muted pinks of the ham create the focal point in a sensual yet silly way. The presence of the unknown around the letter so perfectly perched above the worn-down china. Perhaps in this painting, I saw a true snapshot of life, and that is why I was drawn to it. I saw a simple front with a world of thought and care beyond its pigmented façade. A wine bottle, half full or half empty, perched right next to the perfect ham. A feeling of nostalgia and warmth created by this dull color palette embalms the viewer in a strange grey area of normalcy. Perhaps beyond just a still life painting, Rousseau is showing a still, serene life. A life where the table isn't perfectly set, the china happens to be chipped, and the colors may be dull, but it is still life. Still life … with ham.

Picnic Overlooking the Harbor

Misha Puello Brasil

You can pinpoint the moment
when a man realizes
he has fallen in love with you.

The sky goes dark,
planes get mistaken for stars,
and the harbor crawls out of bed.
Arousal of the feeling comes
into his tearful eyes,
wide with amazement,
and a sprinkle of fear.

Notice the anticipative opening
of the cherry blossom:
his lungs taking in
the thick, unfamiliar air,
his quivering bottom lip.

He's never looked
so unguarded, so honest.

You feel his warmth
almost heal you,
his touch pacific and tender.

He kisses you like a poem would,
all you can do is gloam.

The crickets play
their favorite concerto,
and the buoy heaves.

Finally commensurate, he says,
"I never thought I could love a girl like this."

Small Garden Files

Chardonnae Simpson

Relieve me the way the sun relieves the moon from its night shift

Give me room to breathe and swim around the shark tank

How will I know who I want to be if I'm constantly suffocated by who I was?

I want to reach a new altitude of free

Not having to cross my T's or dot my I's

Dissect my heart and weed out all the dead flowers

Life is an endless opportunity to weed out all the dead flowers

Show me that blossoms like me can and will grow back after they have been stepped on

I owe it to myself as much

I will reach a point where a footprint on my malleable spine won't send me into overdrive

But will strengthen me for whatever is to come

Between the Woods and the Mansion

Emily Jones

My daily life after school was monotonous with barking dogs and gravel still crackling in my head. Every day, I had the chore of taking my grandmother's two little Scotties, with their crusty beards and invincible attitudes, around the gaggle of houses behind my mother's home. If you took a left out past the tall, rickety old fence that was overgrown with weeds and seemed to stretch with the trees in the wind, you would find a long fading strip of grass sprawling down next to the gravel road. The lane was between a row of identical houses with chain-link fences to the left and to the right and dense thickets of oak trees and unknown bushes. It was a government-owned, forgotten piece of home. This became my stage for the adventures in my head and the energy in my bones.

Over the years, a moat had developed, protecting the extravagant homes too big for their own good. The ditch was too wide for me to jump but small enough to seem tempting. A young, slim, black pit bull made his dissatisfaction loud as I ran laps up and down the soft grass with the Scotties following behind. They jumped and hopped as the blades were too big for their small legs to cut through. I did not hold the leash, but they did not think of running away. No flowers dared to bloom in the strip, only little green weeds and bold dandelions. The strip stretched past eight different houses and was considered private, as a sewage pipe center was located by the sidewalk, though I rarely ever saw anyone wandering around. I always felt tiny among the upper-middle class mansions and the ramshackle houses on the other side, past the angled oak trees. My eyes were caught by the light blue of the sky, and my brain wondered how big the world could be.

If you stared down the green lane, you would find it cut off by a black tar road and gray cement sidewalk, surrounded by more homes that blended the more you looked. The Scotties nipped and sniffed at the little lines of grass, attempting to find any bit of information on the area they could; who came, who went, who peed on the tree. Brushing the soft dirt, their beards gathered all sorts of grime and muck crawling with microscopic creatures. Raccoons, deer, a rare fox, and the occasional gopher resided on the woods side of the lane. They were patient neighbors, waiting for the moment to peek their heads out of the green and move on to bigger pastures. I wanted to journey along with them, writing lists of supplies to pack away and preparing myself to trudge to a faraway train station. The woods had become a popular spot because further past some shacks and my house, there was a small creek dug deep in the ground. Ducks and frogs called it home, disturbed only by children who sought to find the rare gemstone or possible fossil lurking within the bed. I lingered in the trees for as long as I could until I felt the pressure to bring my little companions back to their rightful place.

As ticks attempted to climb under my pant cuffs and wool socks, I imagined myself in a place wholly unknown and thought up different threats that lurked on either side with my faithful protectors circling my sneakers. Not wanting to go back, I wished for some journey to embark on or a stranger to investigate. I stared into the treeline, expecting the thump of some giant creature to come stomping down. If I went home, all that waited was my couch that couldn't hold a candle to the green lane offering all kinds of excitement to a little girl. There was no real fear of getting kicked out, but my mind still felt like I was on the edge of some boundary, a place I was not supposed to be. A red trespassing sign, hung by one rusted nail on a telephone pole planted right before the grass began, warned all who dared venture around. The poles ran electricity between the sea of houses with children chattering to their friends about their daily stories. They told each other of spooky eyes looking through their second-story windows, rumors believing the old math teacher to be a possible witch, and what animal they wanted to catch within the boundary of the woods. As I stared within the cracks of the telephone poles, imagining worms or some beetle burrowing deep inside for a home, I caught flashes of electricity running around the wires strung along.

The summer before my senior year, a developer began work on another oversized home next to the gravel path and in front of the green lane, though the area behind was still considered off-limits. Most would struggle to understand the current layout of the strip, but when you're standing between the fading gravel and growing grass, it all feels in order. It was the area I was allowed to trek with no parental supervision. My mother worried that my inability to take out my headphones would make me the ultimate prey. However, they set the atmosphere for my stage. They signaled the background of the stories within my head.

During the night, in my beige bedroom with fantasy novels strewn about, I could look out past the treetops and think of the creatures roaming around, imagining a small deer traversing out down the lane, looking for a place to call its home. These were the hours the inhabitants of the forest could travel, and I was not one of them. All I was allowed was the safety of the far-in-between street lights with my tiny guardians. As I stood under their umbrellas of light, I stared into the darkness beyond, wondering what kind of animals were making their journeys and whether they would let me tag along under the dome of stars. They would say, "Step out onto the dark plane led only by the fires up in the sky and the knowledge of something further beyond."

A Productive Day

Jack Niemczyk

Ruby met me downtown at 1 p.m.

We wanted to do work

It's Presidents' Day so we have nothing, but time

She needed to write her thesis

Me, my novel

—*But he wasn't in Rehab, he was staying with Lilly Bird*

We were quickly derailed

—*And he owes her 8,000 dollars*

We sit, hidden from the glacial wind tunnel that is
Fourth Avenue in February

My chamomile tea fogs my glasses as I hang onto Ruby's
every word

—*Who are we to judge*

We conclude and become immersed into our
prospective work.

The tap of keys erupts over the soft disco that provides
the ambiance for this cafe

Yet just as quickly as it began, it ends

Our eyes lock again and we distract ourselves from the
work we have to do

A sea of *"No way"*

And *"she's married?"*

"With her father?"

Pour out of our mouths as our work becomes a memory
and we indulge in the age-old tradition of gossip

It's 4 p.m. now
Too early for some wine, too late for another coffee
But perhaps we will indulge
For the sake of our work

We order two glasses of red
And some olives
Just to take the edge off

We work for ten more minutes
I finished a chapter, she finished a thought
Just in time for our saccharin beverages arrive
And once again we fall back into the ritual
—*Oh but they will never work out*

B.L.A.D.E.

James La Barbera

(Fall, September. In a room with four walls, a metal object rests atop a table. George, late twenties, on stage, sitting at the table with the object, staring at it and speaking to himself. On a stage, there are rows of chairs where an audience can look through windows.)

GEORGE. Well here we are, sitting here. I'm looking at you and giving you power. Power to do what?

Cause **B**lood to drip because you are sharp?

Cause a **L**oss of time and **L**oss of space from being used?

Cause an underlying Addiction to flare up and be hidden?

Give you power to be **D**angerous or **D**amaging to an already fragile consumer?

Give power to the **E**xperience of disempowerment and **E**xecute a life worth living?

Why is something so small able to cause so much thought behind closed doors, derail a life of growth, and challenge to recruit new ones with past desires?

A pen is mightier than a sword, but a sword can hold much more weight than a simple ***blade*** like you! *(Takes a long breath and starts itching his wrist.)*

Why do I give you power? You are nothing but a piece of metal. I hold you, and there is weight. I toss you around and cut things like meat. You, on the other hand, know exactly when to speak back. Are your wrists itchy again? How's your inner thighs? Do you have that pulsating feeling, are you shaking your wrist out?

Then, drip drip drip, Blood dripping like a broken faucet. I know I am the one in control, and I have the ability to not draw blood, but you're taunting and echoing in my head and praying on my weak mindset.

Then you know I enjoy it, seeing the color red, seeing how thick it is, watching it drip and pour out—the weird feeling of warmth wrapped around me like a hug that *feels nice.*

The feeling of seeing your own blood spill compared to seeing an action or gorey film isn't nauseating and isn't gross, and you know me so well; you are that voice in my head, listening to emotions behind the hurt and the numbness and the desire to feel something. Which is why you call out when I am at my lowest, why I am at the pivotal point of losing a war inside my head. *(Stands up from his chair, walks around the table and starts to circle it.)*

Losing a war inside my head or a general fight every day to just keep up with the normalcy of society. The secrets that no one needs to know you pray on. The long days at work, the joy and warmth I get by helping people or seeing friends—you take it away. The sunshine I hold so dear and the desire to stand there is always blocked when I hear your whispers.

The loss of emotion, the loss of strength, the loss of even hope. You crush everything; you push everyone away. Make everything out of the coldness of your touch and the warmth it brings after. The heat of your hands wrapping around my legs and arms, the need that you make me feel. The need I should get from myself or someone else, but I get it from you. The loss of time and space between the lines Etch-A-Sketch'ed across my arms and legs, similar to the suicide note that was never written and the time that I would have missed out on. *(Loses his tempo and decides to pull out a chair from the table and sit.)*

The Addictive personalities you carry inside my head are terrifyingly enjoyable. Invoking and hazardous. The way a sip of a vodka soda or pull from a joint laced with the potential of silencing your voice, changing your presence around me. The hazy clouds of darkness get brighter and lighter. The bubble of joy comes around for a limited amount of time due to the level of vices I carry. The twelve steps of addition are acceptance and I want to accept you, but I don't know how to accept the elephant stepping on my chest, the nose made of lies and secrets around my neck, the broken glass

I wear as shoes, and even the smile I wear as a mask to hide the person trying to get out.

The biggest addition that you carry, with your compassionate words and the ideology of rescuing me, is that small window of pressure when you collide with my skin, releasing everything that's hiding under the surface, and the magnetic pull to iron coated in red paint. *(Takes a deep breath and looks out into the audience as the audience sits still in silence. He exhales.)*

To say that you can be **D**angerous or **D**amaging is the understatement of all time. The way you can damage the fragility I keep dear. The sanctity of my mind and the spirit within it cry out every time you look my way. The feel in my hand, one slippery slope away from damaging the lives around me. You hold too much power, and the extent of how much I do allow is deafening. That slippery slope is contagious and fun to play with. I sometimes don't realize the depth of your touch, the breath you carry that can even overpower to almost eliminate my own in its wake. The danger you possess is outstanding and remarkable, which makes me question how good you are sometimes and how wrong it makes me feel. The hollowness of the shell you cut into to give way to the glorious reward you seek is at times admirable as well. *Why* does it feel so good but so bad at the same time? That thrill of living on the edge—to know that you really aren't living at all—until that same warm, burning feeling against my already lined skin is so enticing that I won't let you stop pushing me closer and closer to that dark pit. Six feet or six lines—sometimes it doesn't even matter.

(At times, sniffles are heard from the audience in the background. Then George begins to weep slowly as he continues.)

GEORGE. The **E**xperience of disempowerment is gratifyingly sound. The knowledge of how this experience in my life has changed me so greatly created the mask I have worn to hide the crazy truth. Crazy is an understatement. The mechanics of a robot are my living experience the moment I allowed you in it. The darkness that followed and the feeling of emptiness were crushing. The rock that is always in my throat every time I speak a lie to cover up the pain inside and the silence that lingers after I push everyone away. You made me experience what it really means to be alone and how compulsive you are. The desire to be rid of you and to ask for someone to look past the mask and see the real me, or allow the people in long enough to see the scars that line my mind and my body. This is not a wish I want to grant on even the worst of thy enemies. You are like the Executioner's blade of a life that isn't worth living. The executioner that follows you around during the day and holds you into place at night. The executioner that won't allow for any objections from a crowd of one or a crowd of many. I have given you a voice, a body, a feeling; I have made you valid and gave you meaning. The only meaning you've given me in return is to allow you once and for all to do your job. *(Breaks into tears, grabs the blade in hand, rolls up his sleeve and places the blade against his skin, showing everyone outside the room his arms for the first time.)*

How dare you! How dare you possess me, taunt me, and even convince me that you little piece of metal should have a say in my life? You don't own me anymore. After today, you will no longer have a body to call your own or taste the red candy hiding behind the broken shell you've carved into for way too long. I am finished! I choose me! I choose the air I breathe, despite how shallow it can be. I choose the way people want to be in my life compared to walking away every time I say I'm fine when I am not. I choose life! *(Removes the **blade** from his wrist, and throws it across the room; the lights start to dim and the blade hits the ground.)*

I choose life!

Echoes

James La Barbera

(Inside a small coffee shop, open mic night. Henry, mid-twenties, dressed in comfortable clothes, on stage. Lights are on, and Henry walks on stage, sits on a stool facing the audience with a batter bottle in hand, center forward.)

HENRY. *(Takes a sip of water.)* Echoes of a voice are sometimes all we hear when. To have a voice is a powerful tool in anyone's arsenal. It is our one muscle that we constantly use without question, but when we are questioned and put into a box, a corner, and shoved to a point where we no longer can handle what is in front of us, that's when the voice becomes an echo. The echo itself is something that vibrates through your mind, ricocheting through the thoughts and feelings and fears of being mistreated, misunderstood, or considered rude.

But echoes can come in all ways and in all thoughts. Memories, past trauma, happy moments, movie or book quotes, things that resonate with you as a person, and you as the ball of energy people call a soul. *(Takes a breath, drinks some water, and continues.)*

Echoes are memories that keep repeating on and on and on in your head, so much that past conversations become ever-present instead of distant memories that should be closed off or forgotten about. Seconds, minutes, hours, days, months, years—echoes last for an eternity inside the gray matter. Some echoes are louder than others, and then those loud ones become our consciousness alongside dreams. *(Takes a breath, drinks some water, and continues.)*

Dreams have echoes as well; they make us feel this déjà vu moment when scenes recur inside that dreamscape and leak into the consciousness. The fun part is this déjà vu moment, because echoes, like premonitions, can occur in the conscious side of our brains, turning dreams into memories. The darker side of this phenomenon is when that nightmare echoes into your mind and activates your flight or flight instinct. That "dark spirit," "half-lit sidewalk," "empty office with creepy noise" are all echoes from stories you were told, the news you read and watch, the music you listen to, or the movies you have seen. These echoes vibrate at a frequency that makes you question everything. *(Takes a deep breath.)*

Echoes are a normal occurrence that we all hear. Some yodel, standing on top of a hill for you to hear the sound bounce back, like when someone in your life gives you solid advice, creating a core memory to relive. Voice and sound, the vibration of what was, is, and can be. The echoes of the past trauma seeping to the forefront of your life, the voice of a past loved one repeating in your head, telling you, "Keep living on" or, "I love you." Having that same memory or dream repeat inside your head while daydreaming or walking around and continuing your mundane existence in this void of continual sound. Listen. Listen to those echoes, even if it's your favorite song on repeat—that echo can be the most humbling, healing, amazing thought, no matter where in your life you have heard it.

Just listen!

Boys!

James La Barbera

(At a park in the middle of the day, a football team of local college boys are playing. Jacob, mid twenties, shy and alone, on stage.)

JACOB. *(Sits on the bench to watch the game.)* Wow! These guys are really going at it. I mean, I have seen lots of games growing up, sitting on the sidelines and cheering for friends and family. But, OMG, these guys are like... Wow.

What would I do to some of them if I only... I mean if only... I, um, forget it.

Boys. There is something about the male physique that just screams lick me, bite me, smother me with chocolate and devour me. I know how that sounds, so don't judge me. I get that enough from too many people. Oh look, theres the quiet kid, the gay kid, the fag. Can a muscle man with two brain cells come up with anything more original? I would love one boy in particular that doesn't make fun of me when it's just the two of us in a science lab or library studying, or even over coffee when we talk about the latest action movie that came out. Which is the reason why I'm sitting in the park, watching an amateur hour-long game of muscles grabbing at each other. The reason is one really nice guy.

Nice guys always finish last, but he is coming in first. This is the first guy that I think I might fall for, the guy that I can trust with anything and the guy that I can call on. He is such a boy when it comes to other things like shopping for clothes, video game, or movie choices, and his excessive need to always be the clown in the room, even when it's just us. I don't know if it is a good idea. The best ideas I've had in the past were to never trust the inner workings of my mind or gut. My gut has gotten my heart hurt, and my mind was all twisted and broken. Trust has been easy and I've given it to guys that were undeserving, crude, and hurtful, that I defended to everyone in my life, just to feel alone.

I don't understand how easy it can be in their world, falling for woman after woman. Sleeping with whomever they want without it being weird or awkward or feeling uncomfortable after. Boys like them can breathe without anyone questioning who they are, questioning if they are gay, if they're staring too long, or simply looking in their general direction. But boys are also so sensitive, like when they ask if you're okay after you get tripped with your books in hand. They are vulnerable at times, like when you're alone talking about life, the future and the clouds in the sky. Oh, and when they keep eye contact when you are speaking and they are just sitting there listening... Uh, definitely the most attractive thing ever!

But back to the game. We are winning, obviously. El is doing everything possible to make sure of it and kicking ass. He doesn't want to disappoint anyone who's here to possibly scout him. I'm just here to make sure he doesn't overdo it and get hurt. I mean, I would be here for that reason if I were more than just his guy friend. El is both harmless and dangerous at the same time. He makes the world tip off its axis, and it's so interesting how I let a boy make me feel this way.

Boys! They are crazy, funny, adorable, dumb, and yet they know how easy it is to make your heart race and your body to respond. Ooh, just like that tackle. Got to go!

I Have Nothing to Write About

Alena Williams

Life since graduation has been direly meek.

My parents attempt to stress me out and nag, "Do something! Get a job!" Yet I have never felt more relaxed in my life.

Somehow the four years I spent slaving away at an accredited institution amid a global pandemic meant nothing. Nothing to my parents nor to the hundreds of jobs I was applying to every week. I was burnt out. Just tired. However, my time was limited and sleep was not an option in my parents' eyes—I was on the clock. With two minutes left on my mother's clock and even less time with the Almighty, I was seconds to insanity.

Unbeknownst to him, my younger brother would soon be betraying me, as he was about to be off to college himself, leaving me to wilt in my childhood bedroom which seemed to grow smaller and smaller by the day.

As the leaves outside changed from a dull green to an array of reds and oranges, I slowly grew more anxious about making enough money to maintain my standard of living, keep my parents off of my back, and prove to them I wasn't some type of "Gen Z failure." However, concurrently, I refused to sell my soul to some fill-in, dead-end job... So what was I to do?

"Do something! Aren't you a writer? Write something!" my dad's voice echoes throughout my brain. Yet, I have nothing worthy to write about right now... And that's the truth.

I am in a period of rest and rejuvenation. However, it has been deemed completely unacceptable by those around me.

If only they would realize that a butterfly must cocoon before it can fly, and if that cocoon is not fully rested and curated, it dies.

The Bluebonnets

Jack Niemczyk

A cool March breeze
Blows the sea of bluebonnets just in front of me
A rolling wave
that parts the iris bloom to show their green roots
A soft guitar plays in the background
some country song I've heard before.

Do I want to go back to before?
Where my body was simply limp, moving with the passive breeze
When my mind was too naive, simply silent, with no background
And the present of the present was a gift to me
Even my hair, light as a feather, standing at the root
was neutral, not happy or sad, just floating, with no wave

"But who would want that?" the bluebonnets cry with a wave
Grabbing my attention back to where it was before
The hundreds of heads raise to me as if they are trying to escape their roots
Each stem presents ten or twenty indigo bulbs blooming with wisdom that flies on the breeze
and I focus on these blossoms, hoping they can in any way aid me
with the hills of central Texas as a background

"Why so morose as you look to us? As though a somber song plays in your background"

I look at them without an answer. Shrugging my shoulders, I begin a goodbye wave

As I stand to leave, one of the stems jumps to the sky, towering high as the oak trees around me

Its towering blossoms engulf the blue of the sky as though it was not there before

And it raises a voice that moves the surrounding foliage stronger than the breeze

So even the rock I sit upon vibrates its sedimentary center, disrupting my roots

"Nosce Te Ipsum," it yells, and I gaze, confused not knowing its roots

"Sorry," I wilt, "I don't know Latin. It's not my background"

Their presence a monsoon, mine a light spring breeze

Perhaps it knows it frightened me as it shrinks a little, with an apologetic wave

The guitar play plays louder and sings a song I've heard before

It's a sad song, Willie Nelson, I believe, and yet I can hear its beauty, just the flower and me

"I just wish." I open up, just as these bulbs, pollinating the air with the music inside me

"That I wasn't so blue, roots"

Silence washes over the rock, as though everything understood and felt this before

But the bonnets fill the moment, "What's so bad about being blue, it hasn't done us bad yet" and I look up to an oil-painted cloud atop a blue background

And in that moment, as I bathe in the blue of the sky, I have a brain wave

I smile knowing that blue is no different than green, but without the blue, the green stays stagnant with no breeze

When I would have nothing but that neutral light inside me

And I sit nothing more than a character in the background

I sigh. I have changed, and I send kisses to the bonnets. Enough to touch their hidden roots

and they flow back and forth as my kisses tickle the dense ocean, rolling with a capped wave

I am back to before,

but not the same as I sit listening to a blue Willie Nelson make love to the ever-so-blue breeze

Fathoms Below

Jillian Hinz

Thursday, March 14, 2024, 11:29 a.m.

Heartland Travel was the cheapest tour company in Scotland, even cheaper with their discount for the study abroad students.

Sadie from New York had been convinced to go on this trip by her roommates (or "flatmates" as she was so commonly corrected) so they could properly experience the country they were studying in. Olivia from Texas, Libi from Kansas, and Kayla from Wisconsin were all nice girls. That is, until you lived with them.

"It's cheaper for us if you come with," they had told Sadie. "So you can come too... I guess."

And so she came.

Will from Canada had signed up thinking it was a class on the historical Scottish landmarks. He didn't realize they'd actually be *going* to these landmarks until it was too late to get his money back.

Murray the tour guide (from Scotland) didn't care why they were there. He was just glad for the business and that they all had to listen to him ramble while they rode in his van.

It was raining—the usual weather for Scotland. The tour group settled under raincoats and umbrellas as they filed out of the van. Murray had given them three hours to explore the village next to the loch before they were to meet back at the van to head to lunch.

Sadie shared her umbrella with Will as they looked up at the sign that marked the entrance of the village on the western shore of Loch Ness.

"Drumnadrochit," Sadie read aloud.

"Gesundheit," Will replied.

The village of Drumnadrochit was small. Tourists wandered the village like it was Disney World. People wore ponchos with "LOCH NESS" and a drawing of Nessie stamped on the front, children carried around stuffed versions of the monster, and tour groups followed behind tired-looking locals reciting facts about the village.

Tourists could ruin places. She knew from experience. If Sadie had a nickel for the number of times she'd been bumped and bothered by tourists bustling through New York, she could have afforded a much nicer tour van for Murray.

The locals, whose families had called this village home for generations, found themselves outnumbered and overshadowed by the throngs of camera-toting visitors who descended upon their streets each day. Sadie could tell that behind the polite smiles and welcoming gestures lay a deep-seated frustration with the constant invasion of their once quiet and secluded haven. As the population swelled with temporary residents, the quaint charm of the village began to erode, replaced by a commercialized facade catering to the fleeting desires of tourists. Traditional shops and eateries gave way to souvenir stalls and fast-food chains, catering more to the fleeting whims of visitors than to the authentic needs of the locals. The constant buzz of activity drowned out the whispers of nature, leaving the residents feeling like strangers in their own homeland.

Thursday, March 14, 2024, 02:53 p.m.

Will's glasses were fogged and splattered with raindrops despite being under the umbrella. He tugged at Sadie's arm and pointed to a small shop ahead. Its weathered wooden facade bore the name "Nessie's Treasures" in faded gold lettering.

"It doesn't look too crowded," he said. "C'mon, before we drown."

The shop was full of souvenirs. Nessie was, once again, plastered everywhere. Postcards and t-shirts and posters and hats and stuffed animals and figurines and even underwear, which Will pointed and laughed at.

The shop's interior was a treasure trove of curiosities with shelves lined from floor to ceiling with an eclectic array of artifacts and trinkets. At the heart of the shop stood a glass display case, its shelves adorned with an assortment of relics purportedly linked to the elusive Loch

Ness Monster. Framed photographs captured blurry glimpses of dark shapes lurking beneath the surface of the water while plaster casts of enormous footprints hinted at the creature's formidable presence. Sadie looked at them with confusion.

"Nessie doesn't have feet," she said to Will. "Isn't she like... A fish? A big fish? How can she leave a footprint?"

"I thought she was a dinosaur," Will replied as he tried on a baseball cap that read "women want me, fish fear me" with an image of Nessie winking.

Amidst the kitschy souvenirs and sensationalized memorabilia, there was a quiet corner of the shop that held a more subdued charm. Nestled among shelves of leather-bound journals and ornate quills lay an exquisite collection of handmade jewelry.

Sadie picked up a simple silver ring with a deep blue gem embedded in it. She slipped it on her finger. A perfect fit.

"Good choice."

Sadie jumped and turned around to see an older woman peering over a shelf of treasures. Her name tag read "Isla."

"It's pretty." Sadie nodded and slid the ring off her finger.

"Glad you think so." Isla crossed her arms. "Made it myself. Gems like that have a history."

"Really?" Sadie glanced down at the jewelry on display. "That's impressive. I bet you sell a lot of them."

The front door opened with the sound of a bell. In came the rest of Sadie's tour group, chatting and laughing loudly. Libi knocked into a stack of postcards and Kayla started rooting through the neatly folded piles of t-shirts while Olivia spotted Will and immediately asked if he'd been down to the loch yet.

Sadie grimaced at the abrupt change in atmosphere. She cast an apologetic glance towards Isla who did not seem phased. Sadie guessed that she was probably used to loud, disruptive tourists.

"Not really." Isla shrugged. "You lot don't exactly come in here to buy something without the beast on it."

The beast. Sadie's eyes instantly darted to the poster of a blurry black and white image of Nessie with "I WANT TO BELIEVE" plastered over it.

"Guess not..." Sadie mumbled. She looked back down at the ring in her hand. The blue gem seemed to wink in the dim light of the shop. She held it up to Isla. "I'll take it."

Isla raised an eyebrow and looked her up and down. Sadie suddenly felt self-conscious with her rain-frizzed hair and muddy boots. Isla clicked her tongue and headed toward the register. Sadie trotted after her, setting the ring on the counter with a *plink*.

Kayla had made her way over to the register, craning her neck to see what Sadie was buying. She wrinkled her nose at the ring.

"That's it?" Kayla asked. "How much you dropping on that?"

Sadie looked back at the table where she picked up the ring. A small handwritten sign read *£20*, so she started fishing through her wallet for the correct bills. Isla clicked her tongue again and shook her head.

"Just one, love," Isla said.

"What?" Sadie looked up at the woman.

"Just one pound for you." Isla nodded and held out her hand.

"But the sign says twenty—"

"One."

Sadie blinked at the woman. Then she reached into her pocket and pulled out a single pound coin. She dropped it into Isla's hand. Isla pocketed the coin instead of putting it in the register. She picked the ring up off the counter and getsured for Sadie to hold out her hand. Sadie hesitated for a moment before holding out her left hand. Isla slipped the ring onto her finger and patted it softly.

"There we are," Isla said. "Fits you just right, love."

The blue gem winked again.

Thursday, March 14, 2024, 03:55 p.m.

The rain had stopped for now.

Loch Ness emerged from its shroud of mist and drizzle. The air was heavy with the scent of damp earth and pine, infused with the freshness that only a Highland rain could bring. Wisps of fog still clung to the water, giving the loch an otherworldly allure as the sun peeked through the clouds, casting a golden glow over the landscape.

Sadie took out her phone and began taking pictures of the scene. The water, the boats, the trees, the distant hills, and one of Will pointing excitedly at a duck. Libi sighed loudly, taking a bite of the candy bar she had bought at another shop they stopped at after complaining that she couldn't wait until lunch.

"I thought we could have jumped in," Libi said. "I wore my bathing suit under my sweater."

"You guys were planning on swimming?" Sadie looked between the girls and the murky water. "Seriously? Are you even allowed to do that?"

"I looked it up before we came." Libi nodded. "There's no rule that says you can't."

"It's freezing!" Will looked over the side of the railing. "Not to mention deep. Hey, did you guys know that Loch Ness is the largest loch by volume? It has more water than all the lakes in England and Wales combined and—"

"Thank you, professor," Olivia cut him off. "We just wanted a quick dip. Bit of bragging rights to say we swam in Loch Ness. But we don't have time. Murray's gonna be here any minute with the van."

"Speak of the devil." Kayla groaned as they heard the familiar rumble of the engine approaching the parking lot.

Libi, who had been leaning against the railing, pushed herself up as she chewed the last bite of her candy bar. The wrapper flew over the railing and into the water below.

Friday, March 15, 2024, 12:09 a.m.

Sadie was shaken awake just after midnight. Olivia stood over her bed.

"C'mon," she whispered. "Get up. We're going swimmin'."

"What?" Sadie rubbed the sleep from her eyes. "The hell are you talking about?"

"We're going down to the loch," Olivia replied, shushing her. "Quick, or you'll wake Murray. We're all going, even Will. We want you to take pictures."

"How are we getting there?" Sadie asked. "It took twenty minutes to drive and it's late and it's dark and—"

Olivia held up the keys to the tour van with a grin.

"Oh."

Friday, March 15, 2024, 12:47 a.m.

Stealing the tour van and sneaking out of their cottage was the perfect way for them to all get in some serious trouble. Maybe they'd get fined. Or arrested.

Or deported...

Nah.

Libi drove, taking turns way too sharply and going through roundabouts a little too quickly (and occasionally forgetting what side of the road she was supposed to be on). Sadie nervously twirled her new ring around on her finger.

"It's gonna be freezing," Kayla said, "so I say, a quick hop in, snap a picture, then we get the hell out. No way am I dying of hypothermia in Scotland."

"I'll dip a toe in," Will promised. "I don't swim."

"Don't or can't?" Olivia asked.

"Don't!"

"Will can't swim!"

Friday, March 15, 2024, 1:21 a.m.

As the five students made their way out of the van and towards the shore, their feet sank into the mud and rocks with squelching sounds that echoed along with their giggles and whispers.

Sadie noticed the way her new ring glinted in the moonlight. The blue gemstone seemed to reflect against the inky black water, sending shadows dancing across her hand when she moved. She flexed her fingers, watching it with interest until the girls' chatter drew her attention away once more.

It was too dark to properly see anything except the distant lights of a now sleeping Drumnadrochit. Sadie felt as if the dark around her had engulfed them, closing in, suffocating the senses and enveloping all who dared to venture too close to the edge of the loch. Sadie turned on her phone's flashlight, illuminating their path.

The girls stopped next to an overturned canoe on the shore and began to strip down to the bathing suits they wore under their clothes. Will coughed and turned around, opting to just take his shoes off. They set their clothes on top of the abandoned canoe. Sadie suddenly felt a bit overdressed in her pajamas.

"Sadie, get this!" Libi said as she threw her arms around Olivia's and Kayla's shoulders. The girls smiled and posed as Sadie took their photo, pulling Will into a picture, too. Sadie couldn't help but notice they didn't ask her if she wanted to be in any photos. "Okay, now record!"

Sadie switched to a video and pointed her phone at the girls as they counted down.

"Three... Two... One!"

They ran into the inky black water, gasping and cursing at the freezing cold that jolted their senses. Yet, the thrill of the moment outweighed any discomfort, and soon they were swimming with abandon. Will followed them in, wading to his ankles, bouncing a bit to keep the cold away. He turned and flashed the camera a thumbs-up before tiptoeing back to the shore.

"How is it?" Sadie called out to the others.

"Cold!" Libi laughed. "But not bad once you get used to it!"

Kayla hurried out of the water a moment later, her teeth chattering. But she still smiled.

"You get that on camera?" she asked.

Sadie nodded. "Best I could. It's kinda dark but you can see most of it."

"Lemme see." Libi had emerged from the lake, shivering just as much as Kayla was. She took the phone from Sadie's hands and scrolled through the photos and video. "Oh these are cute! Send me all of them. Let's show Olivia."

They all turned to see Olivia still swimming. She had gone much farther out than they expected, backstroking through the loch.

"Olivia!" Kayla called to her. "Come on back! You're going too far!"

"I'm fine!" Olivia called back. "I'll come back in a sec, I'm loving this!"

The surface of the water began to churn, small waves forming in its wake, as if stirred by some unseen hand. The girls' laughter faltered, replaced by nervous glances, each one silently questioning the source of the disturbance.

Why did Sadie's ring feel tighter on her finger?

"I was on the swim team in high school!" Olivia called. She was so far out that it was too dark to see her. All they could hear was her voice. "Don't people swim the length of this thing for competitions? I could totally do that, easy—"

Olivia's voice cut off abruptly.

A long, heavy silence descended upon the once lively shores of Loch Ness.

"Olivia?" Libi called.

There was no answer. Just the sound of the waves on the shore.

Sadie took a step closer to the water, her eyes straining to scan the surface of the loch. There was no sign of Olivia or of those ripples she saw earlier. The ring around her finger began to itch. She shook out her hand, focusing on the loch.

Nothing.

"Did she go under?" Will asked nervously. "Maybe we should call someone—"

"And get caught for stealing the van?" Kayla scoffed. "No way!"

Libi rushed over to the canoe and tried to push it upright.

"Are you joking?" Sadie said. "What are we gonna do with that?"

"We're gonna go out there and look for her!" Libi snapped. "Or do you have a better idea?"

They all looked at each other for a moment. Then, they all stepped forward and helped Libi flip over the canoe.

Friday, March 15, 2024, 1:48 a.m.

"This is bad," Kayla said, leaning over the side of the canoe as she searched the water. "This is really bad."

"Yeah, keep saying it," Libi snapped. "That's helping so much."

"We should turn back," Will said. He stopped paddling. "She didn't even make it out this far. We need to go get help. We'll go to the village, Drum... Druma... Drumadocket—"

"Drumnadrochit," Sadie mumbled. She kept fidgeting with her ring. It itched as she turned it over and over.

"Yeah, that." Will nodded. "We'll go there and get the police or... You think the loch has a coast guard?"

The canoe suddenly rocked, causing them all to stumble and sway. The water rippled around them before starting to bubble, like something was taking deep breaths beneath the surface. The canoe bobbed dangerously up and down, spinning quickly as if caught in a whirlpool.

Without warning, the loch erupted in a frenzy of foam and spray as a massive shape burst from the depths. A shadowy form emerged, its outline obscured by the darkness of the night. A deep, guttural growl echoed through the loch.

They all stared in disbelief as it grew taller and taller, the silhouette of one long, strong neck. Its massive form dwarfed them in comparison. The weight of its gaze upon them, cold and calculating, sent a shiver down their spines that had nothing to do with the chill of the water. In that moment, the illusion of their midnight swim was shattered, replaced by a primal fear that gripped them tightly in its icy embrace. The beast's eyes were the only thing truly visible. They glowed a deep blue.

The same color as the ring on Sadie's finger.

"Go." Will choked out, grabbing his paddle. "Go!"

Friday, March 15, 2024, 1:54 a.m.

Sadie and Will paddled as fast as they could with Libi and Kayla screaming for them to keep going. The beast moved with sinuous grace, gliding effortlessly through the water, its presence commanding attention and respect. The canoe rocked violently as the beast slammed into it with incredible force. Kayla was sent over the side of the canoe by the sudden jolt, landing with a splash.

"Help me up, help me up!" Kayla screeched as she resurfaced. "Something touched my leg!"

Libi rushed over to the side of the canoe, desperately reaching for the other girl. Their hands brushed before Kayla was yanked beneath the surface.

The beast burst from the depths, raining the icy water on them in a giant splash and thrashing its head back and forth. It held something large in its mouth, hanging loosely in its strong jaws. The beast threw it into the air and caught it again in its teeth with a sickening crunch.

Some of the water that dripped onto them felt strangely... Warm. Sticky. Thick. A giant drop landed on Libi's face. Her hand shaking, she reached up to wipe it off only to smear blood onto her hand.

Libi cried out in shock and fell back into the canoe, causing it to rock again. The beast continued to thrash, its jaws making a sickening chomp as it began to dive back under the water. There was splashing and screaming and growling and then—

Silence.

Friday, March 15, 2024, 2:00 a.m.

"Oh my god." Libi sputtered, tears streaming down her face. "Oh my God! Was that the Loch Ness monster? Friggin' Nessie? It— It *ate* them!"

The water began to ripple again and Sadie felt like crying. She kept paddling. They were only a few minutes from shore. They could make it. They could get away…

The canoe spun, caught once more in the whirlpool the beast made as it sped around them. They all yelled again, holding on for dear life as the beast's head emerged. It was even closer this time. They could make out a snakelike face with a jaw the size of their canoe. It stared them down as it raised its head. Deep, heavy breaths blew steam from its nostrils. Could it breathe? Did it? Or was it just another noise the beast made to warn them off its waters?

"Get away!" Libi ripped the oar from Sadie's hands and swiped at the beast. "You stupid ugly thing! Get away—"

The beast got close enough that the oar hit its neck. It snapped right in half. The beast looked down at the lower half of the paddle in the water and blinked. Libi slowly lowered her now broken handle, her hands shaking even more.

They all froze, hoping and praying it would leave them alone. Sadie's ring itched to the point where it hurt, but she fought the urge to adjust it. The beast suddenly sniffed the air and turned its giant head. They all followed its gaze.

Floating lazily past the canoe was the candy wrapper Libi had tossed into the loch earlier that day.

The beast turned its head back to stare at Libi.

"Shit."

The beast's teeth were the last thing Sadie saw before Libi's scream was cut short, replaced by a crunch so loud that it echoed through her bones. The broken oar clattered onto the floor of the canoe, dripping with blood. It looked almost black in the moonlight. The canoe lurched again with the force of the beast's bite.

Will toppled over the side with a shout, taking the last oar with him. There was more splashing and growling and Sadie squeezed her eyes shut, tears streaming down her face as she waited for the sharp bite of the beast.

But it never came.

Friday, March 15, 2024, 2:17 a.m.

Sadie was stranded in the middle of the loch with an oarless canoe and the goddamn Loch Ness monster swimming somewhere below her.

She had her phone. She could call for help. But what would she say? "Dear Scottish police, my friends (or friend, rather) are dead. Drowned and devoured by the Loch Ness monster. Please send your coast guard equivalent to pull this stupid canoe from the water." Sadie looked at her phone. No service.

Sadie was next, she was sure of it. The beast was probably saving her for dessert.

Her ring itched like crazy. She twirled it around her finger. She slipped it on and off a few times. She switched fingers. Still itchy. The blue gem glinted in the moonlight, somehow brighter than before. Sadie shook out her hand as the water rippled again, this time about a yard away from the canoe.

She watched in silent awe as the beast emerged once again, stretching its long neck into the sky and facing away from Sadie. Maybe it was just admiring the moon and it would slink back into the depths of the loch and leave her the hell alone.

Slowly, Sadie reached for her phone again. If she managed to survive this, she needed proof. With shaking hands, she raised her phone and opened up her camera, aiming it at the beast. The picture was dark and grainy, but you could make out the image of the beast in the moonlight. There was no mistaking it. Sadie pressed the button to take the photo—

Click.

The flash went off and that stupid camera noise echoed across the lake. Sadie shoved her phone in her pocket and the beast froze before it slowly turned its giant head in her direction without moving its neck. They stared at each other for a long moment, the beast's glowing blue eyes looking straight into Sadie's soul. Her ring *burned*.

With a jerk, the beast began to glide towards her like it was propelled by a motor. Sadie closed her eyes once more, holding her hand over her head as if it would shield her.

She felt the canoe bob in the water and splash around her. Water dripped on her head as she felt a giant scaly snout bump gently against her hand. She opened her eyes.

The beast was right next to the canoe, its neck craned over to look down at her. Its blue eyes blinked again before it bumped its nose against her hand as if looking for a treat.

Up close, it was monstrously gorgeous. Its body was adorned with dark, glistening scales that shimmered in the moonlight. Atop its head lay a crown of spines, giving it an almost regal appearance. Poking from its mouth was a line of sharp jagged teeth the size of Sadie's forearm. They were stained red with blood. Sadie didn't move. She held her breath as she stared up at it, their eyes meeting.

The beast's eyes were its most striking feature—piercing blue that gleamed with a wisdom as deep as the waters from which it emerged. And it was staring right at Sadie.

It nudged at her hand again, a deep chuffing sound coming from its throat. She slowly lowered her hand in shock. The beast's eyes followed her hand with great interest as it made the noise again.

"Hello," Sadie said softly.

The beast stirred in the water, causing the canoe to shake. Sadie gripped the edge of the canoe to keep herself stable as the beast leaned down to sniff at her hand. She realized it was looking at her ring.

Slowly, she slipped the ring off her finger. It raised its head, letting out a huff. Like it was impatient with her.

"Is this what you want?" Sadie asked.

The beast lowered its head to her height and opened its mouth. The stench was horrible, a mix of low tide and blood.

The inside of the beast's mouth was a cavernous expanse, illuminated by a faint bioluminescent glow that emanated from the depths of its throat. The walls were lined with rows of razor-sharp teeth, ranging from small, needle-like points to larger, jagged fangs, all perfectly adapted for tearing through flesh and bone.

Sadie dropped the ring onto the beast's waiting tongue.

Its jaw snapped shut and it swallowed, eyes glowing brighter for a split second as it made the little chuffing noise again.

"I paid a pound for that..." Sadie said quietly.

Slowly, she placed her hand on the beast's snout. It blinked at her and she laughed at the absurdity of the situation. She had just watched this thing kill four people. And here she was, feeding it jewelry and petting it like a puppy.

The beast pushed the canoe over.

Sadie landed in the water with a splash. The water was freezing, sending a horrible jolt through her body. She resurfaced, kicking madly to stay afloat, and looked around for the beast only to see nothing but her now overturned canoe. Sadie reached for it but felt something nudge at her feet. She held her breath, bracing herself to be yanked under the water to a murky demise.

Instead, she felt herself rising. The beast was pushing her up from below, almost juggling her on its nose as it began to speed towards the shore. Sadie squirmed and kicked, trying to keep her head above water but winding up with bucketfuls in her lungs. About thirty feet from the shore, it stopped. The beast launched Sadie forward, and when she landed she found that she could reach the bottom of the loch. It reached its long neck over and again nudged her from behind, this time with a dark growl, and she didn't have to be told twice. Sadie booked it towards the shore, coughing and stumbling until she collapsed on her knees. She caught the final glimpse of glowing blue eyes as the beast's head disappeared under the water, returning to the fathoms below.

Friday, March 15, 2024, 2:48 a.m.

A soaking-wet Sadie sat on the shore with her knees held tightly against her chest. She stared out at the loch, desperate for another glimpse of the beast. But none came. There was just silence, the water lapping up at the shore.

"Sadie!"

Her head whipped around. An equally soaking-wet Will was stumbling down the beach towards her. He was shivering and missing a shoe. But he was there. Sadie leaped up and rushed to him, grabbing him by his arms.

"I saw you get knocked off! " she sputtered.

"I swam!" Will replied. "It launched me pretty far back, so I swam and wound up on the other side! So I swam—"

"I thought you couldn't swim?"

"I said I don't swim. Not that I can't!"

Sadie just hugged him, exhausted and cold and in shock. He was alive. She wasn't alone. There was someone to back her up.

"I got a picture—" Sadie reached into her pocket for her phone only to come up empty. She looked back out into the loch, realizing it must have sunk to the bottom after she fell out of the canoe. "Dammit."

"How'd you even get out?" Will asked her.

"Fed it my ring," Sadie replied weakly. Will blinked at her.

"Your ring..."

"Yeah."

"You fed it to Nessie."

"Yep."

"And that... Worked?"

"Apparently."

"Okay..."

The sound of a car honking pulled them from their conversation. A taxi pulled up at the street several yards away, and out stormed Murray.

"Sneakin' out, stealin' my bloody van!" he exclaimed. "Where the hell are the others? Why are you two soaked to the bone?"

"They..." Sadie's voice trembled. "They're gone."

"Gone?" Murray repeated. "Whaddaya mean, gone?"

"They're dead," Will explained. "We saw it happen!"

"It was the Loch Ness Monster," Sadie said. "I know it sounds crazy, but it's true! It killed them! It tried to kill us!"

Murray stared at the two of them for a long moment after they finished explaining.

"Yeah..." Murray ran a hand over his face with a sigh. "She tends to do that. C'mon then, the botha ya, back to the van."

Sadie and Will stood there in confusion as Murray headed back to the stolen van, grumbling.

"Damn tourists..." He groaned. "Making my job harder. So much paperwork..."

Dream Girl

Misha Puello Brasil

You think I can't see you.
I can feel your eyes on my flesh,
penetrating my virtue.

You love the way my bouncy curls go *boing*,
Spirals that keep their quality of being untouched
after you affect a sharp tug.

With my large, manipulative, cardboard-colored eyes
and blood-tinted, appetizing, cracked lips,
I gaze at you with the same ingenuous eyes of a bitch
taking a piss.

Hold me tight. I'm the pristine trophy
won by conquering the naive.
The engraving: a pair of baby pink lesions on my knees.

Compliment the tightness of my youth.
I'm soft and unnatural, like a hairless cat.
You love to grip my milk-reliant bones
and the skin they wear like a battered blanket.

I promise to love you forever.
Please don't leave me,
Your Innocent, Little Girl

Gabo

Oriana Galvis Marín

Many years later,
as I faced the nostalgia of my past,
I was to remember
that bitterly cold Friday morning
in which I finally reached the end
of Gabo's enchantment.

The excitement of what was going to be the end
of the Buendía family,
of Melquíades' prophecy,
and the last sentence of a hundred-year story
was the spell that captivated the minds
of a group of students and a Spanish teacher.

Gabo's words transported us to a Macondo
infected by a plague of insomnia and amnesia.
Where death diffused through the pages,
dancing between the borders
of fiction and reality,
of the past and the present.

Gabo's words painted a self-portrait of a country,
surrendered to the disease of forgetting.

The voice that enunciated the words
of the last chapter went through
a metamorphosis of tones and colors.

Shades of yellow dyed the monochrome ink on the page
and let each word fly, like butterflies
marking the way of a lover's grim end.

Time stopped,
but seconds, minutes, hours, kept accumulating.
We were governed under
Gabo's rules
Gabo's time
Gabo's narrative

Trapped in *Cien Años de Soledad.*

Detangling
Kianna Swingle

I. Bangs and curls

I was known for little, intricate braids, perfectly brushed curls, and light brown bangs that never went past my eyebrows because they were meticulously trimmed every other week. The other little girls in my class, and even teachers, were in awe of my perfectly sectioned hair and the ribbons and bands of rainbows that held them together. As a hairdresser, my mother made sure I was always put together. We shared that love for hair. My long curls that were swept out of my face would trail behind me as I walked the rows of the beauty salon looking for a way to help the other stylists. I was happy to grab a broom and sweep away the trimmings. I was often used as a live mannequin for the stylists who were not busy, as they practiced their braiding skills on my little head that grew used to the harsh tugging and pulling. I was probably more of an annoyance at times because I loved playing with the barbicide jars. When the jars were placed out of reach and there was nothing to do, I swiveled in the chair and admired my mother's darker curls and how they flowed as she moved her way around the client she was working on.

I remember watching her as she got ready in the mornings and how she curled her hair with a straightener. I was in awe of the tresses that moved exactly the way she wanted them to. My flimsy purple hair straightener wasn't as nice as hers, but I still danced for joy when I opened it on Christmas Eve. My poor little sisters' ears fell victim to the purple flat iron and my inability to control the clamp fully. Despite the burns on their ears and necks they still allowed me to style their hair.

II. Loose braids and scarves

The days we spent inside watching reality TV are what I remember most. I also remember when my mom would have to run to the bathroom in fear that we would see her get sick. I remember when she was upset my stepfather bought pizza from Pizza Hut instead of Dominoes because they made their sauce too spicy. I remember how much I missed the hotdog stand that was next door to the salon. I remember watching in awe as my mom intricately wrapped her head in scarves. My favorite was the beige one that complimented her tan skin.

My little hands, although inexperienced, were much stronger than my mom's. When I took over the getting-ready routine in the mornings, my sisters were sent to school with lopsided pigtails and braids that were one wrong move away from falling apart. I wanted so badly for them to have the beautiful hairstyles that I sported when I was their age, so I practiced and watched tutorials online. My mom was amazed by how I managed to arrange my sisters' hair in buns that looked like bows. I promised her that when her hair grew back I would do the style on her and we would all match, a memory that still haunts me in the middle of the night. I wish I was able to think she felt as hopeful as I did, but my new found pessimism leads me to believe she bit her tongue at that moment.

III. Split ends

I got the scarves that still smelled like her makeup and the hair straightener that I hadn't seen in almost two years. My tía got her shears and promised I could have them when I was old enough to handle them. My hair grew long and damaged, as the thought of stepping foot in a hair salon caused me physical discomfort. My curls fell out from the damage done to them; I used my mother's straightener everyday to feel closer to her—to make it seem like she was still there doing my hair. I hated my light brown hair, how it was thinner than it used to be and the natural curls had no structure. It was nothing to be proud of.

When I was eighteen, my tía asked if I wanted the shears. I told her no.

IV. Dyed curls

I hadn't stepped in a salon that wasn't inside of a Walmart in almost ten years until I found a salon that seemed to be in my college-student budget and offered mimosas and rosé (in case I needed one). I sat in the chair as a girl with dark curls applied dye to my hair. I breathed in and out, feeling the emotions of the childhood I missed.

I thought of the woman who shared her craft with me. I looked at the trimmings on the ground that needed to be swept when I was left alone to process.

When I got home I stepped in the shower and immediately washed away the blowout the stylist insisted on me leaving with. A familiar but long lost love for my hair washed over me as I used the hair straightener to curl my dark hair. When my sisters complimented my hair, they remembered the times I would do their hair for school. Their faces lit up when they asked if I remembered the bow buns too.

Growing Up: A Playlist as a Time Capsule

Kayleigh Woltal

Shuffle.

I'm five. I'm in my neighbor's basement and she's got her camera. She's filming me jumping over chairs and lip-syncing to Britney Spears. She's making my music video.

Skip.

I'm seven. I'm in my basement listening to my brother's old MP3 player. It's all a mix of my dad's music and songs from cartoons. My brother never added any real songs—music never was his thing. I find some of my favorite songs, even to this day.

Skip.

I'm ten. It's the last day of fifth grade. I'm watching the slideshow video with all the photos taken of the class throughout the year. I'm reminded of how shy I'd been all year and I'm worried there won't be any photos of me, but one comes up of me covered in a powdered donut and I laugh.

Skip.

I'm eleven. I'm in the car on the way home from my cousin's wedding. I was the youngest one there. I didn't dance. I want to grow up more than anything.

Skip.

I'm twelve. I'm in my ex-best friend's living room playing Rock Band. I play the guitar while she sings. I don't realize I will always think of her when I hear the song.

Skip.

I'm fourteen. I'm in my room instant messaging people I met online. I'm getting catfished by some of them, but I don't know it yet. I really shouldn't have unfiltered access to the internet.

Skip.

I'm seventeen. I'm watching from stage left as I wait for the band to finish performing. I'm on deck to read my work in front of my high school. This is my last year doing this, and I feel like I'm going to cry.

Skip.

I'm twenty. I'm laughing with my college roommate in our beds at three in the morning. We talk about how it feels like we're at a middle school sleepover. We don't know that in two years, we won't talk at all.

Skip.

I'm twenty-one. I'm at a concert. I came alone, but I'm seeing the singer I fell in love with at twelve, so I don't feel lonely. I feel like I'm home.

Skip.

I'm twenty-two. I'm graduating in two days. I dance with my friends on a boat to ABBA while the photographer takes our photos. We don't stop to pose.

Skip.

I'm twenty-four. I listen to the boy band I used to love on my way to work. I smile as the memories flood in, the good and the not-so-good. I turn to my nostalgia playlist for more of the feeling and hit shuffle.

Things I Never Got to Say

Chardonnae Simpson

When you find our old silly videos, give me a call, T

Why didn't you take me with you, Grandpa?
I wish you could see me in adulthood

I still have the other half of our BFF mood changing necklaces, G
I still keep the dated letters from when we tried to keep each other from surrendering to premature endings

I hope you hear Evanescence and think of me

When I see men loving their daughters proudly, my eyes search the ground for my father's footsteps

I will never forget painting the Bronx red with you, T

The things I never got to say will become the sky's listening party

Silent whispers of nostalgia
Gnawing regret

My keepsake box is saturated with memories of things I never got to say

Excerpt from Divinity

Jillian Hinz

"I'd say we covered a lot in our last little meeting," Father Rory said. "I can't help but think about what you said to me in the diner."

"Remind me," Shiloh told him.

"You asked me if God answers when I pray," he said. "And when I asked you what you were praying about... Well, I can see you don't have the best relationship with religion."

"What gave that away?" Shiloh asked sarcastically. Father Rory chuckled.

"Oh just a hunch," he said. "And the fact that you're sitting here right now. Never in my life have I ever seen someone look so out of place in a church. I mean, you look like you've seen a ghost."

"I haven't." She sighed and rubbed her eyes. "Trust me."

"I do."

He had said it so earnestly. Shiloh froze for a moment before looking up at him. His green eyes that bore right through her shone in the dim light of the church. He looked at her with a soft smile, and his hand went up to his red hair absentmindedly. Shiloh's eye followed his movements, and for a split second, she saw it again, a black swirl of shadow along his neck. It dove above his white collar like a dolphin jumping out of the ocean. Shiloh jumped up and stood from her seat. The young priest's smile faded as he looked up at her.

"I know that this conversation isn't the easiest." He sighed. "I know religion is a touchy subject for some people. But I'd really like to pick your brain about the way you feel."

"I thought that was my job," Shiloh said, slightly embarrassed that she had leapt up so abruptly. "I ask the questions, don't I?"

"How about we switch roles then?" He gestured over to the far end of the church. "Indulge me, won't you Shiloh Barone?"

Shiloh looked to where he pointed. The confessional was in the far back corner of the church. It stood between two stained glass windows. Rainbow colored light danced around it as if inviting her to step inside and confess her sins, which was the very last thing Shiloh wanted to do.

It was almost as if he could smell her apprehension. Father Rory gave her a warm smile and stood up as if this was a perfectly reasonable request.

"I don't know," Shiloh said awkwardly. "I never liked that part."

She had been inside one of those boxes many times, all as a child. Her mother had made her and her sister go to something called "CCD" after school on Wednesdays. Its purpose was to educate them about religion and prepare them for things like Communion and Confirmation. Shiloh never saw the appeal of it, but she didn't mind that it got her out of school early once a week.

Confession was not an activity she liked to participate in. Shiloh never understood why, at such a young age, she had to go confess her sins. As far as she knew, she didn't have any. She had been a good kid, and there wasn't much to say. But she hated the silence as she sat there in that stuffy box with the priest, a thin layer of wood and screen between them. So she would make things up to fill the silence. Never anything too bad, just things that were believable for a kid. She fought with her sister, she didn't clean her room after her mother told her to, and she stole a candy bar from the store (that one had been true). The guilt ate away at her for weeks. Yet all she ever got in return was the occasional "Hmm" while she spoke and then, "Say three Hail Marys" once she was done.

"It's not that bad," Father Rory said. "Really. You just tell me all your deepest darkest secrets and I can't judge you for any of them or else God will take away my fancy robes and reserved parking space."

She chuckled and glanced towards the confessional then back to him. He was looking at her with those eyes again. Boring a hole right through her. It made her squirm. Maybe she really did need the separation of a dark screen between them.

She was about to protest again when she felt something move through her. It was like she had stepped into a warm ray of sunlight. That pulling, pushing feeling she had felt by the lighthouse when she slipped earlier. But this one was stronger, the warmth spreading across her chest, down her arms. Her palms tingled at the sensation. She turned to Father Rory and nodded.

"Alright," Shiloh whispered. "I'll see what the fuss is about."

Father Rory suddenly looked more tired than before. *Had the bags under his eyes gotten darker?* It must have been the dim church lighting because he grinned and escorted her to the confessional. He opened the door on one side and gestured for her to enter.

"Ladies first," he said.

Shiloh paused for a moment, peering inside the small box. There was a wooden seat built into the side and a window with a screen built into the wall that separated each side. She stepped inside and sat down. Father Rory nodded and shut the door. It was suddenly very dark. A small dim light flickered on above her as she heard the other door open and Father Rory sit on his side.

She could see his silhouette through the screen. His head was bowed in a silent prayer. Shiloh squirmed in the uncomfortable wooden seat.

"I don't know what I'm supposed to say," Shiloh said. She heard Father Rory chuckle.

"Well usually you say 'Bless me father, for I have sinned,'" he replied and paused, waiting for her to say it.

"Bless me father for I have sinned," Shiloh repeated.

"My last confession was..." he prompted her.

My last confession was..." She paused and thought for a moment. "So long ago I can't even remember."

"Good," he said. "Then we'll have a lot to cover."

Shiloh sat there in silence for a moment. She didn't know what to say. What could she confess? That she thinks she's going crazy? That she's seeing things, terrifying and impossible things and she thinks he's responsible for it? But those weren't sins, were they? What could she possibly—

"Tell me about your family."

"What?"

She heard Father Rory lean back in his seat, his head resting on the wall.

"Tell me about your family," he repeated.

"I thought I was supposed to confess my sins, not give you my life story." Shiloh swallowed nervously. The dim glow of the light above her and the smell of incense made her hazy. That pushing feeling was still there.

"You'd be surprised how simply having a conversation can open one up," he said. "We'll get there soon enough, don't worry. Now, tell me about your family. Do you have a good relationship with them?"

"I..." Shiloh thought for a moment. "I'm close with my dad. He and I always got along. He's funny, and always supported my writing even when he didn't understand it. My mom... We don't always get along. I know she loves me, that she normally means well but there's just some things I can't wrap my head around about her."

"Like what?" Father Rory asked.

"I don't know, it's hard to explain." She shook her head.

"Any siblings?" he asked.

Shiloh's mouth clamped shut. A lump automatically formed in her throat. She coughed quickly, trying to send it away. She didn't want to talk about this. But against her own accord, her mouth opened.

"Yes."

"How many?"

"One."

"Older or younger?"

"Younger."

"Brother or sister?"

"Sister."

"What's her name?"

"Her name was Lizzie."

It was Father Rory's turn to get quiet. She heard him sit up straight again and could practically hear the gears in his head turning as he carefully thought out his next words.

"You said 'was,'" he said softly. "I'm sorry, does that mean—"

"She died almost four years ago." Shiloh swallowed the lump in her throat the best she could. "She was eighteen, I had just turned twenty-one. And she was... We weren't close. It wasn't like we hated each other; we got along fine. We were just two very different people with not a lot in common dealing with different things. She and my mom didn't get along at all. They had a fight one night and Lizzie just stormed out of the house and drove to... A friend's place. She didn't make it there. Some drunk asshole hit her head on. She didn't even make it to the hospital."

Shiloh reached up and wiped away a stray tear that had managed to slip out.

"I'm sorry for your loss," Father Rory said. "Can I ask why she and your mother were arguing?"

"I'm still not entirely sure." Shiloh shrugged. "I was up in my room with the door closed, so I didn't hear all of it. But I'm pretty sure it was that my mom didn't want Lizzie to leave."

"Why not?" he asked.

"The friend that she wanted to see," she said. "Well, she never told me exactly, but I don't think they were just friends. She lived in some fancy part of Brooklyn. They met at school and hung out all the time. Lizzie came out to us when she was in high school. I was cool with it, my dad got used to it... My mom never did. That was the only time I heard her properly talk about religion."

"Really?" he asked. "Could that be why you feel so strangely about it?"

"Maybe," Shiloh considered. "I know people use it as an excuse to hate the way certain people live their lives. No offense."

"None taken," he said.

"But it's just the way my mom would say it," she said, "That it was a sin. But I never understood it. This was Lizzie she was talking about.

119

Her daughter, my sister. She told her she would go to hell. And... And when she died, my mom blamed her for it. If she was different, it never would have happened. She said that to me at the funeral. I sat in that church alone, just hearing her say it in my brain, over and over again while I stared at her casket. My sister was gone, and my mother blamed her for it instead of mourning like the rest of us. But what I worry about is, what if she was right? There's no way for us to know where Lizzie went after she died. We just listen to what our faith tells us is true or not. But what if it *is*?"

"I'm so sorry," Father Rory said. "I can assure you your mother is wrong. I bet your sister was lovely."

"She was," Shiloh said. "Lizzie was smart and she was funny and talented. She used to joke that when my book got published, she wouldn't read it because she hated reading."

"Did she like your book?" he asked.

"She never got the chance to read it."

Another silence overtook them. Shiloh pulled at her sleeves, the tingling in her palms growing stronger. She took a deep breath.

"I dedicated it to her," Shiloh said. "I think she would have liked it. I... I was working on revisions for my editor the night she— She had asked me to drive her after her fight with our mom. But I told her I was busy. If I had driven her that night, if I had just put down my work for one second—"

"It isn't your fault," Father Rory said firmly. "Not at all. It wasn't her own fault either. It was just—"

"If you say it was God's plan, I'm going to punch through this screen and choke you."

Shiloh hadn't meant to say it so cruelly. She sniffed and wiped her tears on the back of her hand. But she heard Father Rory chuckle.

"I believe you," he said. "But you caught me. I was going to say that."

"That's what I don't get," Shiloh said, her voice rising. "God's plan. Why would the plan include getting rid of someone so innocent?

Lizzie didn't do anything wrong, no matter what my mother might think. She was going to make something of herself, she was gonna pursue music. Lizzie wanted her name in lights, and she deserved to see that come true. If 'God's plan' is so great, why couldn't he have given that to her? She was gonna create something to be remembered for, and now all she's remembered for is how my mother saw her."

Shiloh's voice shook. She paused and took a deep breath, closing her eyes for a moment as she collected herself. She didn't want to cry. Not here.

"How is she supposed to have a legacy if her life was cut off before she could even start it?" she asked. "People die every day, and almost every single one won't be remembered in fifty years. Time passes, and people move on and forget them. They become names on headstones people don't even glance at. We look at religion for answers, but all it gives me is more questions. Faith is good to have, but I just don't have any. I need real, hard proof in front of me. I want to know if Lizzie got heaven or oblivion."

The tears were falling faster now. Shiloh hugged herself, talking faster and growing angrier. The confessional booth walls felt like they were closing in on her. She stared at Father Rory's silhouette. He didn't move.

"We live our lives for what?" she spat. "To be another name on another headstone. The few who manage to be remembered, those are who matter. God's plan or not, religion or not, they matter but aren't remembered. My sister mattered. She deserves to be remembered, to have a legacy. That... That's what I want for her. For myself. More than anything else in the world."

"A legacy?" Father Rory asked, sounding interested.

"Yes," Shiloh nodded despite the fact that he couldn't see her. "I'm terrified of living my life without making one for myself. Lizzie didn't get one, and that scares me. I wanna honor her, I do, but my mother's voice in my head holds me back. So since Lizzie never got her name in lights, I got mine in print. I made sure her name was in the dedication. It's the only way that her name can live as long as mine."

Shiloh caught her breath. She hadn't expected today to go like this. That pushing feeling was luring the words out of her until they tumbled from her lips like water from a faucet.

"And I think I'm going crazy," she said, her voice barely a whisper. "Ever since she died, I've felt different. When I got to Numen, things got worse. This place was supposed to help me. But now, I'm going truly, properly crazy. Father Rory, I'm seeing things. Something is wrong with Numen Island. People are dying and I swear, I see them. I swear you were there too. Felicity Sheridan said that death follows me, yet everyone else is dropping like flies. I'm starting to believe her. How the hell am I supposed to finish my book like this? Keep my name out there? Death terrifies me, and now I'm scared that I'm next. All I have to my name is one book. How am I supposed to continue a legacy if it can be cut short so quickly? How can I do anything if I'm insane?"

Shiloh curled up into herself with her face buried in her hands and started to cry. That pushing feeling was now a dull throb in the back of her head. For a moment, there was no sound but her muffled sniffs and sobs. Then, Father Rory spoke.

"There it is..." His voice floated through the screen that separated them.

Shiloh lifted her head and wiped her eyes. She looked at the screen but could no longer see his silhouette.

She was alone in the confessional.

The walls were suddenly too close and the smell of incense was too strong and the light overhead was too harsh. Shiloh began to sweat, furiously wiping away her tears and running her hands through her hair. She shook out her hands, but the tingling sensation wouldn't go away. She needed to get out. She stood, bumping into the wall and reaching for the door.

It swung open before she could even touch it.

Father Rory stood there looking like he hadn't slept in a week. He didn't look this tired before. Somehow the bags under his eyes were even darker. But he loomed in the doorway like he was waiting for something. Shiloh stepped forward to exit the small space but he stepped inside.

"You aren't crazy, Shiloh Barone," he said quietly. "Quite the opposite, actually."

He leaned forward and brushed away a tear that streamed down her cheek with his thumb. Slowly, he brought his thumb to his lips and pressed it to them. His eyes never left hers.

"You are of completely sound mind." He reached for her again, this time tucking a curl behind her ear. "And body." He moved his hand and held her chin, tipping it up so she could look at him. "And soul."

Shiloh couldn't move. The pushing feeling went from a dull throb to an electric shock running through her body. It shocked her well enough to root her to the ground. She felt like she was having a strange out of body experience, like she was looking down at herself from above and watching this strange scene unfold.

"As much as I try, I cannot control your faith," he whispered to her. "But we both deserve legacies. More so than others. We can overcome oblivion. We can help you with that..."

He pulled her closer to him by her waist, his other hand moving from her chin to cradle her cheek. She didn't fight. Her brain was in a fog. This felt like a dream. The pushing feeling made her palms tingle, and she raised her hands like she was a marionette puppet. She rested them on his chest and he smiled.

This close to him, Shiloh couldn't see the black tendrils that danced across the veins in his neck.

"We can show you how, darling..." He breathed in deeply, like he was in pain. "If you'd let us."

For a split second, Shiloh could have sworn that his green eyes were golden, but there was no time to know for sure because he was closing his eyes and leaning towards her. That pushing feeling wouldn't let her move. He was closer and closer and—

"Father? Are you here?"

Shiloh was pushed backwards. She stumbled right back into the uncomfortable wooden seat inside the confessional booth. Father Rory turned around and stepped out of it casually.

"Mrs. Sheridan!" She heard him say. "What a delightful surprise. What can I do for you?"

"Is someone in there?" Felicity Sheridan's voice rang in Shiloh's ears.

"Just Shiloh Barone," Father Rory said simply. "Showing her around. She was curious."

She heard him knock on the side of the confessional, a signal for her to come out. The pushing feeling was gone now, like it never affected her at all. Slowly, Shiloh stood and poked her head out. She saw Felicity Sheridan standing there with her arms folded haughtily across her chest. Father Rory stood beside the door, a smile on his face as if nothing had just happened. He offered a hand to her to help her step out. She didn't take it, but he reached forward and took her hand anyway. Felicity looked between the two of them with a frown on her face, her eyebrows narrowed.

"I came to discuss this Sunday's mass and the prayer service for those we've lost recently on the island," She said. "But I can see you're... Busy."

"Not busy at all!" Father Rory waved her off. "She was just leaving. Weren't you, Shiloh Barone?"

Shiloh looked at him with wide eyes but was met with that same polite smile. He didn't look as tired suddenly. His eyes were still the same green. Shiloh nodded dumbly.

"Your coat's in the sacristy," he told her. "I'll see you soon, yeah?"

Shiloh didn't answer him. As quickly and casually as she could, she left out the back door.

When she passed the gravestones behind the church, she made sure she looked at the names.

Subverting Expectations of Race, Gender, and Sexuality in the Gothic Genre

Misha Puello Brasil

Gothic texts have a running theme. They serve as an outlet for the unspeakable in society. Gothic literature manages to shed light on and emphasize the hidden American culture and its history with race, gender, and sexuality while also keeping it hidden from the plain eye. The genre uses symbols, motifs, and characters with new motivations and backgrounds to redirect the mainstream literary canon.

Race can be a sore subject within the United States because the history of the country's racism has to be discussed. Racism goes as far as to infiltrate the legal and judicial system, politics, and citizens' behaviors. One of the groups that has experienced extreme racism within the United States is Black people. The United States has packaged slavery into a digestible moment in history so that school children learn of the fact but never understand the extent to which the brutality went. The topic of slavery or racism can be taboo and is sure to kill the mood in any social gathering. Toni Morrison says more about how race has been implemented into literature in her speech titled, "Unspeakable Things Unspoken: The Afro-American Experience in American Literature." She says, "The 'race' aspect is as severe as it is because the claims for attention come from that segment of scholarly and artistic labor in which the mention of 'race' is either inevitable or elaborately, painstakingly masked... Thus, in spite of its implicit and explicit acknowledgment, 'race' is still a virtually unspeakable thing." In Gothic literature, race can be discussed freely, primarily if the horror within the themes and motifs is based on real life.

Beloved by Toni Morrison follows the story of Sethe as she deals with the ghost of her infant daughter in her house and recalls her days as an enslaved person at a plantation called Sweet Home. Naturally, the book covers topics of racism and tragedy that plague Sethe's life and that of the other characters. However, through the details provided, readers get a much deeper look into the various troubles that plagued people during and after being enslaved. Horrific details and circumstances that arise from enslavement and trouble the characters endure are not dwelled on, but instead shared matter-of-factly and even made to be seen as the natural state of things. When describing the men's anticipation for the arrival of thirteen-year-old Sethe, acts of bestiality are seen as a better alternative than the first option, raping Sethe. The book says, "All in their twenties, minus women, fucking cows, dreaming of rape, thrashing on pallets, rubbing their thighs and waiting for the new girl" (Morrison, 13). By stating this information and then moving on, readers are made aware that such situations may not be as uncommon as people like to think. The use of animal imagery here and the phrase "thrashing on pallets" reflects the brutalities of enslavement, detailing not only how others viewed the men, but also how they were taught to view themselves. In the eyes of the White people on or around the plantation, the men are no more helpful or meaningful to them than cattle. Enslaved men are seen as less than. The use of animal imagery reoccurs when discussing Sethe and her stolen milk. Just as the men do to the cattle, the boys do to Sethe and stole the milk she had produced for her babies. Not only do they treat her as sub-human, but they deprive her of her one desire to be a mother and nurture her children.

The loss of individuality when subject to the cruelties of slavery is another theme that is discussed in Morrison's *Beloved*. Paul D recalls his time enslaved in a Kentucky plantation, where he and other men were chained together to walk and work. No distinction is made between one man and another, as they do not get the opportunities to form deep bonds and the men in charge do not see them as equals. Because of their circumstances, the men are made to obey, as one man falling behind would affect the rest directly. The book says, "If one pitched and ran—all, all forty-six, would be yanked by the chain that bound them and no telling who or how many would be killed. A man could risk his own life, but not his brother's" (Morrison, 129). Not only is there a loss of individuality, but conformity is also pushed upon them. While subject to these conditions, the men are responsible for themselves and the people around them, making any form of rebellion dangerous for the entire group. When the mud structure around the men collapses during a storm, the men are left to die and need to figure out for themselves, in the dark while bound to one another, how to get out.

Instances like these are complicated to talk about and difficult to listen to, as we see with Sethe and Paul D. Sethe, who already is dealing with her inner conflicts, is fatigued from thinking of her past and seems tired and almost irritated when Paul D wants to share his stories with her. This could strain family dynamics. Families already affected and pulled apart by slavery and racism now also had to deal with the aftermath and traumas that plague them. The effect of slavery on families and motherhood is another topic heavily discussed in *Beloved*. When Sethe shares her passion and love for her children, Paul D finds it to be one of the riskiest things a Black mother can do during those times. The book says, "For a used-to-be-slave woman to love anything that much was dangerous, especially if it was her children she had settled on to love" (Morrison, 54). This notion highlights how families were split apart to work on different plantations, and mothers had to choose between sacrificing their children or subjecting them to a life of slavery. Anything that held value could be used as a weapon and taken away. This created a loss of innocence in children and adults, subjecting them all to surreal atrocities.

The true horror of *Beloved* lies in the fact that the disturbing facts and details included were a genuine possibility and outcome of slavery. The pain characters in the novel experience are traumas many real-life people dealt with. The nuances of slavery and racism that go unspoken about in society and may generally make people uneasy are explicitly discussed and explored. The Gothic is known for making you feel uncomfortable and causing bodily reactions. Morrison uses real-life circumstances and realities that people have been subject to to create an eerie world in which the characters cannot escape their past traumas, no matter their efforts. Whether it comes to animals or chains, the imagery highlights the darkness of the times still being pushed down today.

The topic of gender is not as taboo, historically, when compared to race, but the nuances of the subject can be, especially when intertwined with factors like socioeconomic status or race. Women in particular have been seen as less than men and have been expected to be quiet and subservient. Women are placed on a pedestal in a hidden place, expected to be happy, to be loving, and to serve a husband and family while not being thanked, and they are expected to keep their own suffering to themselves. Traditionally, even in Gothic literature, women were cast aside, and all their characters served as objects of tragedy or devices to continue the story. As more female writers become recognized within the Gothic genre, this trend of shedding light on the unspeakable continues. Female writers in the Gothic genre aim to rewrite and reclaim stories about women and use their day-to-day experiences and traumas to write their Gothic tales.

In the short story, *The Bloody Chamber* by Angela Carter, expectations of the female in the Gothic genre are entirely subverted. The protagonist is not lured or thrown into dangerous circumstances; instead, she is allured by the possibility of change and danger. The mother is another figure who works against the woman's usual position within the Gothic genre. When her daughter is in danger, it is not a male character—who may be a love interest or a father figure who feels the need to protect her—that saves her—that saves her; it is the mother who rides in on horseback, wielding a gun. She acknowledges the performativity of gender and being a woman and uses it in her character's favor. Carter mutates expectations, as we see in *The Bloody Chamber,* and it continues in her work regularly. In Emma Pi-tai Peng's article in *NTU Studies in Language and Literature*, she says, "The Gothic deals with these themes as a space of horror; Carter deals with them as a theatrical site, a fearful space where people transgress the boundaries but are reflexively conscious of the theatricality of their fear, and the paradox is, though the fear is theatrical, it is no less genuine." (Pi-Tai Peng 2004, 31).

The Yellow Wallpaper by Charlotte Perkins Gilman and *The Husband Stitch* by Carmen Maria Machado are both similarly written by feminist female authors. Their writing often talks about the nuances of being a woman and the different crushing societal expectations and conditions that women have been subject to over time. *The Yellow Wallpaper* follows a woman who is held hostage in a room by her husband after she has a miscarriage and falls into a depression. The woman is told what is best for her, and her husband and brother, who are both Doctors, refuse to listen to her or take a closer look at what is going on, and her condition worsens. In *The Husband Stitch,* a detached tone lingers over the piece as events unfold and the small injustices women experience from girlhood, onward are highlighted and explored. As the title of the story suggests, when giving birth and in a vulnerable state, her husband opts for the husband stitch, which is when an extra stitch is placed in the vaginal opening for a "tighter" feeling.

In the true Gothic style, these female authors use the genre to speak on the fears of a generation, speak of the unspeakable emotions and experiences women are subjected to and expected not to talk about, and redirect the craft of creating female characters to make them reflect real women.

Sexuality can be another taboo subject, though the severity depends on what period one focuses on. Homosexuality, on the other hand, can be a complex subject to discuss even in today's climate, where we have made great strides in comparison to ten years in the past. Homosexual women are sexualized, fetishized, or not believed, and homosexual men are seen as sinners, lesser men, and promiscuous. Women or men who loved the same gender were previously persecuted under the law and are still being treated indecently today. In the 1800s and 1900s, this was especially the case. Though Oscar Wilde was not speaking of America, *The Picture of Dorian Gray* is a perfect example of Gothic literature serving as an outlet for the unspeakable.

Oscar Wilde, a poet from the nineteenth century, is best known for his playwriting, novels, and imprisonment in 1895 under the United Kingdom's "gross indecency" laws. While Wilde spent most of his adult life married and had two children, he had a love affair with Alfred Douglas that ended with Wilde in prison. At his trial, they used his writing against him, arguing that there were underlying homoerotic tones. He spent the rest of his life after imprisonment in exile and with little money to his name, despite all his accomplishments and the successful life he had lived before. Wilde knew that homosexuality was seen as sinful and was punishable by law, but even when in court, he never apologized for his actions, as they aligned with his philosophies as an artist and a lover of beauty no matter the form. In Wilde's work, *The Picture of Dorian Gray,* we see homoerotic tones and themes sprout throughout the novel. There is no homosexuality anywhere explicitly in the book, only heterosexual relationships, because otherwise, the novel could not have been published, but Wilde found a way to include homosexual undertones.

In a scene between the two men, Basil pleads to Dorian to listen to what he is about to say without judgment, as it may affect their friendship and how Dorian views him. Basil then confesses what seems to be an infatuation with Dorian, but can also be perceived as a love confession.. He says, "I was dominated, soul, brain, and power, by you. ... I worshipped you. I grew jealous of everyone to whom you spoke. I wanted you all to myself. I was only happy when I was with you. When you were away from me, you were still present in my art. ... Of course, I would never let you know anything of this" (Wilde, 114). This passage could have been seen as a reflection of reality, where, because of the lack of labels or understanding at the time—the concept of homosexuality had not been solidified—Basil could not name his feelings and chose not to express them out of fear of repercussions.

The portrait of Dorian painted by Basil can also be seen as a representation of the repressed homosexual desires of Dorian. In her paper, Alexandria Wohlford says, "Victorian society has placed social and legal obstructions to any engagement with same-sex relationships, causing Dorian to view his homosexuality as something sinful and grotesque. These attitudes are projected metaphorically onto the portrait, resulting in the horrid image that emerges. Thus, the portrait can be viewed as representing Dorian's fear of his repressed desires—deep down, he suspects that his same-sex desires make him as gruesome as the artwork has become, and this fear is what is reflected in the portrait" (Wohlford 2023, 7–8). Following this idea, homoerotic desire was the fear or "monster" within the novel. If it were not for the societal pressures of the time, the fear may not have ultimately consumed Dorian and led to his and Basil's death. The Gothic trope of the double or the uncanny serves perfectly for such metaphors of desires that must be repressed out of fear that they are ugly.

The Gothic has also been used as a weapon against the "unknown." Anyone different can be labeled a monster. In *Gothic Studies*, George E. Haggerty says, "Gothic motifs of dark and threatening passages and looming hooded figures jump out from descriptions that hint at a deeper haunting than even Gothic novelists achieve. This author uses conventions that are familiar in Gothic fiction to render the threat of the sodomite psychologically more disruptive than it might otherwise be...the notion that they might be masquerading as respectable members of society makes them doubly vicious" (Haggerty 2006, 39). This is true not just of sexuality but of race, nationality, and more. Despite this, today's writers are paving a path in a new direction and using their voices to amplify different stories and struggles.

Whatever subject rings true to the author or the time, Gothic literature serves as an outlet for the aspects of American society that are left ignored or pushed aside by creating characters with different motivations and backgrounds and by utilizing motifs and symbols to speak about the unspeakable. The Gothic genre dares to push against societal norms, rewrites stories of those who could not tell them themselves, and sheds light on the dark corners readers may not have been able to talk about or read.

Works Cited

Carter, Angela. *The Bloody Chamber: And Other Stories, 75th Anniversary Edition*. Penguin Classics, 2015.

Gilman, Charlotte Perkins. *The Yellow Wallpaper*. Virago Press, 1981.

Haggerty, George E. "'Dung, Guts and Blood': Sodomy, Abjection and Gothic Fiction in the Early Nineteenth Century." *Gothic Studies* 8, no. 2 (November 2006): 35–51. https://doi.org/10.7227/gs.8.2.3.

Machado, Carmen Maria. "The Husband Stitch." *Her Body and Other Parties: Stories*, 3–32. Graywolf Press, 2017.

Mattawa, Khaled, and Vicki Lawrence. "Unspeakable Things Unspoken: The Afro-American Presence in American Literature." Michigan Quarterly Review, June 22, 2021. https://sites.lsa.umich.edu/mqr/2019/08/unspeakable-things-unspoken-the-afro-american-presence-in-american-literature/.

Morrison, Toni. *Beloved*. Vintage International. Vintage Books, a division of Random House, Inc, 2017.

"Oscar Wilde." *Queer Portraits in History*. Accessed January 15, 2025. https://www.queerportraits.com/bio/wilde.

Pi-tai Peng, Emma. "Angela Carter's Postmodern Feminism and the Gothic Uncanny." *NTU Studies in Language and Literature* 13 (June 2004): 99–134.

Wilde, Oscar. *The Picture of Dorian Gray and selected stories*. Signet Classic, 2007.

Wohlford, Alexandra. "Dorian and the Double: Repressed Homosexual Desire in The Picture of Dorian Gray," 2023.

Vassell, Nicole. "Stephen Fry Says Oscar Wilde's Story Made Him Fear 'A Cursed Life' as a Gay Man." The Independent, August 8, 2023. https://www.independent.co.uk/arts-entertainment/tv/news/stephen-fry-gay-uk-oscar-wilde-b2389332.html.

My Favorite Red

Jack Niemczyk

I brought a bottle of my favorite red wine
For us to share

We bathe in the autumn sky in Central Park
The leaves falling around us
But not dying
just resting for a small period as we all need to do

It's a sparkling lambrusco
he doesn't usually like red
So it is a little lighter
Just like he likes

We enjoy it in our mismatched mugs
as we pretend that nothing and everything is about us
Silent
With each other

A child scrapes her knee, her orange corduroy pants
speckled red
A nanny loses control, she embraces a tone similar to
Ms. Doubtfire
A couple fights, their roars echoing and turning heads
A tuba plays a polka, childish and divine in its popping
melody

We sip
We watch

'Til it's all gone
The only memory of the bottle
Seeped inside the cork
Enough for me
Enough for him
Enough for us

"How about some dinner?"

I love this

Servitude

Chardonnae Simpson

Women are taught early to water dead plants.

Give it some light to soothe your inner melancholy
Give it some water,
It could satisfy the parched entity that is your heart

Drained by him

Women are taught to be eternally empathetic
To diminish their feelings and cater
to someone who will never cater to us.

We clean tables, do dishes
        Sweep
    Mop

Give the babies a kiss
tears welling in our eyes
Kill each other for the male gaze

No tips
        No appreciation
    No love

We should have more "closed" signs for men with
entitlement
But the door will always say, "open."

Machu Picchu

Misha Puello Brasil

At eleven years old, I went with my mother
to visit her father's homeland, Peru.
Too young to appreciate the history
petrified in the beige city walls and stone roads,
I was intrigued by the culture and strange, colorful
sights.

We traveled from morning to dusk
in a van, sticky from heat, with blue carpeted seats
that held onto memories from past travelers
in the form of mysteriously shaped permanent blobs.

When we arrived in Cusco, the air felt thin and difficult
to breathe. My brain rattled around the inside of my
head.
I didn't like being distinguished from the natives—
We shared the same blood. My mother and I decided
to scale a grand mountain and climbed toward the
infamous summit:
Hours spent in the thick forests and steep ascents
where fresh air had never seemed so unattainable out of
doors.

Dogs barking for rest, we reached our destination,

a sight I knew I would never forget.

Sun-dried grass and oddly-stacked, disfigured gray bricks.

The gaseous smell hit first, and then I saw it:

A llama had created the most beautiful structure:

A mountain of soft Milk Duds, the pile half a foot high.

Summer Breeze

Madhuri Pawar

You came in like a cool breeze of summer,

took away all the impounding sickness from my heart.

You healed me in ways I never knew were required.

Kissing my scars, perfecting my insecurities, holding my heart, caressing my yearning.

You saw me for not what I had done, but for who I was.

The embrace that we shared perfectly seeped into my frame, knocking on my core to announce, *you aren't alone.*

You came in like a cool breeze of summer,

took away the fog that the dark winter nights brought.

You shone like the brightest star, poured all the vibrant colors,

yellowing my Blues, greening my Grays, whitening my Blacks.

You besotted me like never before,

holding onto my hand whilst I was tumbling into iniquity, kissing away my tears, filling me up with your aroma.

You came in like a cool breeze of summer,

took away all the blistered slices that the frosting brought.

You read my mind in a tongue I'd never heard of before,

you taught me your dialect, and I began to speak to you.

Entangling your fingers with mine, stroking my palm with your thumb, making sure I felt every trace on my heart.

You came in like a cool breeze of summer, but why did nobody tell me that summer too, is just a season?

Why did nobody tell me that the breeze that grazed my face had to go beyond?

Why did nobody tell me, the shinier the days, the darker the nights?

Why did nobody tell me that it's the rain that follows the summer?

Why did nobody tell me that the rain that follows the summer gets thunderstorms along?

Why did nobody tell me that there would be no more cool breeze of summer, but the thudding of windows?

Why did nobody tell me that I would have to protect myself from the rain?

Why did nobody tell me that I would be left alone in the darkness?

Why did nobody tell me that summer, too, is just a season?

Now I'm lonely, under the table, catching a glimpse of myself in the mirror, while the lightning flashes my face with a gush of rainy wind.

Now I have to yearn for you,

yearn through the rains,

yearn through the winters,

yearn through the spring,

yearn for the summer.

The Color Blue

Alena Williams

Blue is serenity. Blue is pain.

When I think of the color blue, I think of the ocean.
The vast, uncharted waters that hold the souls of my
ancestors.

I often think of the spirits that float in the sea, forgotten
by many minds, but on a loop in mine... I think of the
strong, blue waves as my fighting ancestors, trying with
all their might to crash their way back onto the shore
of the physical world, whisper in my brown ears at the
beach.

Perhaps there's a magical world under the sea where the
bodies of our ancestors are finally free; a world where
they're at peace and their hearts swim with love for
what never came to be: grandchildren never created,
dreams never fulfilled, and flowers never blossomed.

Blue clings to my skin like earthy sea salt. It flows
through my Black blood and crashes through my blue
veins. Eyes, though brown, cry blue with the thought
of my grandmother's grandmother; my grandfather's
grandfather, and all of those who came before them.

Blue is the color I feel. Blue is serenity, and blue is pain.

Glass Eyes

Misha Puello Brasil

Koan sat alone on the pavement at the bottom of the grassy hill, looking over the water and swinging his worn Converse above the rocks. To the north were the mysterious islands he liked to imagine were inhabited by a lost community of runaways fed up with corrupt governments and the cruel mediocrity of every twenty-four-hour day. Koan's shoulders hunched forward, and his jaw tightened. He scowled. He allowed the cold to affect his hands, enjoying the rigid feeling in his fingers. He envisioned himself as a puppet. Not the sock-puppet type with the bland button-eyes and a hand up the ass, but the sophisticated kind of puppet with human features manipulated by invisible strings. His favorite puppets were the ones with wide, lifeless glass eyes and motionless facial expressions. He felt a certain kinship.

Koan stared at the high rocks to his east that had climbed up from the water. They formed a staircase to a beautiful view overlooking the neighboring country club's beach. He believed the club's water only looked so enticing because no one could touch it. He didn't like to sit up on the rocks anyway. He always thought about how he and Amber, not even three years ago, used to sit on that peak together and discuss what they'd do in college and plans for the future. They had the same conversation every Friday, but Koan looked forward to their walk to Davenport Park after school, coffee, and a donut from Dunkin' Donuts. He thought about the last time they spoke up on those rocks three years ago.

"How many people do you think have fallen off this rock and into the water?" Koan asked, dangling an empty Dunkin' Donuts cup over the edge.

"All-time? Probably a couple hundred. This year..." Amber checked her phone. "It's only March, but the general public looks especially stupid this year, so I would say maybe twenty?"

Koan gently lifted his fingers one by one, starting with his pinky, off the clear plastic cup. He heard the brief sound of ice jangling before the cup disappeared below the rocks. Koan counted silently,

"One Mississippi, two Mississippi, three Missi—" Then he heard the faintest *splash*. "I would say about 50 percent live," he said to Amber.

Amber glanced over at him, mouth ajar, then laughed. "I'm going to miss our Davenport talks next year." She grabbed her coffee cup, shrugged, and chucked it into the ocean. "It's already polluted," she said to Koan.

"What will you miss?" Koan asked. "Freezing our asses off, polluting the water, or the thirty-minute walk uphill?" Koan uncrossed his legs and adjusted his jeans by the rip designed to be on the knees. The fabric bunched at his pelvis from sitting on the rough surface of rocks.

Amber shrugged. "I mean, this is our place." She placed a loose strand of her black and blonde hair behind her ear. "Remember our middle school field trip here? We became besties on that trip. Or..." Amber snapped her neck like an owl, looking directly behind her, her massive gold hoop earrings perfectly placed to make her look like Dumbo. Then, pointing to the right, she smiled. "Or our first acid trip under those trees. That was a good time."

"You're the one moving. What's so good about California anyways? The heat makes you obnoxious to be around." Koan stared at his mysterious islands. He wished he could swim off right then.

"Hey, don't be rude. I get obnoxious, and you love it. You know, I've been working towards this for a long time. I haven't gotten into UCLA yet." She smiled, but Koan's eyes looked away from her and back towards the water. Amber stared at the faint dye on the back of Koan's neck from coloring his hair black. "Koan, can we please talk about this?"

"Can we not?"

§

Koan sat alone on the pavement at the bottom of the grassy hill and swung his battered Converse with as much force as he could gather into the rock directly behind his heel. He didn't like to think about that day with Amber. He hadn't sat up on those rocks since his and Amber's last conversation three years ago. He didn't know that would be one of the last conversations they would ever have, that their friendship would end before graduation. Koan rummaged around his inner jacket pocket until he found the large white envelope. He stared at the envelope in his lap. *I'm so sorry, Amber,* he thought to himself.

Koan could remember the moment when he and Amber became friends. They were in the same grade but always in different classes until middle school when test scores grouped them into the same class. Mr. Nunez had taken a teacher's development course that year that suggested exploring nature would promote learning in children. This influenced him to take the entire class for a field trip to Davenport Park, a twenty-minute walk uphill from school. Koan had no idea that this area of New Rochelle even existed, hidden amongst the country club, mansions, and gated communities, but he instantly fell in love.

Koan kicked the metal flag pole that stood on top of Davenport's hill with his dirty Vans. The black had washed to charcoal, the white stripe had turned gray, and pills covered every inch of fabric. The rest of Mr. Nunez's eighth-grade class scattered amongst the trees around the edges of the park, but Koan's feet and eyes stayed glued to the metal.

Koan felt a soft material hit the back of his head, causing him to narrowly miss collision with the flag pole. "What the hell!" Koan turned to find an open, empty Sprayground backpack with a painting of a crazy old man with green foam oozing out of his mouth. Koan felt almost as angry as the man in the picture.

He snatched the bag off the ground, and two classmates ran up to him, shoving each other along the way. "Shit. Sorry, man, that's my backpack," said the scrawny boy with thin hazelnut hair. Koan looked at him and decided that he could take him if it came down to it. He'd finally get to practice the choke slam he saw on WWE. Koan looked down at the backpack and locked eyes with the crazy old man.

The short boy said, "It was meant to hit him." He pointed to the larger boy with black hair standing beside him.

Koan ignored them, lost in the old man's gaze. *He looks like a wicked puppet master,* he thought.

The larger boy waved his pale hand in front of Koan's face. "Dude, can he have his bag back?" Koan looked up at the blonde-haired boy, the mean expression leaving his face once he realized the boy was looking down at him; he had to be at least six feet tall. Many boys had growth spurts that year, but this kid was massive.

"Who is this guy?" Koan asked, pointing to the backpack.

"That's Rick, from *Rick and Morty*. You've never watched *Rick and Morty*?"

"Obviously he hasn't watched it if he's asking who it is, dumbass." The bigger guy shoved the smaller one by the shoulder, causing him to stumble back.

"Whatever. Can I have my bag?" The shorter boy had enough and extended his hand forward. Koan reluctantly handed him the backpack, only because the blonde-haired boy had become physical.

In the exchange, the scrawny boy dropped a square rustic gold wrapper. It was a condom wrapper covered in dirt. The larger boy quickly swept the condom off the floor and hid it in his hand. "Ha! It's mine now," he said.

"Fuck!" The shorter boy said to himself, zipping up his backpack. He tightened his lips and focused his eyes on Koan. "This is your fault man, I found that shit, and you made me lose it."

Koan rolled his eyes. *Why would anyone pick up an old condom off a park floor?* "That has to be expired," Koan said.

"What?"

"Condoms don't expire, dude," said the blonde-haired boy.

"Sure. Whatever, man." Koan's attention had started to move past the conversation and over to the odd culmination of stones by the left end of the park.

"What do you know anyways, freak," the blonde-haired boy said, already shoving the condom deep into his jeans pockets. The other boy followed close to him, bookbag and ugly expression in hand.

"They're so stupid," a higher voice said from behind Koan.

Koan turned to his right to see a short girl with black hair and a fuzzy pink sweater thicker than his winter jacket standing beside him.

"Aren't you hot in that?" he asked.

The girl ignored him. "I saw them find the condom earlier; it was under a rock."

"Okay," Koan said. *Figures. I hope he uses it.*

"I don't think you're a freak," she said. "It was so mean of everyone to think you're the reason Jeremy went missing. It's not your fault. Pure coincidence, I think."

Koan thought of Jeremy, the hamster. The class pet. The hamster was large for its breed and had golden fur. Koan admired the chocolate patch of hair that grew from his neck and spread to half his face; he thought it looked like a mask. His eighth-grade class had adopted and named Jeremy on the first day of school. Koan hadn't voted on the name Jeremy, though; he had liked the name Morningstar instead, but nobody voted for that.

"I didn't kill Jeremy."

"I didn't say you did! Boys are so stupid." She looked to Koan for a response, but none came. "I don't think you're stupid or a murderer."

He looked her straight in the eyes. She and Koan had never spoken before; Koan habitually kept his distance from most people. "Why not?" he asked.

"Why don't I think you're stupid?" she asked, tilting her head to the side. Her black hair was plaited into two pigtails, tied off with pink bands. Her ears were decorated with two small gold hoops. "Cause you stay away from everyone else. I would if I could, but..."

"But what?"

She shrugged. "I don't know." She looked down at the ground and pointed aggressively, her charm bracelet packed with the whole rainbow of color jingling. "I like your shoes."

Koan looked down at his tattered shoes, which were coming apart. He didn't like change, and they were comfortable. "They're raggedy," he said.

The girl in the pink fuzzy sweater put her hands on her hips. "If they're raggedy, get new shoes," she said, huffing and then putting her arms back down at her side. "Your shoes are worn; It makes them look cool and comfy. You should learn to take compliments because I like to give them out a lot," she said, looking at Koan. She seemed to be waiting for an answer.

Koan smiled; His teeth were small and slightly crooked. He always kept to himself in his classes. He thought it was best to refrain from speaking if your words would be misconstrued. The only people he was close with were his two older brothers, but they didn't get to talk much since they were both in training for the military. *She could be different*, he decided. "You're Ember, right? Cool name."

She smiled back, "Amber, but thanks."

"Amber. That's cool too. I'm Koan," he said.

"I know your name, I pay attention." Amber tilted her head sideways, this time in the opposite direction. Her pigtails followed. "Has anyone ever told you that you look like the Once-ler from The Lorax? No offense or anything," she said.

Koan smiled, authentically this time. "None taken. No, no one's said that before. I see it, though," he said, thinking of the same comment his brothers made all the time.

"The Once-ler is like a baby tree though, tall and still stick thin. You're more like a nicely shaped and trimmed bush," she said. Koan had no idea what she was talking about, so he decided to keep it that way and ignore it.

Amber started trotting over to the small gathering of rocks to the west. She was wearing linen shorts, and Koan stared at the scratches on her calf. He followed after her like they were attached by a string. "That's the Shakespeare Garden. The fifth-grade class from Trinity donated it like twenty years ago or something. It's pretty, but it's just rocks and flowers arranged in a pretty pattern with *one* bench in the middle. I mean, I guess there's these like stone benches that you could sit on, but my butt would hurt after sitting on that for a while," she said.

"My thing is, why would you only put one bench in the middle of the thing?" As they started getting closer to the garden, Amber turned around and started walking backward. "It's cute and all, and there is the factor of how much they could afford, but if the city wasn't so cheap, then maybe they could have expanded the garden or something," Amber said as they reached the edge of the garden.

It was just as Amber had described it. No more than about thirty rocks arranged in a pattern that almost looked like the hippie peace sign. In each of the sections, the pattern created was a pathetic arrangement of flowers that was devoid of red color. *Plant Vampires.* Three wooden stumps and two stone stumps were oddly placed around the perimeter. It looked more like Mother Nature's bedroom floor than a decorated garden. In the very center was a single wooden bench, identical to the ones on top of the park's hill where Amber and Koan stood earlier.

"What do you think? Kinda pathetic, right?" Amber asked.

"I love it," Koan said, "It's awful."

"Right! That's why I like it too," Amber said, smiling.

§

Koan preferred to remember all of his and Amber's best memories. After their meeting at the flagpole and their journey to the garden, Koan and Amber became close friends. The day of their trip, while walking back to school, they grew closer over conversations about the different attitudes of their peers—whose personalities were ever-changing. They talked about their favorite movie-to-book adaptation, *Cruel Intentions* (1999), both agreeing that the book should be evaluated separately from the film.

When Amber's black hair and pigtails changed into an emo shag, Koan remained friends with her while her other group of friends laughed. The two continued their friendship when Amber became mainstream again, sporting her shiny, thick lip gloss and long, hot pink acrylic nails. When Koan's father passed away, Amber held his hand and gave him a safe place to cry. Koan had come to trust Amber like no other.

Koan tucked away the envelope, placed his hands on the warm pavement, and jumped to the rocks. It was low tide, perfect for a walk. Koan started to move across each rock as slowly and animatedly as physically possible, practicing for his puppet future. He thought about where it could have gone wrong.

Koan never had many friends at school. He was always regarded as odd, even in elementary school. He always said the wrong thing. In middle school, his father died, and relating to other children got harder. They never wanted to talk about heavy topics like death or even be reminded of it, but Koan didn't have much else to think about than mortality. The latest episode of *SpongeBob SquarePants* or the most attractive girl in the grade was not interesting to Koan, and soon, he developed the idea that it was below him. By freshman year of high school, he had worked past his pain enough to be at peace during the day, but his anxieties and his distaste of classmates never entirely disappeared. He couldn't be blamed. If any average person was to listen in on a thirteen-year-old's conversation, they would also be abhorred.

At age sixteen, his junior year of high school, his brothers died, meaning Koan had to relive everything that he had gone through with his father's passing. He spent countless nights awake, unable to sleep without having uncomfortably vivid dreams of his family. He was convinced he caused misery to everyone around him; Even his own mother had become a husk of a person, prescribed so many medications that Koan began to think the government was experimenting with zombies.

Koan used to dream of himself as an old doctor, so immersed in his own retirement that he started to grow mad. Every dream was the same: the doctor wore the same lab coat and conducted his own experiments until he finally ran out of test subjects and started taking his concoctions himself. The doctor called himself The Puppet Master.

When Koan's father passed, his dreams changed, and The Puppet Master finally stopped using himself as a subject for experimentation. The Puppet Master had started creating his own human-like puppets, starting off with Koan's dad. When Koan's brothers passed, The Puppet Master had acquired two more subjects to work on.

Each dream started the same. The Puppet Master held the three men in a dark, damp room below ground. The light fixtures on the high ceilings flickered, and the buzz of electricity filled the room. The ceilings and walls had gray moss overtaking every visible surface, except for the white tile floors, which The Master regularly cleaned.

The expansive room held five cement slabs to the far right, with three of them occupied by Koan's father and brothers, who were chained, standing up and gagged at the mouth. The odor was putrid; it smelled of years of accumulated human excrement that didn't just pierce through your nose; it invaded and swelled, taking over your sinuses and creeping down your throat. Whenever Koan had these dreams, he held his breath, convinced he could feel the fecal matter particles in the air entering his mouth.

The Master would operate on the men individually on his operating table in the middle of the room. He would lay the men down on the metal table and slice them open directly in the center, from the top of their skull to the bottom of their ball sack so that it lined up with their ass crack. The screams of the men came out almost muted. What seemed to only increase in volume was the sound, *drip, drip, drip,* that came from the cracks in the ceiling. *The moss is peeing on me,* he thought, as the inevitable end of the dream came.

The room flooded with the murky water, and Koan washed up in front of a stage where The Puppet Master put on his new production. Koan sat chained to a stone chair and gagged at the mouth with bloody bandages, unable to move or scream, as he waited for his father and brothers to perform on stage and do a little dance.

Koan was convinced that *he* was the reason that The Puppet Master put on this show. He believed *he* was why his family was up there, and he didn't have to guess who those two extra stone slabs were for: his mother and Amber.

Koan had never told anybody about his dreams. As much as he trusted Amber, he believed it was unlikely he would ever tell her about them. He didn't want to cause her to run away. She was one of the few consistent good things in Koan's life. He promised he would never leave her; to his content, she promised the same.

Koan couldn't help but think of where he went wrong.

He continued walking, mimicking a puppet as best he could, turning and looking toward the top of the highest rock where he and Amber had their last conversation. It was time to confront this. Koan lifted his arms high above his head and converted his hands into sharp claws, running bow-legged, slightly hopping side to side towards the rock, screaming as loud as he could. If anyone were around, they would think the Vikings had come back. Koan used so much force in his steps that he could feel the jagged rocks on his feet as if he were stomping towards the earth's center. He arrived at the bottom of the rock and started to climb it carefully, enough adrenaline having left his body from his scream that he was clear-headed and proceeded with caution.

§

Amber held the large white envelope in both her hands. She wore the same pink fuzzy sweater she wore four years ago on that field trip; this time, her black hair was detailed with chunky blonde highlights. Koan sat beside her with his feet touching the edge of the cliff in his raccoon-striped shirt and brand-new Converse that Amber had gifted him in anticipation of graduation. He stared at his mysterious island intensely, readying himself for Amber's decision letter to be opened.

"Koan, can we please talk about this?" Amber said, placing a hand on his shoulder, urging him to turn.

Koan shrugged off her hand and crossed his legs so he would no longer be at the cliff edge. "Can we not?"

Amber withdrew her hand from Koan's shoulder and stood up, waiting for Koan to turn around. Koan stared at the clearest tree in sight on the island. It was the tallest, but its branches were strong and shaped differently than the others.

Amber started fidgeting with the envelope, bending it back and forth as she paced along the rocks' edge. Koan's tree was then blocked by a pink fuzzy sweater, and the wind blew little pieces into his slightly open mouth. She looked down at her black boots and then up at his face. Amber had her hands on her hips.

Amber sighed. She dropped her hands and crouched so that she and Koan were eye-level. "I'm serious, Koan. Can you please be happy for me? I want to share this moment with you," she said.

"What is there to talk about, Amber?" he said, staring at the envelope still clutched in her hands. You're the one who's moving all the way to California for college and then asked me not to go

150

with you." Koan knew he was acting like a child, but she was the one breaking their promise. "Why do you want to go, anyway?" he asked.

"UCLA is a really good school, and it'll let me start over completely new. I can't live in the same house with my parents anymore. Haven't you ever wanted to just start over?" Amber asked.

"I just don't see why you have to do that without me," Koan said.

"Can you please not be that way?" Amber adjusted herself, and Koan noticed she was getting tired of crouching. "I'm not trying to push you away; there are so many ways to stay in contact. We already text every day. I just don't want you to plan the rest of your life around me. You need to branch out and find what you like to do," she said.

"I know what I'd like to do. I'd like to go to California with my best friend. I'd like to just focus on getting a job and making some money. I'd like for you to not push me away!" Koan said. He had almost been yelling. Amber was betraying him.

"I'm not pushing you away!" Amber said, sounding desperate. Koan only glared at Amber; his eyes had glassed over. She tossed her envelope onto the rocks. "You need to grow up, Koan! You can't chase me around forever," she said.

By the time Koan finished processing Amber's words, he had already grown cold towards her. Amber's mouth opened, but no words left her mouth. A moment passed, and then Amber said, "I'm sorry, Koan. I was angry, I didn't mean it." She placed her hand on Koan's knee.

"Get off me!" Koan said, grabbing Amber's hand and pushing it away from him with a force he had not expected to exert. Amber attempted to steady her footing and started to stand, but she lost her balance and fell backward into the rocks and water below.

Koan's mouth dropped open and locked in place. He could feel his breathing stop and his heart drop past his stomach and straight into The Puppet Master's room. *What did I just do?* He quickly got on all fours and lay flat on the cliff, trying to get as secure as possible before peering over the edge. Koan's eyes searched and found Amber's body lying flat on the rocks below. He stared intensely, searching for a sign of blood. In what had been seconds but felt like hours to Koan, he caught sight of the pool of blood forming a steady stream down the rock where Amber's head lay and into the water.

§

Koan reached the top of the cliff where he had witnessed Amber's death. Residents of New Rochelle hardly climb toward the very top of those rocks anymore. It turned out that Amber had been the first in several years to fall off of the rocks and die. However, nobody believed Koan when he said it was an accident. It was the same with Jeremy. Koan had only tried to give him a sweet chocolate treat.

His dreams now included Amber, and he saw her perform every night. She was dressed as the prettiest ballerina, and the Master gave her the most beautiful glass eyes. Koan was jealous. He couldn't wait to go on stage and perform with Amber. He missed his father and his brothers, who got to dance with Amber and help lift her during Swan Lake. A part of him was grateful that now Amber would never leave.

It was time to finally open the decision letter and determine if Amber had gotten into UCLA. Koan stared down at his worn-out Converse, where holes formed in the soles. He took a deep breath before creeping into his jacket pocket and pulling out the envelope. The envelope was worn over time, and the paper had become soft. The envelope was dirty around the edges from being held and moved so many times. He reached back inside his jacket pocket and pulled out a letter opener. He was prepared for this moment. His chest hurt. He could feel his heart beating and gliding up his throat while he opened the envelope and took out the contents from inside. His hands were sweating, and his fingerprints left damp marks on the single white sheet on top of the promotional content packet.

Koan's eyes scanned the top of the page, and he read the words: "Amber, we regret to inform you…"

Complain and Simple

Jack Niemczyk

Have you ever been told, "Your kiddo is such a ham" or, "He is such a natural?" On your child's report card, does it say, "She loves to express her ideas every chance she gets!" After hearing this twenty-two jillion times, you may think to yourself, *maybe I should channel this energy into something productive.*

One way to home in on your little Lamenting Linda (or Larry) is through complaining! While you can literally find a peewee football team on every corner, and every homo sends his or her fruity child to the arts, another activity is sometimes overlooked: complaining! Now, as newcomers, it may be hard to navigate how to get your child involved in complaining, so here are some tips from moms who have been through it that may help.

1. How to tell if your peewee has a gift for grumbling

The first sign that a child may be unhappy is the presence of colic. Though doctors say there is no real reason they are crying, an artist's—nay, a cynic's—point of view is that they are simply unhappy and want to let you know. A good mother would take this as the first sign and begin to train her baby. For the younger folks, the training is as simple as buying extra hard bottle nipples or feeding them just too little or perhaps too much. This slight uneasiness will hone their skills and give them problems in their otherwise pleasant lives, which is wonderful fuel for complaining. For many of the weaker ones among us, that constant turmoil you see in your precious baby can be too much, and many mothers are unable to successfully get their complainer through the young years. We know it may be hard, but don't forget, Mom; if the baby is crying, it's just practice. A wonderful motto to follow!

2. Do research on studios

Once your child has reached the ripe age of about two or three—just as he or she begins talking—find a local studio that specializes in vocal lessons; no, not lessons in singing (only the queers would pay for their children to do that) but lessons on being vocal. Your child should have at least one lesson a week with activities ranging from *Getting the Wrong Meal at a Restaurant* to a simple-a-thing like *The Weather*. Most major cities have wonderful classes that all ages can take, but in the rare case that there isn't a studio near you, simply put your children in an unair-conditioned room with your in-laws, and they should become experts.

3. Specialty Schools

While not all mothers agree with this tip, if you find your child getting bored in studio classes, think of sending him or her to a specialty school. Not every child needs it, but a good mother—nay, a smart mother—would realize that putting her child through the stressful environment that is a concentrated school will only help the child be a better complainer. The prestigious institutions include Whining Academy, Moaning Montessori School for the Angered and Annoyed, The Bellyaching Institute of Bali, and, of course, Harvard. Many more schools offer fabulous programs to get your youngling to work. No matter how much it may cost, in the end, it will help your kiddo!

4. Create a Daily Schedule

One of the most valuable lessons I learned from an older comParents (it's what we call our message board—isn't it just a riot?) is that creating a daily schedule will help your child get the practice needed in real-world experience, especially if enrolled in an institution like the ones mentioned above that specializes in written complaining. (It's good to get some in-person experience). For example, my Karen's schedule goes as such:

6:00 a.m.—Karen's alarm goes off, and she means to snooze but accidentally turns it off.

8:35 a.m.—Karen awakes, late for class.

9:00 a.m.—Karen's eyebrows are slightly uneven.

9:05 a.m.—Karen grabs fruit for breakfast, but only oranges (she hates oranges).

9:10 a.m.—Karen misses her bus.

10:00 a.m.—Karen gets to school after tons of traffic.

10:15 a.m.—The teacher calls on Karen when she doesn't know the answer.

11:45 a.m.—Karen opens her lunch box to find nothing but an orange.

12:30 p.m.—Karen forgot her gym clothes and has to wear used ones.

12:45 p.m.—Karen's team loses the game unfairly.

1:30 p.m.—Karen is called on again.

2:45 p.m.—I pick Karen up from kindergarten late.

Now that is only a sample; I have every minute of her day planned out. Remember ladies: our job as complainions (what the message boards call us—so clever!) is that we must add fuel to the fire so that your child has plenty to complain about. Though it may seem tedious, setting her alarm wrong every day and posing as a student to steal her gym clothes from her locker, don't worry, moms... The shoes on your knees get more comfortable.

5. Always be prepared

Preparation is key! The world may be an awful place, but not enough for your child. If you want to challenge your kid, you must be prepared. Children should feel as if the world is against them. Call a bomb threat into a store before your child enters, hand him or her an umbrella when it isn't supposed to rain (and vice versa), and make life a difficult one. Then the true beauty of their complaining will be exposed.

6. Trust the Process

I feel as if I don't even need to tell you ladies this—it would be an insult to me—but the saying goes, "No pain, no complain." (Once again from the message board—so clever!) You will not see any progress if you do not challenge your child. Though he or she may struggle, falter, fall, or contemplate suicide, don't let up and keep pushing.

7. Do it for the right reasons

I mean, c'mon, moms—we know this. We have all had a bad day at complaining, whether our phones somehow worked correctly or there was nothing wrong with the service at lunch; there is no reason to then force your child to follow in your footsteps. Complaining should come from the heart; it should be something that your child is passionate about. Let them be who they are, whether that be a complainer, a football star, or a theatre kid. They are all beautiful.

8. Trust your gut

You've got this, Mom! Remember that you are not alone. It is difficult to raise a child to be a complainer. Your child may be mean, nasty, and straight-up disrespectful, but remember that you are suffering for him or her. So power through that crying and get that kid to complain.

We moms need to stick together, so if any newcomers need any advice, feel free to post any questions you may have here! The life of a complainer is no different than a theatre kid, a jock, or any other child; it's just a little bit more work to build your child's talent. You got this, and if you ever feel lost, just remember our motto, "It isn't that hard, it's complain and simple!"

Hopeless Romantic

Chardonnae Simpson

I looked for love in all the wrong places
Found joy in all the wrong faces
Proved myself in all the wrong cases
I was spineless
Smiling with snakes
Swimming with sharks

My heart yearned for telepathic connection
A love like no other
My love had capacity for Mr. Wrong and Mr. Right
As if these two types could ever coexist comfortably
As if I could decipher who was plain sighted poison and
who was sly simple syrup

My moral compass was darting in every direction *but*
rational
I thought my love could patch up the big gaps in the
hearts of the heartless

I was mistaken
I was then misshapen

Where do you go when the whole town has a piece of
your heart like a collectible?

MotorTrend Magazine

Jana Lewis

MotorTrend Magazine is widely known across the automotive community because of its in-depth articles and honest reviews. The magazine was a starting point for the MotorTrend Corporation, which encompasses nearly all areas of media to reach millions of customers. The structure of the magazine has changed over time and continues to evolve to make the experience better for readers. The revenue generated from ads is geared toward what customers would find useful in the maintenance of their vehicles. Select few non-automotive related products are also promoted. The magazine is printed on high-quality paper that helps the page layouts look crisp, clean, and eye-catching. What started as a small special interest magazine has now become a large-scale empire supporting motorheads across the world.

MotorTrend Magazine released its first issue in September 1949 in hopes of being "the magazine for a motoring world." Their main audience is men or women interested in all things automotive, from performance sports cars to luxury and every-day family cars to heavy-duty trucks. Motorcities.org states that "Motor Trend is the number one magazine in the automotive consumer market because they create the right content featuring what consumers are looking for when making new automobile purchases."

MotorTrend's first issue was a two-color, 32-page magazine with black and white photos, heavy text, and ads for car dealers, car parts, and service companies. It has become the best-selling automotive magazine in the world with high value placed on its content and reviews of various vehicles. According to the magazine's 2022 media kit, *MotorTrend* readership is predominantly men in their mid-thirties, though the past two years have seen an increase in female readers. Though it started out as a monthly magazine, it recently moved to a quarterly publication resulting in a one hundred page issue. The magazine features items that are more directed toward a male audience, but it has never completely excluded women and does not feature them solely as eye candy. The October 1949 issue highlights a female racer in its article about the first races to allow imported cars.

Another article in the magazine covers the process in designing a car in which a man is seen taking measurements of a woman sitting as she would behind the wheel of a car to find optimal seat dimensions. While women are not prominently displayed in images and articles, *MotorTrend* does give them recognition as drivers as well as racers.

The layout of the magazine is standard. Initially, issues were about 25 percent ads with the remaining pages filled with articles, but times have changed and now, over half the magazine is dedicated to ads. Initially, the magazine's table of contents only listed the articles and their page numbers, but this later changed to list feature articles and a small section of articles by department all on a single page. Since 2001, the table of contents has been split in two, with feature articles first and a second table of contents with the specific departments that appear in each issue a few pages later. These sections include "Editor's Letter," "Intake" (a section about the important things going on in the automotive world), "Technologue" (discussions about technology that is being utilized), "Your Say" (customer comments), and "The Big Picture" (discussions on a broad topic in relation to cars). One final piece is "MT Garage" which focuses on existing cars and includes small updates on what a manufacturer is doing or updates on previous articles. *MotorTrend*'s coverage of new models of cars lists about every specification you could think of and provides readers with the information they need to make informed decisions.

In March 2021, *MotorTrend* introduced the concept of using a QR code to start a free trial of their app to stream "Top Gear America." In current issues, the QR code can be used by readers to get more information on a topic, sometimes including added video content.

To keep a magazine going, ads must be purchased to help fund the cost of creating the magazine and to keep the sale price down. *MotorTrend* is no different. It is known all over the world and offers multiple avenues of advertising for customers. The first issue contained ads that were all car-related: dealerships, companies and products to modify a car, and car parts. Today's *MotorTrend Magazine* has expanded to include ads for specific vehicle models, aftermarket accessories, products for cleaning your vehicle, radar detectors, tobacco products, racing schedules, car events, and the occasional male-enhancement product. *MotorTrend* offers advertisers high visibility between print and digital offerings, with print alone seeing over seven million readers. Not only can ads be posted to the print and online magazine, but there are also *MotorTrend* sponsored events, a successful YouTube channel, and various other social media platforms. These expansive offerings can create successful advertising packages for clients. Several ads can be seen in multiple issues of the magazine, meaning there are often deals made for ads to be placed in multiple issues. This works for the client and the magazine, as the magazine has a paid ad that they don't have to wait to be submitted, and the client can get a discount on placement in multiple issues.

In terms of the physical product, the quality of materials is important for the longevity of the magazine as well as its attractiveness. Most issues of the magazine are printed on lightweight, most likely supercalendered paper. The paper is bright white and smooth, with high opacity (level three) that allows it to hold heavy ink well. Most, if not all, pages include images and color blocks that fully bleed with little ghosting on the adjacent page. The paper is thin but prepared enough to hold a lot of four-color ink, and the cover is slightly thicker. Note that this pertains to a subscription version, and weight may vary for newsstand versions.

When *MotorTrend* moved to a quarterly publication, one alteration the magazine made was increasing the weight of the paper. The cover has more flexibility than cardstock and has a glossy coat that emphasizes the cover image. The increase in paper weight gives the illusion that the magazine is much bigger than the monthly edition, as it is twice as thick but is only about sixteen pages longer.

Overall, the magazine has done a fantastic job of reaching its customers and providing content that tells readers what they want to know. I'm not sure that the splitting of the table of contents layout was such a promising idea, though. For someone who doesn't read every issue, it surprised me to stumble across a second table of contents for feature articles. Combined with that is the fact that the page layouts for both table of contents pages look a lot like an ad, so I almost missed the content because I thought it was just another ad. Most of the revenue for MotorTrend Group seems to come from digital products, but print ads are still prevalent in the magazine. Even though the magazine is reducing its frequency of publication, the readership is vast and the content is well-known and trusted by many people. For this reason, I believe that the magazine will continue to be printed as long as it has loyal customers.

Works Cited

"Motortrend Magazine: September 1949." *MotorTrend Magazine.* September 1949. https://www.motortrend.com/magazines/motor-trend/issue/574852/.

"MotorTrend Media Kit." MotorTrendGroup. Accessed May 5, 2024. https://www.motortrendgroup.com/new_car_media_kit.

Tate, Robert. "Motor Trend Magazine Is an American Automotive Industry Icon." MotorCities. September 7, 2022. https://www.motorcities.org/story-of-the-week/2022/motor-trend-magazine-is-an-american-automotive-industry-icon.

The Story of a Month

Mia Ilie

When Marjorie first met Pandora, it was the first of August. They were both at a secluded beach in a small town located in Massachusetts. It was a small place, hidden a few miles behind the trees that surrounded Marjorie's home, so only she and her family had known about it.

This beach was only a few acres of mainly rocks leading into sand that led into water. Marjorie always thought it was beautiful how this deep, dark forest that was filled with dirt, trees, and leaves could slowly turn into rocks with different colors and patterns on them, then soft sand, and finally, a cold blue-green body of water. Marjorie wondered if maybe that's why she always returned to this place when everything else in the world felt wrong.

When the days felt dark like the color brown—not the pretty type of brown that's seen in fall leaves that land on the grass, adding different colors to the once solid green, and not the brown that is the color of the logs in the fireplace that keeps the house warm and cozy in the bitter-cold winter—the type of brown that stains on the ceiling when it's raining too hard, the type of brown like mud, once solid dirt but now sloshy and slippery like the thoughts in Marjorie's mind. When the days felt like this, she returned to the beach to see that brown turn to orange and yellow and blue-green ocean.

The day she met Pandora was a sloshy, muddy brain day, and she desperately needed the salty air coming from the ocean. She needed to dive into the water and swim until her feet could no longer touch the ground and she could bring her head underwater, where it was peaceful. The loud crashing sound of the waves on the shore and the sounds of the world never seemed to quiet—because there are billions upon billions of living things, everywhere, always making noise—but when she was underwater, it was silent for the first time ever, and even though she couldn't breathe underwater, it felt like she was finally able to breathe after months of not being able to.

But on this sloshy, muddy brain day, fate had other plans. She stopped in her tracks when she spotted white-blonde hair elegantly blowing towards her while the other woman stood facing the ocean, wrapping her arms around her chest to keep warm.

Marjorie was unsure of what to do. No one had ever been here before. Was she supposed to just ignore her and dive into the water like she normally did? Or was she supposed to say hello and introduce herself first? Before she had a proper chance to think the two options through, her metallic water bottle slipped out of her backpack—which she had thrown haphazardly on her shoulder and never properly closed—creating a loud clanging sound against the rocks.

Pandora turned around at the noise, her white hair hitting her face, and she frowned at Marjorie. Before Marjorie could apologize for startling her, Pandora left.

§

Marjorie spent the rest of that day thinking of the girl with the long, white hair. Even when she was underwater and everything was silent, the image of her tall figure and pale skin would not leave her mind.

Marjorie grew up in a small town. The type of place where everyone knew everyone, and they all had a routine that kept their small world spinning. Every person in this town knew who they were, what their roles were, and that they couldn't leave. That this town was it for them. The finish line. The last stop on the local train line. Either heaven or hell, depending on the person.

Needless to say, Marjorie knew every face in this town. She knew her neighbor Louise, who always brought her parents potatoes from their garden on Sundays. She knew the old round lady who was always in some shade of purple, had fraying gray hair, wore lipstick that always somehow stained her chin, and always went grocery shopping on Tuesdays, the same time Marjorie finished up the local park cleanup and would grab a sandwich from the store. Whether or not she wanted it, she knew everyone, and everyone knew her.

But she didn't know who was at the beach and how she found the spot that was meant for Marjorie and only Marjorie.

Marjorie went back the next day at the same time in hopes of seeing her again. She was unsure if she actually wanted to get to know

163

the girl or if she wanted to grab her by the shoulders and yell at her to get the fuck out of this town before it was too late.

She pushed through the trail, brought her sandaled feet onto the end of the rocky path, and made her way on the sand.

Pandora was there once again, facing the ocean, white hair blowing back with her arms around her chest. Marjorie dropped her small, blue bag and towel down quietly and walked to her, as if in a trance.

She walked up to her so they were shoulder to shoulder, a few inches between them. Neither of them said anything at first, but Marjorie knew the girl was aware of her presence by the way she righted her posture.

"You're not from here," Marjorie stated.

Pandora dropped her arms from around her. "Seems that way."

There was only silence for about a minute.

"Why would you come here?" Marjorie asked as she turned to face Pandora. She was still looking at the ocean.

"It was too loud."

"What was?"

Pandora turned to her then. Her soft brown eyes met with hazel.

"Everything."

And from then on, Marjorie knew what was meant to happen. She was meant to introduce herself properly. Say something like, "Hi, I'm Marjorie. I like to paint, and I like nature."

And then the girl would smile at her and respond with, "Hi, I'm Pandora. I like to travel, and I like dreaming about the taste of stars."

And then, oh, and then... Marjorie would tell her she could help with the volume of the world. She would tell her about the magic of this secret place and how it could make the world stop for at least a moment, how it made even the never-ending ringing inside one's ear stop for a moment, how it showed you what silence—something meant to have no sound at all—truly sounded like.

When Pandora would ask her how this one place could do that, Marjorie would bite her lip to hide a smile and then shove the white-haired girl into the water. That would be when Marjorie would hear the most beautiful noise she ever would: Pandora's laughter.

It would be an absolutely horrible, ugly laugh. She would snort and wheeze like her grandmother's old tea kettle, and her face would get all red from lack of breath. But it would leave Marjorie feeling like she was the one who was breathless just from the sound alone.

Marjorie loved silence more than anything else in this world until the day she heard Pandora's laugh.

After Marjorie would hear that laugh for the first time, she would join her in the water. And then she would tell Pandora how she often dreamed that she could breathe underwater, the way that Pandora would dream about the taste of stars.

They would swim for a while, sink underwater for a bit.

That is what happened that day. And Marjorie could safely say she once again knew everyone in town and that they knew her.

§

The next week the two women became attached at the hip.

Marjorie showed her all of the things she painted. Pandora was unaware that Marjorie had never shown anyone her art before. And Marjorie made Pandora take one of her brushes, a blank canvas, and a bottle of paint and paint whatever she wished.

Pandora painted something awful. It was all yellow. Everything was so very bright, and she had absolutely no idea how to paint. It was a yellow blob, many of them, and one black spot. It was horrendous, truly.

Marjorie told her she would frame it.

While they were under a tree eating strawberries, Pandora told her that she was from Texas and was staying with her grandma because there was too much happening at home and she longed to be able to breathe without her chest hurting. She told Marjorie that she was unsure how long she was staying but didn't want to think about leaving. Then she threaded her fingers through Marjorie's and squeezed her hand.

Marjorie told her that she might never leave. No one here ever does. Pandora squeezed her hand again and said nothing.

The rest of the week was filled with swimming at their spot, picnics, talking, painting, reading, singing, dancing, everything, everything, everything.

At the end of the week, they lay with their backs on the sand and watched the stars. One of them turned on their side to face the other; the other woman turned and did the same. Then, at the same time, they moved forward, and their lips met, and some sand tickled their cheeks and even got on their lips.

When they pulled away, Pandora told Marjorie that she finally knew what a star tasted like.

One week passed. And then another. All filled with love, sand, excitement, and a romantic silence.

They slept at Pandora's grandmother's house. Pandora was staying in her mother's old room. The beige wallpaper was chipped, and the brown-red rug was ugly, but everything was beautiful to Marjorie.

They went to bed and kissed. They woke up and kissed. They ate meals and kissed. They loved and loved and loved.

Marjorie had always had a routine. She'd do the same thing every day and see the same faces every time. Pandora was something new and something wonderful. Marjorie decided she knew how the sun felt when the moon would finally match its path and create a solar eclipse. That's what Pandora was to her, and she told her as such. That made Pandora smile and kiss her again.

Another week passed all the same, never boring, never for a moment. September was approaching and the women were happy.

On the morning of August 31st, Pandora received a letter. She stood up from the breakfast table and read it to herself. Something happened as she read the letter. She fixed her posture like she did the first time Marjorie stood next to her and wrapped her arms around herself.

When Marjorie asked what was wrong, Pandora went upstairs for a while and then came back down and grabbed her hand.

"We should go to the beach."

So they walked to the beach in silence. But not the kind that Marjorie savored. The kind that was loud.

When they got to the beach, Pandora held onto her hand until their toes met water, then she turned to face the ocean. It was then that Pandora told her everything.

She was from Texas, her family used to be rich but was losing their money, and she was to be married to a man who could fix that. She told Marjorie that she was engaged and had been for about a month. That she left, temporarily, to breathe and never expected to find someone with an unlimited supply of oxygen.

Pandora told Marjorie that she had to go.

Marjorie asked her not to, begged her not to. She was ready to get on her knees and plead and plead and plead.

"One day he may die," Pandora told Marjorie when the first tear slipped from her eyes. "One day he may die, and I will pack my things so quickly. I will leave the house within the hour and come back to you."

"No one is supposed to leave here," Marjorie told her, hoping, praying, aching.

"Seems that way," Pandora whispered as she placed her soft lips on Marjorie's forehead.

She left after that.

Marjorie stood in the same place for a long time, hoping that if she looked behind her, Pandora would still be standing there. But she knew that wasn't true, so she didn't dare to look. Eventually, she stepped forward.

She walked into the ocean, letting the cold water sink into her burning skin. She went until she could no longer stand. She put her head underwater.

She wished again that she could breathe underwater.

When Marjorie met Pandora, she had no idea she would experience life for the first time. She met the world, the moon, the girl who wished to taste stars, and she lived with the rest of the world muted. She felt like she did underwater, like she could breathe for the first time. But this time, it lasted longer than when her lungs burned for air.

It didn't last forever though, for she was a star, the brightest star. She was the sun and Pandora was the moon. And an eclipse is never meant to last forever.

The longest eclipse ever recorded had only ever been seven minutes—Pandora and Marjorie's lasted a month.

The Last Day/Public Service Announcement

Alena Williams

PSA:

I am no longer your sounding board,

your listening ear,

or a face for you to vent to.

I am no longer a friend only in your times of need,

or a shoulder to cry on only for you to leave when the tears dry.

I am no longer yours to keep,

yours to have,

or yours to hold.

I am me.

I am myself.

I am mine.

Ain't I a woman?

A woman that is no longer yours.

Downtown 6 Train to Grand Central

Misha Puello Brasil

"Stand clear of the closing doors, please."
Marigold and tangerine benches set an ominous tone
on the three-stop ride to Grand Central. Heavy
humidity seeps through the naked aluminum doors
while exhaustion envelopes the lower-middle class,
who stare intently at "no internet connection" screens.

Strangers stand at opposite sliding doors. Dilapidated
winter jackets—one gray, one beige—differentiate the
two men
from their fellow passengers. The man in gray studies
his comrade
and knows they are akin. Fast friendships form on the 6.

"Make it pop!" he yells,
"Make it pop. Make it pop!"
then throws the individually wrapped candies of the fun
gummy variety at the sleepy man in beige.
Contemplating,
then complying, the drowsy man concentrates, squints,
then squeezes
the dollar coin-sized wrapper with both his hands, then
POP!

POP! POP! POP!
One after the other, both candy and wrapper fall
to the stained yellow train floor. Red, blue, and green
debris
litter around his feet. A pile forms.

A smile emerges from the man in gray—he has been recognized and understood.

Laughter emerges from the foundation of his chest

with the likeness of a child; his hands clap together clumsily as he becomes giddy.

"This is Grand Central." The passengers exit the train, but the two

strangers stand still, now having to divorce. The giddy man salutes

his new friend in beige as he watches him depart.

Turning the bag over, he lets the remaining candies clatter to the floor

POP! POP! POP!

"Oh shit! They're shooting!" he says.

      "Stand clear of the closing doors."

THEY'RE WATCHING, THEY'RE MOCKING

Madhuri Pawar

I thought the craziest dumbfounding noise would be in
a crowd of fifty-thousand people.

Ironically,

it's in a room full of objects,

a room full of thoughts,

a room full of photographs,

a room full of silence.

The silence is so *deafening*, it splits my ears.

I can feel them looking at me.

The objects.

The fan.

The vase.

The couch.

The cushions.

I can see them smile at me.

The non-existing.

The curtains.

The rugs.

The walls.

The mugs.

None of them talk, but they all smile.

None of them walk, but they all ride.

They are welcoming me into their world.

A world full of stillness.

A world full of grime.

A world full of silence.

A world full of void.

It all seems beautiful.

To not use your voice box and hush.

To not move an inch and lather with grime.

To not move your lips and be a shrine.

To not feel anything and be paralyzed.

They're all mocking me.

At the fact that I am a human.

At the fact that I can feel.

At the fact that I can love.

At the fact that I am as helpless as them.

Pages from *Bastseker's Patrol Notes:*
The Arrow of Avarice
S.B. Black

It's about time I came up for proverbial air. I don't know how many will see this, but I need some sense of normalcy in all this craziness that has been going on over the past few years. Getting some admin tasks done for this blog should help with it. Hopefully Lapis, my hero best friend, sees this and gives me some sign of life. She's never been radio silent for this long before.

To those who have stumbled across this meager blog or have decided to randomly check your old bookmarks, welcome. I am Bastseker, one of the admins of The Extraordinaries' superhero team blog and founding member. Now, why not Psycat, as the old posts have? Let's just say that brand recognition was more of my concern earlier in my career as an unregistered superhero. Psycat was more recognizable to most, but after the DC incident, I finally stopped putting up with it. Now you get my actual call sign, and you will from now on.

My worries about my best friend in herodom and general clarifications aside, being a superheroine patrolling the west side of Houston, Texas has its ups and downs. The ups: being more in touch with my community and helping with mutual aid requests. The downs: being chased by the Superhuman Registration Agency (SRA) and their parolee supers, and feeling crippling anxiety about handing over cases to registered informants. But there's always a weird component to my patrols in some form or another. One from this week definitely had that in spades.

Now, Tableau (a friend and fellow Houston superheroine) and I have gotten a mutual aid network for the city up and running. I am only one woman, and Houston's the size of Connecticut, so having more people to keep the streets safe is always good, especially if it represents the diversity of the city. We call our network the Cross-Town Initiative, or CTI. Several heroes, both registered and not, have signed up, and I'm proud to answer a call if I'm available.

I was having a quiet patrol on an afternoon off work. The repairs to Barker Reservoir's dam looked solid after we'd been hit by Hurricane Hugh six months ago in August of 2017. I had just finished an aerial flyby over a neighborhood on Akersedewet, my flight platform. Hovering over the mall, I was lazily considering if my wallet could afford lunch at the food court when my com earpiece beeped.

"One o'clock and all's well," I said upon tapping it.

"Heh, well, that answers my question about what movie you were watching last night," Marcus, my confidant, co-admin of the blog, and logistics manager of the team, said in my ear.

"Sometimes I get a hankering for nostalgia, you know. Much like the hankering for crab that I've had off and on for months. But bills and duty first."

"Maybe we can make a boil out of the next team meetup."

I smiled. I did love getting to see everyone when we weren't pressed to serve. "Got an ETA on that?"

"The same as last week. Extraordinaries business aside, you know that newbie super you inducted into the CTI a few months ago?"

"Not really."

"Ledgermain ring any bells?"

"Oh yeah, the magical calculus guy."

"I got a request for aid from him at Bush airport."

My smile faded. Ledgermain was primarily a street-level superhero who patrolled Bellaire and Chinatown. For him to be active outside of his area...

"Tell him to hold on, I'm on my way. Patch him in direct if need b-be. Is it a low level request?"

"From the sound of the background, no."

I flicked down my clear riding glasses and muttered a prayer to Bast and Wepwawet. "Putting this as a priority. I'm gonna punch it."

"All right. Ride like the blue blur, Em."

"Heh. *Kheperu.*" I mentally willed Akersedewet to accelerate and leaned into the air pressure, going ever faster as I dodged power lines on my ascent. Once I cleared the high-tension transmission lines, I leveled off and made a beeline for my dad's old workplace, Bush Intercontinental Airport.

§

The smells of the city were exhilarating as I rocketed towards the airport. I had the terminals in my sight in about twenty minutes.

What also graced my gaze were the white SUVs of the SRA's task force parked near the fence to the terminal tarmac. Great, I'd have to deal with their assholery, too.

"So, where's Ledgermain at? Inside or outside?" I asked once I had killed my speed enough to hear Marcus again.

"Gate C43, outside, next to a pretty big jet," he said after a moment.

I stimmed on my jeans' texture. I know what a jet engine can do to an unsecured person on the tarmac if they're not careful. That bit from my dad's study materials used to give me nightmares as a kid.

C'mon Em, you gotta help the guy! I thought and mentally stepped into my hero bravado as I stood up on Akersedewet for maneuverability. If this was anything like when I got dragged across my patrol borders, I would need it.

"All right, keep in contact with the FAA and Houston Airport Authority. Coming in from the southwest at thirty miles per hour."

"Roger, whiskey tango foxtrot. Ledgermain's still kicking, too."

I shook my head and smiled. "It'd be a shame if he weren't. Now if I remember right, it's the terminal right next to the circular hotel."

"Fuzzy memory and cat costume parts, meet a website map. It's southeast from the hotel, along the walkway to E."

The tang of jet fuel wafted around me as I made a sharp right at the hotel. "Too bad it wasn't C42. I could've made a good joke about that one."

"You and every other person that went through that gate."

"At least it's empty. But hoo boy, that is a big 767 at C43. And it just *had* to be dad's old airline, too."

"Wait, you can tell by looking?"

"Dad geeking out about planes is one of the few ways I got to bond with him. Tail's easy enough, but I can't make out specifics."

"I'm surprised that you even care to remember it."

"I'll explain later. For now, I best be getting into federal airspace."

"All right, keeping them abreast. Hopefully they aren't peeved about it."

I took a deep breath and then flew over the first arm of terminal C. I scanned the ground around the 767, noting that while the jetway was connected to the plane, it was torn. Some bags were scattered on the tarmac, and the crew was nowhere to be found. I thought I saw an extra engine under the left wing, but it was hard to tell. Then I spotted Ledgermain, the Vietnamese, math-genius superhero, hiding behind one of the nearby baggage carts. Time to drop in.

"So, what's the situation?" I asked once I got within conversation distance.

"It's about time you got here," he said as he crouched down, clutching his coin shooter. "You're ten minutes late, according to my calculations."

I shook my head. Of course a super calculator would say something about it. "Look, I don't always have my game face on when in route, ya know. But seriously, what's up?"

Two scenarios ran through my head: either he had been in the area and a situation demanded him go hero, or he was pulled across territory boundaries by something.

He considered me over his shoulder. "I heard chatter about a robbery at a seafood market, and when I arrived—"

"HAHAHAHA!" a high-pitched male voice sounded from somewhere around the left wing.

I peered over the luggage cart. A guy with white-blond hair in a crab-like vehicle harassed a ramp worker holding a box.

"—*That* cackling motherfucker was stealing cash and crabs. I chased him all the way up here before I called it in."

"He looks kinda run of the mill. But then again, I could be off."

"I'll show you then." He popped up and took a shot, the abacus hanging at his waist glowing. The coin bounced off of the man's white coat harmlessly.

"See? Even with my accurate calculations, my shots aren't having any effect."

Well, fuck.

"Okay... And he's not amenable to coming quietly?" I asked and crossed my arms.

"Do you think that I'd be shooting if he were?"

I sighed. Another look over the cart told me the ramp guy had dodged one of the arms. I opened my mouth when the sound of gunfire cracked the air.

I ducked, then cautioned a gaze over the cart again. SRA agents in uniform tan and white suits were shooting at the villain and getting about as far as Ledgermain had.

"Hahaha, your guns are no match for me, Professor Pincer!" the villain said, then turned to sweep a few agents with a robot crab leg. At least two were yeeted back into the jetway stairs before he turned back to the worker.

"Welp, that's about as bad a match-up as Team Rocket versus Pikachu. Either of you got any ideas?"

"I'm fresh out," Ledgermain said. "But then again, I don't know your kit that well."

"Too busy keeping a jumpy FAA agent calm here," Marcus said over the com.

It looked like I would have to do the formulation. "It's a bit risky, but Marcus, I'm gonna pull a Dogula."

"A what?" Ledgermain asked.

"Fuuuck. Just be prepared, okay?" Marcus said.

"Yeah, even I hate it. But we gotta get him subdued." I turned back to Ledgermain. "I'm going to draw his ire while you figure out his weakness. Then we can use it to pacify him."

"And if I can't?"

I winked at him. "Everyone's got a weakness. You're smarter than my psychic-butt. I have faith that you can come up with something."

He looked at me, amazed. "I'll do my best."

I nodded, steeled my nerves, and then sped out to the wingtip while concentrating on a Ka strike. I had to get his attention away from the worker and the SRA agents.

When it was ready, I tossed the purple ball of mental energy at him. It flew past, inches from his face.

"Hey Wiley Egg, how about you douse that attitude in butter and stick it," I yelled, giving him the finger.

His head whipped to face me. "Well, if it isn't the infamous Psycat," he said.

My gaze tightened at the portmanteau. "It's Bastseker, jerkwad!"

"I was wondering if you would show up. Screw you and your butter!" He was fast in that crab tank and was on me in a second.

I definitely had his attention. I did my best to dodge the leg aimed at my head.

"I ain't gonna take my lumps from some robo-seafood," I said with a wry smile.

"Crabs are the ultimate life form, having evolved separately at least five different times. I will not suffer your insolence about them!" He swiped at me again, grazing my leg.

"Well, someone's sour," I said, blocking another shot while trying to concentrate on a Ka strike. "Almost like you got doused in lemon juice."

"I'll show you sour!" he snarled and tossed me back several yards off my board.

As I reeled from being knocked off Akersedewet, I painfully sat up to see Professor Pincer smack the box of crabs out of the worker's hands. The sluggish crabs inside spilled onto the wet tarmac and got excited from the hydration. He then pulled what looked like a toy ray gun, and a light issued forth at the crabs.

"Em, are you okay?" Marcus said as I stood.

"Shit, that stung," I said, rubbing the back of my scraped arms.

Out of the corner of my eye, Ledgermain was staring at Professor Pincer intently, likely doing whatever deep calculations he needed.

Movement from the crab tank caught my attention, and I spotted several growing crabs with blue pincers. The embiggening ray had turned them to the size of loveseats.

"Show the fat hero who's superior!" the Professor said, and a few crabs charged at me.

Ah, hell no. I did *not* want to end up being a Texas blue crab's dinner. I got a running start and telekinetically pulled Akersedewet to me, clearing the ankhs around the rim and landing on the deck. I corrected my forward motion and tossed Ka strike after Ka strike at the crabs.

It wasn't having as much of an effect as I'd hoped. I barely missed my leg getting crushed as I looked around for another option.

There's one! I threw a heavy, hard-sided pink bag at the nearest crab, and it landed with a crunch. The crab tipped over and its legs waved uselessly in the air.

I thought I was gaining ground when another crop of enlarged seafood swarmed around me. One pinched my butt before I swatted it.

"Ugh, why do crabs gotta be sexual harassers?" I said and knocked a wide arc of them away.

"I'm not going to say what I'm thinking with a federal agent on the other line," Marcus said over the com. "Anyway, patching Ledgermain through."

"You okay? You look like you're tied in a crab trap right now," Ledgermain said.

Now I understand why most villains get annoyed at my puns. "Yeah, playing keep away with gumbo ingredients is getting old, though."

"I saw that he's got some sort of size-change gun."

"Ya think?"

"Come on, no need to be snippy."

I ducked a crab pincer.

Ledgermain continued, "When he pulled it out on that last wave, I got a good look. It's got a shrink setting, too."

That we could use. "Now to get it away from him."

"Exactly. Once we do, we can get to the weak point I observed on his back."

"All right, then let's get this rolling."

I rammed the suitcase into the crabs, clearing a path.

Another gunshot rang out, this time burying itself in the Professor's crab tank. Several SRA agents were back up and either wrestling with the megacrabs or keeping the Professor from hurting the worker.

I raced through the narrowing path of crustaceans, getting as close as I dared to the Professor. I had to have eyes on the gun, but where was it?

The crabs parted momentarily as the Professor said, "You overfunded government dogs are no match for my pretties." He leveled the ray gun at a smaller crab that the worker was chasing. *Dua Wepwawet for opening the way to victory!*

"Thank you," I said and yanked the contraption out of the Professor's hand.

"You!" he raged.

"Aw, no need to be crabby about it," I said with a smirk before tossing Ledgermain the ray.

Get them back to normal size. We won't have as much pressure with them small, I telepathically said when I caught his gaze.

He nodded and went to town on the bloated crabs.

"You and those government dogs ruined everything! My lab, my funding, my research, everything! I'll make you pay!" the Professor screeched before he swiped at me.

I noticed that several SRA agents helped the worker get the now normal-sized crabs back in the box; figures they would make me do the heavy lifting.

I gathered a Ka strike and threw it at the Professor. It caught him in the shoulder, and he snarled at me.

From out of nowhere, a huge stone crab claw reached out toward me from the Professor's lab coat. I barely dodged it, thanks to my Khu net, but damn did the feedback smart.

The Professor's coat and shirt were in tatters, revealing grafted crab claws onto his sides, similar to a certain arachnid superhero's villain from comics.

"Check, you salty bastard!" Ledgermain said right before the coin pierced his back.

The Professor grimaced, clearly not used to taking damage. "Fuck you!"

I leaned in, ducking another claw before I caught his gaze. "Boil over it, asshole," I said with a sneer and shot him a migraine.

"I will not be denied!" he said, straining against the sound of his voice.

Ledgermain took Professor Pincer's swing at me as an opportunity to get another shot in.

Just then, a plane on a nearby gate fired up its engines. I covered my ears, not wanting to risk hearing damage.

The Professor also covered his ears and screamed, but it was too much for him. He slumped backward, out cold from the noise.

I let out a tense sigh as soon as I checked him. It was finally over.

"Thanks for your help," Ledgermain said as soon as the taxiing plane was on its way out.

"Don't mention it," I said with a weary smile. "Let's just get things cleaned up and get the hell out of here."

"Gotcha," he said.

We both tossed the rest of the crabs back into the box, including one that had made a break for the runway. Once the last crab was fettered, the SRA guys, who were on Professor Pincer like ants on a sandwich at a picnic, noticed that we were finished. Seeing as I have a reputation with these jerks and Ledgermain is undecided, we both split before they could turn on us.

"Hey, Marcus?" I said once I was on my way back to his place.

"Yeah?"

"Thanks for dealing with that jumpy FAA agent. I didn't hear everything, but at least we didn't have to deal with a plane coming into C42."

"It's okay, but I'll have to watch for no-fly lists for a while."

I shook my head and hurried back along the freeway's path.

This was one of the weirder villains that I've had to deal with in quite some time. However, I'm glad that the CTI is working as intended. Now, if only I could make enough money and get more time off to focus on my patrol routes.

See ya!

Bastseker

The Nobleman

Misha Puello Brasil

The unease never seems to go away,
lingering in all the abilities I don't have
cultivating nature, art.

The pavement feels uneven and rugged,
standing barefoot at the barren corner waiting for you,
overflowing with the anxiety of possibility.

I'm cemented in adolescence,
awaiting your return so I can resume
the aspirations we shared.

You ran towards your sweet peach.
Down the verdurous road
with all my permissions and regrets.

Land, kept barren by the Lord
who returns simply for his taxes.
Your insatiable nature depleted my resources.

The Devil is My Melatonin

Chardonnae Simpson

I have my demons
Some days they play with my hair and whisper sweet
nothings in my ear

Other days they decide the devil's pitchfork will dig
directly into my shoulders
It depends on if I tick them off or not
Somehow I always tick them off

Then they pity me and play nice
I tune them out, dulling my senses

The road to recovery isn't always face masks and
positive affirmations
The road is dark and muddy

You're going to slip and slide, clinging to your sanity
The endless cycle of highs and lows is the bitterest pill
to swallow

Your demons force-feed you then tuck you in and tell
you to get some rest
Sweet dreams

The Running Kind

Liz Abrams

A list, in no particular order, of the select few things Lana cares about as she works her way through her routine stretches:

- The half-eaten pan of brownies waiting for her at home, if she can get to it before her siblings' wandering hands cause them to mysteriously disappear.

- The fact that she forgot a sports bra. Track is an unforgiving sport and her chest will undoubtedly be sore before the end of practice.

- Finding the time to do the various worksheets tucked haphazardly into her backpack between school, practice, and the test she needs to study for; surely, there's room somewhere in her schedule if she cuts out something menial, like two of her seven hours of sleep. Or breathing.

The list of the many things Lana does *not* care about as she balances precariously on one foot with the heel of the other pulled up against her butt so that her hamstrings are forced to loosen:

Well, that list would span multiple pages with no margins and teeny, tiny font.

It's only the first week of the season, and they won't have any meets until the end of the month. When they ran timed laps yesterday, Lana had only been slightly disappointed in her results; she isn't as in shape as she thought she was, but it's still pre-season. She won't have to race for another three weeks, and it'll be at least as long until she even needs to *think* about Katherine Yates, let alone worry about facing her again.

Of course, Lana's luck is nowhere to be found when she needs it.

The sight of Katherine walking up to Coach in all her insurmountable, annoyingly composed glory almost sends Lana to the ground. She stumbles, slapping her palm against the wall before she can tumble to the hall floor. There's a split second where she's convinced that she's wrong—shoulder-length black hair and tan skin are common traits, after all—but Lana has spent an infuriating amount of time staring at Katherine's back. She remembers how that hair looks escaping from a braid it's almost too short for and how it moves against her back in time with her steps.

Lana switches legs absently, pulling her left foot behind her with one hand and gripping the wall with the other. It's definitely her, out of her distinct green and white uniform and looking uncomfortable under the fluorescent lights.

Katherine talks to Coach for a moment, unaware of the way Lana's eyes are boring holes into the side of her head. Coach beckons someone over. Audrey, the team captain, bounds over to him and joins the conversation enthusiastically.

Practice has always been a safe space for her, something that the other parts of her life can't spill into and corrupt. It's where she can focus on something other than the due dates constantly looming over her head. It's where she can push herself without the pressure of a race weighing down her heels, where she can be as serious as she wants without coming off as hungry for a win that won't mean anything ten years down the line. It means more to her than competitions ever have. It's the only place she can *breathe*.

Audrey takes Katherine by the wrist and starts introducing her to people, casual as anything, like she belongs here and not two towns over. Lana's brain stutters over itself. She can't reconcile her teammates with the girl being led through them. Audrey catches her eye as she passes by. The look on her face makes it clear that she and Lana are going to need to have a talk.

Lana turns away. She joins the group of girls filing through the double doors to begin the day's run before the room runs out of air.

§

Lana manages to go the next three days without interacting with Katherine beyond the short, awkward wave she gave when Audrey introduced Katherine to the other seniors on the team. Her bad luck catches up to her again on Friday, as she's about to start a run that will take her to the edge of the next town, a neat five-mile round trip along the canal. She's ready to spend the next forty-five minutes mentally drafting an outline of her AP Lit essay.

Audrey asks her to lead Katherine through the day's route, and the request drops on her plans like a shoe on an unsuspecting ant.

"You've got to be kidding me."

Audrey's eyebrows go up. She looks distinctly unimpressed by Lana's outburst, and Lana takes a moment to question *why* she lacks a filter between her brain and mouth when it's most important. She takes another to mourn the sprint-jogs she's probably going to have to do later.

"Sorry," she says before Audrey can tell her to take a few laps and come back with a better attitude. "I know you want us to get along, but does it have to be me?"

"She's the only one that comes close to your times for runs. You guys should be working to push each other. Coach agrees with me." Audrey considers her. "It's not like she spit in your face. You guys are just different people. Don't let it get in the way of functioning as a team."

The "or else" is left unsaid, but Lana hears it loud and clear. Coach had let several people go last season for in-team fighting. The idea of being kicked off the team in her last season scares her more than she thinks it should. She's not going to do anything that risks her position, and Audrey knows it.

"I'll try not to let it be personal, I guess." The words taste bitter in her mouth. It is personal. Even though Lana tries to not let it be. Even though Katherine probably didn't even remember what she said.

Lana remembers it well enough for the both of them.

Audrey claps her on the shoulder. "Good. Now get out there and show Katherine the ropes."

Lana lets herself roll her eyes. The air around them is more relaxed, more like two peers talking to each other than a captain scolding a misbehaving teammate. "She knows how to run. I'm not exactly teaching her rocket science."

Audrey rolls her eyes right back. "Just lead the run."

"Yeah, yeah, I got it." Lana makes her way into the crowd of distance runners getting ready by the door. Katherine is talking quietly to an underclassman but looks up when Lana approaches. "Hey, you're with me today. You ready to go?"

Katherine nods, arms crossed over her chest.

They set off at a jog while Lana lists directions to the canal trail. It hasn't snowed yet, so they don't have to worry about the path being clear. "From here on out it's pretty simple, straight out until we hit the little waterfall at Swift's Landing and then back."

"Okay."

They run in silence, mostly. Lana points out the tree with a yellow streamer tied around it that represents both the quarter and three-quarter mark, but otherwise, the only sounds are the cinder crunching under their feet and the wind whistling through the trees. She starts thinking about her essay again, wondering if she could get away with saying nothing until they return to the school.

"I know you don't like me."

Lana tries not to let her surprise show when the relative silence is broken, but she isn't very successful. She trips over her own feet, interrupting the steady stride they'd worked up. When Lana recovers enough to look at her, Katherine is smiling in a way that contradicts her nervous tone. The amusement falls from her face when she sees Lana looking.

Looking at her is irritating, like if Coach switched her events at the last second and left her fumbling to get to the starting line on time. Ignoring her is tempting, but cooperation is the order of the day, so Lana plays along. "I probably don't hide it that well," she says evenly. It's easy to avoid looking at Katherine when the excuse of watching where she puts her feet is readily available.

"You don't," Katherine confirms. She seems to take a moment to think. Lana listens to her breath. "Is it because I place above you at meets?"

The question is carefully neutral, like Katherine thinks Lana might suddenly start raging if she brings up something they both know is true. The assumption makes Lana rankle.

Katherine continues before Lana has a chance to reply. Her voice is less controlled now, held aloft by anger or discomfort or something equally messy. "That's kind of shallow, isn't it? It's just track."

"Just track," as if being on a team isn't a good enough reason to *care*. God, she can't stand Katherine.

Lana makes a show of taking a deep breath. Getting worked up right now is a terrible idea, not only because she's supposed to be making an effort to make nice (make neutral?), but also because at the pace they've set, she doubts she has the lung capacity to start shouting. "That would be shallow," she agrees. "And sure, it's frustrating to be behind you every time, but that's not the reason you get on my nerves."

"What is, then?"

Lana thinks about being bent over in the bathroom stall before a meet, wishing she could throw up her nerves with her lunch. She remembers crying at Finals because they lost second place by two points Lana could have scored by moving up a place in the two mile. She feels the weight of the team on her back. She knows that she's not carrying it alone, but she struggles to balance it right on her shoulders.

Katherine's voice echoes in her head. *It's just track.*

"I don't want to talk about it."

"I do!"

Lana speeds up. Katherine matches her pace. The clearing with the waterfall is two hundred meters down the trail. "Well that's just too bad, isn't it? This isn't therapy!"

They skid to a stop next to a yellow sign with a duck on it. They're both breathing heavily, shoulders heaving. Lana's cheeks burn from anger or exertion or both.

"Coach said we're going to be paired together for the rest of the season. Shouldn't we be able to get along?" Katherine raises her voice. Lana tells herself it's so she can be heard over the rushing water.

It was already a mistake to let the conversation get this emotional. The sooner she ends it, the better for both of them.

"Getting along doesn't mean we have to be friends. I'll stop holding a grudge for something you obviously don't remember, you'll stop asking me about it, and we can get through the season and go our separate ways."

Katherine just looks at her. She looks like she has more to say, but she stops herself from speaking. Eventually she shakes her head and takes off towards the school. It's not an agreement, but she doesn't try and pick the conversation back up, either.

Katherine is quiet for the rest of the run, and Lana lets her be. She's said her piece, and she still thinks Katherine's attitude is annoying. If Katherine wants to do anything with that information, she'll have to do it on her own.

Lana's done more than enough putting herself out there for today.

§

Running in the winter is, to put it lightly, bullshit.

It's not the cold that makes her reluctant to go out, or the early darkness that forces her to run farther, faster. It isn't even the icy wind that dries out her skin and whips right through her no matter how many layers she piles on—though it certainly doesn't make her more eager to face the elements.

No, the worst thing about running during winter is the *goddamn sidewalks*.

"Shit," she mutters as, for the third time on this block, her legs threaten to slide out from underneath her.

Half a step ahead of her, Katherine glances over her shoulder. In silent agreement, they come to a stop on the sidewalk, and Lana takes the opportunity to stomp her feet to clear away the snow caught in the treads of her sneakers. If they keep to the sidewalks, they won't make it to the end of the street before she's back to sliding around every time she pushes off. Katherine's no better off; they're only halfway through this run and she's almost wiped out twice.

"Fuck this," Lana says, stepping into the street. Brown sludge and melting road salt create an unappealing slapping noise against the soles of her shoes, but at least she has traction.

"I thought Coach said we aren't allowed to run on the road," Katherine says, still standing on the sidewalk. She hasn't bothered to knock the snow out of her shoes. Lana wonders if Katherine thinks that's unimportant, too.

"We're not," Lana says, and starts running again.

Behind her, Katherine scrambles through the snow. Lana hears it crunching flatly under her feet. She can also hear the distance between them increasing, which is how she knows Katherine is going to join her on the road before she steps off the curb.

"Coach is going to kill us," Katherine says when she catches up.

"Do you want to spend the next half an hour trying not to fall on your ass, or do you want to cut the amount of time this run is going to take in half?"

Six miles isn't the farthest either of them have ever run, but the cold air has made her thighs numb. The sky is gray and cloudy above them with only a suggestion of the sun lighting their way. Running on the street is against the rules, but hell, if it isn't easier. With both of them on the asphalt, they'll be able to pick up the pace—maybe even push themselves in the last mile or so. Katherine either agrees with her and doesn't want to admit it or decides it's not worth arguing about.

It usually ends up that way when they talk. They've had a couple meets by now, but they haven't been in the same race yet. Maybe it'll feel different now that they've had more than a handful of conversations around the starting line. Maybe it'll feel just the same since most of those conversations have been arguments.

By the time they get back to the school, Lana's cheeks are bright red and numb from the stinging wind. Despite wearing leggings under her sweatpants, she can feel the telltale itch of windburn on her thighs. They're the first ones back, and although her knees are stiff from overcorrecting in the snow, she's satisfied.

She and Katherine trudge into the school through the propped double doors, tracking in melting snow and salt. Katherine pulls the hat off her head, revealing her frizzy braid and flyaway hairs. Lana watches her shake the snow out of her shoes and wonders if they'll ever agree on anything.

§

They finally get put in the same race. Coach wants them to take second and third in the mile. First, if one of them can snag it.

Coach pulls Lana aside when Katherine wanders off to warm up. "Stick to her like glue," he says.

He's told her the same thing before every race for the past two years. Lana lets herself imagine, briefly, pulling Coach's disgusting mustache out. She knows he's trying to encourage her, but the implication that she's been *letting* Katherine get away from her makes her shoulders tense up.

His words work her up a little more than he probably means them to. She goes out quickly when the starting pistol fires, takes first and holds onto it tight for the first lap. She can't keep that pace, gets bumped back to second by a girl from another school, and then gets bumped into third when Katherine passes her.

Katherine pulls into first on the last lap. Lana's barely got enough energy to sprint thanks to her eagerness at the beginning, but she manages to put the previous front-runner behind her on the final stretch. The extra points bump the team's total to tie for first place.

From her place in the throng of racers catching their breath, Katherine catches Lana's eye. Katherine smiles, and it's a smile that says *I thought you had me for a second, there.*

Oddly enough, it doesn't feel like an attack. Lana smiles back, though she's sure it looks more like a grimace. She props her hands up on her hips and tilts her head back to take in the dry air of the indoor track. The stitch in her side burns as her chest heaves.

§

It's mid-way through January before Lana's nerves get the better of her and she throws up at a meet.

There's nothing in particular that sets her off. Midterms have just passed—she's been extra stressed, recently. It's a new year, but she's as tired as ever, maybe even more so. Graduation comes closer every day and with it a host of changes Lana isn't ready to make. She's felt buzzy all day, like someone stuffed her head with cotton and wasps are buzzing in her ears.

She lingers at the edge of the group as her teammates mill around the halls outside the indoor track. The nearest bathroom is around a few corners, and she drags her hand along the wall as she makes her way there. Her fingertips are cold.

A long line of stalls runs along one wall. Girls crowd around the sinks, using the mirrors to put up their hair or tie ribbons into their ponytails. Lana drifts past them, feeling vague and warped as she pushes open the door to the stall furthest from the door.

She clenches her hands in her lap as she retches. A hand lands on her back, not hard but unexpected. She forgot to lock the stall door. Lana jerks, then gags again when the motion encourages the contents of her stomach to make a spirited reappearance. Someone swings her ponytail over her shoulder, holding her hair out of the way as she empties her stomach. She's grateful, but she really hopes the person touching her is a teammate and not a stranger—who follows someone into a stall when they're clearly puking their guts out?

The nausea settles after a long moment, one she spends spitting and trying not to look at her own mess. The hand on her back disappears, but the person behind her says nothing. Lana reaches up and flushes the toilet.

Behind her, there's the scuffle of rubber soles on gritty bathroom tiles. Katherine stands behind her, looking distinctly awkward. "Uh... You okay?"

Lana sniffles, rising to her feet. "I'm fine."

"Do you want me to go get someone? I could find Audrey."

She shakes her head. "No, I think I'm done here."

Katherine nods. She steps out of the stall, looking back at Lana as if she's unsure what's next.

Lana doesn't know what she should do now, either. What's the protocol when someone you've just started getting along with rubs your back as you throw up in a public bathroom? Talk about an awkward situation.

"You did better than last time," she says, because her brain to mouth filter is once again offline.

"What?" Katherine looks lost.

Lana can't even appreciate the absence of her usual serious look, because she's busy panicking. She's managed to avoid putting her foot in her mouth up until now, but she just threw that streak on the ground and let it shatter into a million pieces.

That doesn't stop her from trying to backtrack. "Nothing. Sorry, just... I meant to say thank you."

"No, wait, tell me what you were talking about!" Katherine brushes aside her excuses, watching her face intently as they walk back towards the side-hall where the team dumped their bags.

Lana sighs. She feels more present now, less like a bottle rocket seconds away from launch. "It's stupid."

"I don't care. You're always so cagey, and I just want to know what your deal is." Katherine watches her kneel to dig through her duffle bag for her water bottle. "I want to know why we can't be friends."

Lana takes a minute to swish water around in her mouth. It doesn't completely get rid of the taste of bile, but it's better than nothing.

"The first time we raced against each other, I worked myself up so much that I couldn't focus at all. I completely blew the race and came in pretty close to last."

"I'd forgotten about that. Didn't you—"

"Throw up on the track? Yeah. They had to put sawdust on the track and push back the next race so they could clean it up." Lana laughs sardonically, running a hand through her ponytail. "And it was embarrassing, sure, because there were so many people there and they all kept asking me questions. But you said something that stuck with me, even though it was just an offhand comment. 'It's not worth it to run until you throw up. What's the point?'"

"I thought you had the flu or something. I didn't understand why you would make yourself sick just to run a race." Katherine sits next to her on the ground. "I guess I don't understand why you would do this if it makes you so nervous that you puke, either."

Lana pulls her knees up to her chest. Around them, people come and go; family members stop by to see their kids, girls leave to get ready for their events, people from other teams look for friends. She imagines herself in their midst, walking away from this conversation until she's so far away that Katherine's voice no longer rings in her ears. "It usually doesn't. Sometimes I let myself think too much, and I get caught up in my head."

Katherine leans forward. "Why do you care about track so much? I can't imagine staying on the team if I felt like that, but you still try so hard."

Lana winces. "I've been doing it since middle school. I can't really imagine stopping, especially now. What's one more season?"

"You shouldn't stay just because it's senior year. If it's fucking you up, it's not worth it."

"Track is the only thing I can control. I can study all I want, but that doesn't mean I'm going to get an A. But if I work out every day and eat right and keep myself healthy, I get better. Even if I don't place well in every race, I still feel like I'm making progress."

Katherine doesn't seem to know what to say to that. Lana is glad. She digs around in her bag again, looking for her folder. Her event isn't for another forty minutes, at least, and calculus is boring, but it'll help her keep her mind off of things. She plugs in her earbuds and jams one into her ear. She leaves the other out, just in case.

§

The two mile is, objectively, terrible.

It's twelve minutes of dizzying competition, each lap a blur of adrenaline and paranoia that there's someone ready to overtake her at any moment. Lana's too focused on making sure she breathes deeply enough and regulates her stride to think about much more than catching up to the girl in front of her.

Katherine isn't any more than a hundred meters in front of her. Lana closes that distance, bringing them closer with every lap. She widens her stride, getting close enough that she could pass her in the last stretch. Sprinting is hard; Lana feels lightheaded and can barely see enough to direct her numb legs towards the finish line.

They cross the finish line, so close she can't tell who came first. They'll have to wait for the official's judgement, but for now, it's all she can do to keep breathing, gasping in air despite the pain in her ribs.

The end of the season is coming fast. By the end of March, they'll start training for outdoor track, and Lana will face her last sports season. Graduation is no longer a vague speck on the horizon. But she still has a little time.

There will be other races. For now, she's content to give her teammates high fives with wrists that are still floppy from exhaustion.

The Ferry Zone

James La Barbera

(On the Staten Island Ferry on a Thursday night, the clock is stopped at 7:30 p.m. George, 49, male, enters. Frank, 79, male, present. Bianca, late thirties, female, Frank's dead wife, out of view.)

GEORGE. *(Speaking loudly)* Hello, Sir! Is there anyone sitting there?

FRANK. Sorry! *(Annoyed)* I can hear you. I am not deaf!

GEORGE. *(Points to an open seat with a purse on it)* Oh, I'm sorry. Is there anyone sitting there?

FRANK. No. Not that I can remember.

GEORGE. Okay. Thank you! *(Walks over, grabs the bag, sits down, rests the bag on his lap, takes a pause, waits to say something. He then decides to extend his hand.)* My name is George.

FRANK. I'm Frank. *(Grabs George's hand and shakes.)*

GEORGE. *(With a smile)* It's nice to meet you.

FRANK. What do you mean, it's nice to meet me?

GEORGE. It's just a saying. I'm sorry to bother you.

FRANK. Not a bother. Just surprised.

GEORGE. *(Concerned)* Surprised about what?

FRANK. We haven't spoken in years, and you now say it's nice to meet you. We already know each other.

GEORGE. I'm terribly sorry, but I don't know who you are.

FRANK. Yes! Yes, you do!

GEORGE. No, I think you are mistaken.

FRANK. *(Angrily)* I am not mistaken! I know who you are!

(George goes to get up and sit somewhere else, and the purse falls to the floor.)

FRANK. Hi, I'm Franklin, but people call me Frank! *(Sticks out a hand to George.)*

GEORGE. *(Confused)* I'm George, but people call me G or Georgie. *(Reaches out and shakes Frank's hand.)*

FRANK. *(Sighs.)* This ride feels like a lifetime.

GEORGE. It sure does if one sits for far too long.

FRANK. *(Looks down at the purse.)* Is that yours?

GEORGE. *(Mirrors Frank.)* No, I thought it was someone's when I first sat down.

FRANK. *(Shocked)* Oh! You sat here before?

GEORGE. Just a minute. *(Reaches down to grab the bag and places it on the seat next to him.)*

FRANK. What are you doing?

GEORGE. Just sitting here.

FRANK. No, I meant with that purse. It's not yours!

GEORGE. Do you know who this belongs to?

FRANK. *(Upset)* Yes... No... Maybe.

GEORGE. Well, which is it? *(Concerned and angered)*

FRANK. *(Yells)* Fuck you, Frank and your shitty memory!

GEORGE. Is everything okay?

FRANK. No, everything is not "okay." *(Slight pause like a sigh.)* That—that purse reminds me of my wife. She had one just like that one when I first met her.

GEORGE. I'm sorry to hear that. *(Pause.)* May I ask what happened?

FRANK. We met when we were young, here, even when the boat was first open and then... *(Stops when he sees his wife come walking over to grab her purse.)*

BIANCA. Oh, Frankie, you are a gem! You found my bag. You are the sweetest man I've ever met. *(Grabs her bag sitting next to George, then she and the purse disappear.)*

GEORGE. What the fuck?

FRANK. Hunny ... Wait!

GEORGE. Frank!

FRANK. Frank who?

(The ferry starts to dock at the Manhattan terminal but neither man gets up, frozen where they are. Lights fade out. Lights then shine on Frank and George sitting where they already were.)

GEORGE. Frank, are you okay? Did you take the purse? Where did it go and what just fucking happened? *(Pause.)* Frank!

FRANK. Sorry, sorry George. I missed her again... I mean, I miss her.

GEORGE. Again? *(Pause.)* If telling me the story is hurting you, you don't have to continue.

FRANK. Nonsense, I'll continue. She was wearing this beautiful blue dress and white hat, sitting exactly where you are and... I couldn't help but stare at her, she had a wild spirit, she was the one that said the first words...

(While Frank is speaking, his story is being acted out right next to them when the purse reappears.)

BIANCA. Excuse Me! What are you staring at?

FRANK. Oh, sorry I couldn't stop but stare at a beautiful work of art.

BIANCA. Oh?

FRANK. How rude of me, my name is Franklin, but people call me FRANK. You are the most beautiful woman I have ever seen. *(Extends out his hand and waits for hers.)*

BIANCA. Well, thank you Frank. And it's nice to hear someone say I'm a work of art! My name is Bianca. *(Extends her hand. Frank kisses it.)*

FRANK. Where are you off to?

BIANCA. To visit some family in the city. Where are you going?

FRANK. I don't know yet, I just wanted to see the new way of traveling.

BIANCA. They had boats before.

FRANK. Yes, but nothing of this magnitude, where cars and people can travel across the river.

BIANCA. You have a point, but it's nothing out of the ordinary.

FRANK. Well, I apologize for not being too original for you then.

(Frank and Bianca both laugh)

BIANCA. Isn't that amazing?

FRANK. What?

(Bianca gestures to the window as they pass the Statue of Liberty.)

FRANK. Oh, wow that is very amazing!

BIANCA. Wouldn't it be amazing to one day be able to climb inside that tower of hers and look back at the city and New Jersey?

FRANK. I sense you have a thing for adventures?

BIANCA. I do, but you didn't answer my question.

FRANK. *(Chuckles.)* It would be nice to view things from your eyes and from that tower.

BIANCA. You are very smooth Franklin, very smooth.

FRANK. Thanks! *(Pause.)* So, why are you truly going into the city, because I don't think you are just visiting family?

BIANCA. Ha-ha, you caught me! I am exploring the city, and my family is back there on that island.

FRANK. I thought so! Would it be rude of me to ask to come with you?

BIANCA. I thought you wanted to stay here on this boat?

FRANK. I do, well, did. I feel like I met someone wonderful and don't want to squander my time just sitting here.

BIANCA. Well, I don't see why it's not a good idea for you to come. *(Pause.)* I think you should accompany me into the city.

201

FRANK. Excellent! *(Pause.)*

(Focus shifts back to Frank in the present, telling George the story.)

FRANK. Then the boat docked. We got off, went exploring the city, exchanged pagers and landline numbers. After a few stops in certain parts of the city, we traveled back together. *(Pause.)* After that we went our own ways, didn't see each other for a few years, and then bam, we were back in the same place and decided to go out. And then, well, we got married and had a child, then she... She got ill and passed away after a full life of exploring everything together.

GEORGE. Wow what a wonderful story. Is that why you are on the boat now?

FRANK. Well, yes, to try and remember her. It's sometimes hard to remember certain aspects of my life now.

GEORGE. I can relate to that. My own memory sometimes goes without even asking for permission.

FRANK. I see you have a suit on and that man purse of yours.

GEORGE. Man purse? *(Looks next to him and a light blue purse is sitting next to him again.)* This isn't mine. Where did this come from?

FRANK. It wasn't there before I was telling you my story?

GEORGE. No, not that I can remember.

FRANK. That is the same bag Bianca had when we met, the same bag she had when we met again, and had before she passed away. My son George and I buried her with it.

GEORGE. Your son's name is George?

FRANK. Yes, we fell out of communication after she passed. He now lives in the city Bianca and I were going to when we met, as I told you.

GEORGE. Oh, wow! That is just amazing. *(Pause.)* Doesn't that look amazing?

FRANK. What does?

GEORGE. Look, the statue at night with the flame all lit up.

FRANK. It does, doesn't it? *(Pause.)* So, George, where are you going currently?

GEORGE. Oh, I don't know, I sometimes come and take the ferry at this time to remember my family after work.

FRANK. Oh, and where do you work?

GEORGE. I work... I work... Somewhere near Broadway.

FRANK. Ah Broadway, where dreams are born and adventures are held everywhere in time.

GEORGE. Exactly. That's how I fell in love with the city and my job. The desire to explore was always in my blood.

FRANK. Now who is relating to who?

(Frank and George both laugh.)

FRANK. Tell me something, George, are you in love with someone?

GEORGE. No, no, no. I am happily in love with the city right now, not ready for commitment yet.

FRANK. That is understandable. I wasn't either 'til I sat right there with Bianca.

GEORGE. She got you moving a lot, huh?

FRANK. She sure did. *(Pause.)* So, enough about me, tell me about your family.

GEORGE. Well, my mom died when I was young, and my father raised me all on his own. The best were the stories of her, especially this one about... My father said she had this beautiful smile, and contagious laugh, so he decided to take her to ...

(While George is speaking, his memory is playing out next to them, just like before.)

FRANK. I want to take you to see this comedian on 21st street and Broadway.

BIANCA. Oh, a show on Broadway! How wonderful! When, and what should I wear?

FRANK. How about tonight?

BIANCA. Does that mean we are taking our ferry into the city?

FRANK. Yes, Dear. And I read in the newspaper that they are lighting the torch tonight as well.

BIANCA. Oh, Franklin, I am so excited. We should get ready right away to catch the 7:30 boat.

FRANK. Hun, it's only 3:30 in the afternoon, I have other things in mind to do before we leave.

BIANCA. Oh? And what do you have in mind Franklin?

(Frank and Bianca laugh, and the laughter becomes distant as the focus shifts back to the present.)

GEORGE. He told me she had a beautiful time, and they fell even more in love when they saw the torch all bright at night.

FRANK. That sounds like a wonderful memory.

Gorge. That is why I decided to work on Broadway, to feel closer to her.

FRANK. I wish I was still able to see her and tell her how much I still love her and...

(Frank stops again, and Bianca comes walking over. This time, George can see her.)

BIANCA. There you are my darling boy.

FRANK. Oh, my love.

GEORGE. Oh, mom.

BIANCA. I think it's time to get off the boat, Franklin.

FRANK. Dear, I have been waiting all this time to hear you say those words.

BIANCA. Oh, Georgie, I think it's time for you to also get off the boat and live the life we set out for you.

GEORGE. Mom, I can't get off, I miss you so much. I don't know Frank. He's not Dad.

BIANCA. Oh, Georgie, you have been sitting in the same seat I did, speaking to the man who misses his son so much.

FRANK. Bianca, sweetheart, George is at home studying for his exams. He's not here.

BIANCA. Franklin, Dear, we need to go now. The boat is about to dock.

FRANK. I can't move, I'm stuck!

BIANCA. Grab my hand, Franklin.

GEORGE. Wait... Don't go. The boat isn't docking, Mom. Frank, don't leave me alone.

BIANCA. Goodbye, my sweet Georgie. Don't forget, we are always here for you.

(Just as the bells ring for docking, Bianca, the purse, and Frank disappear, and people start appearing.)

GEORGE. Wait! No! Mom! Dad... Dad!

(Lights fade out on George sitting in his seat with a blue briefcase at 8:00 p.m., just as the boat is docking.)

VOICE OVER THE LOUDSPEAKER. Thank you so much for riding the Staten Island Ferry. Watch your step in The Ferry Zone.

Stu's Brew

Misha Puello Brasil

Boris and Stu lived together in the same home for ten years, being each other's best companions. Boris had inherited the two-bedroom, single-story home, leaving him lonely and with no external motivation to establish himself as a respectable member of society. For ten years after his mother's death, circumstances hadn't changed for Boris. He was still collecting disability checks from a fall that broke his leg during his three-month-long job as a personal-care aide for the elderly. His leg had been in working condition for years now. He still had no warm-blooded friends.

Boris leaned into his antisocial tendencies, neglecting his daily showers and weekly hair wash, causing his dark blonde hair to look plainly brown, and yelling at any passing stranger who dared step on his dying, dried grass. Boris would have been left utterly alone if it weren't for Stu, the red-frilled lizard. His orange-brown body was three feet long, and he only weighed about a pound, but he was Boris' best friend. Boris only had two passions in life: Stu and beer brewing, beer that Boris would spend Stu's whole life trying to perfect.

The house changed. His mother's room had become Stu's room and now contained a 120-gallon tank surrounded with an array of green flora to make the room look overrun with trees so that Stu would feel at home and be able to explore. Sitting at a consistent 85°F, the room was filled with heat sources for Stu, areas to hide when feeling unsociable, and paths made from faux branches so Stu could easily travel from one high area of the room to another.

Boris' old room, directly across from Stu's new room, had become his brewing den. At the beginning of his brew-master journey, Boris would buy the ready-made containers of pale ale—his favorite—and only have a hand in the boiling and fermentation process, but over time, he became more involved. Boris' disability checks were split in half to cover the cost of Stu's happiness and Boris' home brewery. Boris' room, once filled with only a bed, dresser, and a fading-orange lampshade, was now overtaken by empty and filled glass bottles, cardboard boxes, labels for "Boris Ale," and an eight-foot fold-out table with his fermenter, wort chiller, and various tubes and thermometers for the actual brewing process.

As his passion grew, so did his efforts. Boris dedicated the entirety of his backyard to growing his hops so that he could control the process from start to finish. With a work ethic he had never felt before, Boris raised multiple twenty-foot trellises and planted his hop strains. His backyard smelled immaculate—a garden of beer.

As the Bineyard grew in size and Boris pimped out Stu's and the brew room, the rest of the house started to slowly be ignored.

The living room now served as Boris' room, containing everything he needed: a stained mustard couch to sleep on, a record player *only* for listening to The Beatles, a box TV to watch and fall asleep to, and a window to yell at teenage biker "gangs" out of. From the age of twenty-one, Bois, a beer enthusiast, collected all the cans of different beer brands he had tried and, without rinsing them, flattened the cans in his mother's driveway wielding a baseball bat, then mounted the accomplishments on his wall. The eight-by-ten wall had been covered in beer cans and wore labels of all colors of the rainbow, some still exuding that wet cardboard smell.

The dark, damp living room smelled of growing mold. The true source of the smell was debatable. The floors went without mopping, only receiving the occasional vacuum when substantial cracker crumbs hit the floor. The filth of the room was covered by soft orange lighting that allowed only the most dire stains to be visible. The kitchen went untouched except for storage or microwave usage.

Early in the morning, Boris sat on the floor of his beer den with his stubby legs stretched out before him. He was hugging his fermentation jar, which, in this position, was just as tall as him. This was the perfect brew; he just knew it.

Boris had had his best harvest of hops to date; he recalled the smooth drying process and the bittersweet, earthy aroma of the chartreuse pine cone shaped flower. He had sterilized every square inch of any surface or container his precious beer would touch. He researched the best pale ale malt for days, then spent the last of his savings ordering a fifty-pound bag. He had used water perfected in quality by the best reverse osmosis filter his now depleted money could buy. His countless experimentations had aided him in perfecting the conditions for the ideal wort: boil at 149°F, be generous with the hops within the first hour for bitterness, be unsparing with the hops added during the last hour to release the sweet, fruity aroma the hops held hostage.

Boris reminisced on the sugary, sweet, liquid wort that made his pale fingers sticky when he dipped them in and brought them to his crusted lips for a taste. It was the best wort he had ever produced. He had remembered to infuse the wort with oxygen while transferring it to cool and cooling it immediately—his best time yet, twenty minutes flat—and he remembered to triple-check his hydrometer for the density number. Boris had provided his latest beer batch with the best yeast for pale ale, US-05, and had immediately airlocked the jug.

Now, two weeks later, the beer was ready to be bottled. Boris was sure this would be the brew to change the trajectory of his life. With a perfected beer brewing recipe, Boris could finally be real competition for other breweries, get his brewer certificate and licenses to sell his beer and start his empire. All he needed to do now was bottle the beer at its peak and let it carbonate for another seven days.

Boris wanted to share this moment with nobody other than Stu, his best friend.

Boris gave his fermentation jar a sweet, light kiss, then slid the jar under the table and carefully backed away from the scene so as not to accidentally tip anything over. Once he had made it over the threshold out of his beer den, Boris ran with as much force as his swollen ankles and broken leg could muster and excitedly opened Stu's bedroom door to find him and have him join Boris in a celebratory taste. Boris scanned the room, short of breath, to find his beloved red-frilled lizard, but Stu was nowhere to be seen.

Boris carefully walked over the green moss-covered mats he had bought for Stu. He looked for him in all the usual places: under the lamp that heats to 90°F in his tank, under the huddle of dracaenas by the painted black window, and finally on the growing eucalyptus tree behind the door.

There lay Stu behind the door, his frills compacted to his neck. Startled by Boris' sudden and forceful entrance, Stu, in his old age, jumped towards another branch and missed, causing him to fall to the floor. Tired, Stu didn't hurry back up on his feet but instead enjoyed the texture of the thoughtfully bought moss mats. Boris concluded that he had slammed the door into Stu and caused his death.

Boris stood in place, stunned, and stared at his red-frilled lizard. His heart raced, and he became overwhelmingly sweaty. He didn't acknowledge the room's temperature; he believed he was about to have a heart attack at the age of forty-one.

Boris thought there would be no better place to die than next to his best friend. He clutched his large chest with his hairy, sweaty fingers and sat on the mossy floor. He lowered his head so that he and Stu could lie together and curled into the fetal position. He was ready. Stu did not like the invasion of personal space, so he propped himself up and waltzed through the path of decorative logs into his tank to make it just in time for the timed mist. It was hot in here.

Boris' eyes followed Stu the whole way, and upon seeing Stu enjoy his light shower, he immediately shot up from the ground.

§

Boris and Stu returned from the vet feeling heavy from the unfortunate news they had received. Stu had not sustained any damage from his startle or his fall, but the vet had found a tumor in Stu's liver. Stu was nearing the end of his lifespan, with only five more years to go, but complications had recently started to arise. Boris had noticed Stu's declining mood and appetite, but he figured Stu was being angsty.

Worst of all was the bill. The visit to the vet had left Boris with a balance of seventy dollars. The medication for Stu would cost over a hundred dollars, depending on how quickly he received his surgery. The surgery to remove the tumor that had caused so much inconvenience was estimated at only three hundred dollars. Still, travel to the nearest reptile surgeon would easily cost him more. Boris simply did not have the funds.

Of course, Boris blamed himself. He thought of all the times he brought Stu along to try his latest brewed beer and gave Stu a second sip even after Boris claimed one was his limit.

Boris walked over to Stu's room, let Stu out of his carrier, and closed the door. Boris sat on his mustard couch and started to cry. Where would he find the money? He had spent the last of his disability checks on the ingredients for his perfect brew. The rest of his money was tied up in either beer or Stu's room—all non-refundable. He was willing to give up his disability checks, but he couldn't get a job. That would take weeks, and Stu needed help now. He couldn't sell his beer yet, not legally at least. He could bar himself from getting a license before he even tried. He knew that if he had the opportunity, his latest brew would cover the cost of Stu's surgery and more. It comforted Boris that even if he couldn't help Stu in time, he would still have his dreams come true in a week.

He thought over how he used to make a quick buck when his mother was still alive and he had seen a gift he wanted to get her on the TV infomercials. Instantly, a great idea came to him. He would collect cans and plastic bottles. Having lived off his mother's life insurance and disability throughout his thirties, Boris had no real gauge of money.

Boris stood from his couch and shuffled over to the dark kitchen. The windows were covered with blinds and curtains, and Boris hadn't bothered to replace the light fixture's bulb when it went out weeks back. Next to his empty and unplugged fridge—Boris only ever ordered take-out—was a bag designated for beer cans. He quickly snatched up the bag, hoping to hear the clunk of empty aluminum cans, but the bag was empty. He had emptied the bag just yesterday and used his baseball bat to flatten them all in his driveway. He enjoyed smashing the lesser beer vessels in the name of his glass bottles.

Glass bottles will do, he thought, and he looked over at the other side of his refrigerator to find a tall paper bag completely overfilled with beer bottles. Usually, Boris would reuse these since he was the only person ever to drink his beers, or he would line them up around the living room's perimeter, though there was no longer any room. Boris grabbed a garbage bag under his unused yet stained sink and transferred all the empty bottles he could find into the garbage bag. He carefully carried the bag over his shoulder, yelled, "I'll be right back!" to Stu, and headed out the door to his Corolla.

Arriving at his local bottle deposit station, Boris placed his garbage bag of beer bottles on the floor, opened it up, and placed the bottles in the machine one at a time. The monster of a machine towered over Boris' five-foot-seven stature and had black lips that, when the light turned green, unveiled the esophagus full of teeth like thorns on a rose. The light would then turn red, and instead of the expected roars of the machine, he heard his deposited bottle clink at the bottom of the machine.

He would try the next one, then.

Ten bottles were deposited into the machine, and ten bottles were spat out. Boris had chosen the non-recyclable ones. He deemed "recyclable" labels unnecessary; anything could be recyclable. The words "recyclable" and "reusable" had the same meaning to Boris.

Boris looked over to his right. He had refused to look past the floor and the machine he was using on account of not wanting to talk to anybody. A lanky White woman was rummaging through the garbage of bottles and cans that could not be recycled, usually due to missing a cap or being misshapen. The woman snatched a water bottle from the trash, blew air into the open top to reform it, and then placed it into the large shopping bag she held in her other hand.

He would have to resort to the efforts of the homeless. Boris thought of the homeless population as nothing more than lazy junkies who didn't care to bathe or eat but instead only focused on their next fix. He hadn't seen the irony.

Boris dropped his garage bag of beer bottles at the feet of the lanky woman and quickly walked past her, darting back to his car. He drove around the corner to the main road of town. He was to slowly drive to each trash can and find enough plastic bottles to collect to save Stu. Even receiving various honks to speed up or being angrily passed by the car behind him, Boris drove slowly, scoping the sidewalk for his first trash can.

Finally, he came across one. Boris put on his emergency lights and hurried around the car and over to the large green garbage can to find his first hostage. He found two water bottles and three soda cans. Boris found a second trash can and a third not a block later. He collected ten water bottles, seven soda cans, nine beer cans, and two soda glass bottles. At this rate, he was sure to make enough within the week.

While rummaging through his fourth trash can, located right in front of the Blind Pig Pub, Boris was interrupted. He felt a kick to his shin.

"What the hell do you think you're doing?" someone said.

Boris turned around to see an old Black man staring at him. His lips were curled into each other, and his nose was scrunched tight. His most prominent feature was the few short white curls on his otherwise bald head. He clutched a bag of bottles and cans in his left hand.

Stunned, Boris didn't respond, so the man kicked him again.

"This is my territory." The man showed Boris his few remaining teeth.

Boris could think of nothing other than to mirror him, so Boris parted his lips and snarled.

This only angered the old man, whose grasp on his plastic bag became tighter. He lifted his right hand, ready to hit Boris.

Boris' eyes widened, and before he was even aware of it, he had dropped any cans he had found in this fourth garbage can and was back in his car.

"That's right, you bum! Find your own street." the old man yelled while picking up the cans Boris dropped during his escape. "Colonizing bum."

§

Boris arrived home feeling defeated. After trading in his bottles, he was only able to make two dollars and thirty-five cents. The payout of collecting bottles seemed much higher when the goal amount was much lower. He would have to resort to selling one of his few prized objects.

Anything related to beer was not for sale. He couldn't sell his couch; it was multifunctional and served as his bed. He didn't know what he would do without his TV to fall asleep to. It was settled then; he had to get rid of his record player. He would no longer be able to listen to The Beatles, but he would have to do without it and hope they played on the TV music channel.

Boris logged onto Craigslist using his phone and prepared to sell his records. He looked over similar items for sale and tried to determine his price when he got sidetracked. Remembering that Craigslist could help you find an odd job and hoping not to have to sell his record player, Boris searched for something that might suit his talents.

He started looking under the "Domestic Gigs" tab, hoping to find something that was not too strenuous. And he had experience being an aide to his mother, after all. He browsed through countless posts asking for cleaning services, tutors, pet sitters, or some midnight company. Boris was not willing to do any of this. His efforts seemed to be in vain until he refreshed the page and found a post from two minutes ago that caught his eye. Only a five-minute drive outside his town.

QUICK THOUSAND DOLLARS. PLAIN MAN WANTED TO PICK UP AND DELIVER PACKAGE.

Without a second thought, Boris selected the post and hit reply, saying he was both plain and interested. The person replied immediately with the name of a diner Boris had never heard of. Leaving his house for the third time—the most he usually traveled outside his property line was once a week—Boris started his Corolla and headed off to Big Buck Diner.

Boris followed instructions to meet in the woods behind Big Buck Diner and parked in the space closest to the entrance to the trees. From what he saw of the parking lot, it was empty except for a couple of cars parked in the employee parking spaces. Then he took twenty "big boy" steps into the woods—as directed—and sat on the quite large, cut-down stump between two particularly thick trees.

Boris fiddled with his fingers as he studied the lime-green leaves. He listened to the birds chirp as he waited for the package. He thought about buying a gun and learning to shoot.

The sound of someone clearing their voice caused Boris to turn quickly and fall from the stump, causing a *thump* to be heard.

"Oh shit, man! Let me help you up, my fault." The teenage boy hurried to Boris and helped him back onto the stump. The boy looked at Boris expectantly, but Boris just started back.

The boy couldn't be any older than sixteen. Baby fat still clung to his cheeks and neck. The eyebrow piercing he was sporting tried to age him, but his eyes had a certain sparkle that only somebody who didn't pay taxes had. *This is why,* Boris thought, *politicians seem so trusting.* The boy was definitely high. He reeked of marijuana.

"Well, are you gonna let me sit, man?" The teenage boy motioned with both his hands for Boris to scooch over. The boy held out his hand, but the bright, neon-green zip-up sweater swallowed his whole hand in the process. "Oh, my bad, man. I wore this for camouflage and shit, you know?"

Boris simply nodded. He was not a big fan of speaking, especially to teenagers, but he would stick this out for Stu and that large sum of money.

"Are you mute or something, man?" the boy asked and continued without waiting for Boris' answer, "Man, that's rough. My cousin was like selective mute n' shit. He said it was 'cause of trauma and shit but I think he's just a pussy. Damn, you got trauma, man?"

"Do you always say man when you speak?" Boris replied. You couldn't distinguish his speech from a grunt.

"Huh? Speak up, man."

"Don't call me man!" Boris barked.

"No problem, man—I mean, dude. Dude." The teenage boy nodded to almost no end, and his brunette bangs started to fall into his green eyes. Boris couldn't help but roll his eyes. This teenager was one of those emos he'd heard so much about. Best to make this quick and stay far away.

"Don't call me dude, either. Where's the package?"

The teenage boy smiled mischievously. "I'm the package." Boris turned his head and scrunched his nose. "Here's the thing, Boss," the boy started, and Boris' ears perked up at that. Maybe this emo wasn't so bad. At least he knew how to show respect.

"I can do Boss," he muttered.

The teenager smiled again; he seemed to be getting excited. "No problem, Boss Man."

"I said don't call me man." The teenager shot his hands up in defense. "Just explain," Boris said.

"Alright, Boss, so here's the deal. My girlfriend's parents are like... Stick up their ass strict. Super Religious," he elongated the U in super. "They won't let me see her 'cause of some stupid rumor at school. I don't even think it's true but that doesn't matter because they grounded her and now I can't see her."

"So, Boss, I want you to drive me to her house and distract her parents long enough that I can get in."

Boris could not care less about the problems of a teenager in love, but he needed money and fast. "Okay, what's the address?"

Boris and the teenage boy packed into Boris' Corolla. Making their way out of the diner parking lot and into the road, the boy began to speak.

"Should we have a code word, Boss?"

"Sure," Boris grunted.

"How about Victor?"

Boris blinked in response, his face keeping his emotionless stare.

"Cause that's my name, so like, I'll know you're warning me."

Boris couldn't help but roll his eyes. He watched as supermarkets and laundromats turned into large estates with multi-story homes for one family. Boris' Corolla became one of a kind. After about a forty-minute drive, they arrived at their destination. Boris' part of the plan was simple. All he had to do was keep the parents occupied for a couple of minutes until the teenager could sneak in the back.

Boris exited the car and shut the door, walking to the house.

As Boris knocked on the door, he saw Victor place the envelope in the car seat and send a thumbs up. Boris just had to give Victor enough time to sneak in successfully, and then Boris could start to make his way out. Promptly, a middle-aged Hispanic woman answered the door. Her husband was sitting in the chair just a few feet behind her.

"Hi," Boris started. "Do you have a minute to talk about the true God?" He handed over the flyer Victor had provided, which had just the word "Harold" written on it and an address.

The woman's face morphed into a new one full of youth and joy. She looked about ten years younger now.

"Harold!" the woman yelled, peering over her shoulder to look at her husband. She violently waved her hand, motioning for him to hurry over. She said something in a language Boris couldn't understand, and the woman's husband looked just as excited. "Finally! We were wondering when someone would answer our flyers."

Boris stood at the threshold, confused. Victor had told Boris to ask about God, but he never mentioned why. Before Boris could gauge the situation, he was being pulled by the wrist to follow the woman outside.

The couple walked Boris to their shed, which, instead of behind the house, was several feet directly to the right. It seemed newly built; and the paint on the outside did not have a single blemish. Once inside, Boris regretted his decision.

The shed was converted into some sort of worship bunker. Bright white lights caused Boris to start sweating, and he followed the line of purple pillows lining the walls. He could feel sweat beginning to form around his forehead and neck. A built-in shelf on each wall held candles, and what looked like an altar loomed at the room's rear. In it were pictures of the woman's husband, Harold. It sent shivers down his spine. Boris had seen enough.

Slowly backing up with a giant smile, Boris thought Victor must have had enough time by now and started running away as quickly as his legs would allow. Harold and his wife screamed after him, but he couldn't understand through the haste. He arrived at his car out of breath and in sheer panic, but as he changed gears into drive, he saw the yellow envelope in the passenger seat. Boris was smiling as he sped away.

§

Boris arrived home, reveling in his victory. He had made an amazing amount of cash; his lifelong dream would come true in just a week when his beer was done carbonating and he had the money to save Stu. He made a beeline towards Stu's room and shared the good news.

His long day of hard work deserved to be rewarded with a rest on the couch and the company of the beer channel on TV. Boris lay back on his mustard couch, then turned on his TV which was always set to the news or the beer channel. He let himself relax as he watched advertisements for the different yeast brands and learned of the newest fermenting devices.

Boris' eyelids started to become heavy. The wear of his long day and his hours in front of the television strained his eyes. As Boris rapidly blinked, trying to remove the sting from his eyes, his attention turned to the current advertisement for beer-making classes and certificate bundle, license earned separately, "On sale now! Half price at one thousand, two hundred dollars." Boris' eyes began to water. This had to be a sign.

Boris punched in the numbers that appeared on the screen onto his phone. This was the opportunity of a lifetime. Certificate classes could range from 2,000 to 5,000, and Boris felt he would never be able to save that much. Now that the classes were on sale, he had the chance to afford the classes. The only problem would be that he would need to use the money he had earned for Stu. And where would he get the last two hundred dollars? Craigslist might be a good source for another odd job.

Boris' head fell into his hands, and his fingers massaged his temples. It was an impossible task to choose between his best friend and his life-long dream. Stu had been his best companion for ten years to date. His mother wanted Boris to learn to care for others, but Boris was sure his mother would want him to succeed professionally as well. His leg bounced as he weighed all his options and the possible outcomes.

Stu only had about five more years to go, less if any other complications arose. Stu's veterinary bills would perpetually drain Boris' bank account for the next few years. He couldn't wait another five years to be a brewmaster. He would be almost fifty.

Boris solemnly walked to Stu's room and slowly opened the door, searching for the red-frilled lizard. Stu lay under his heat lamp as the timed mist started to appear. Boris searched Stu's face for an answer, pleading with his eyes for a result. "Tell me what to do Stu. Give me a sign," Boris said.

Stu lifted his head to look at Boris, and Boris could've sworn Stu winked at him.

Of course his best friend would want him to succeed. Stu wouldn't dream of holding Boris back. Stu knew how much this meant to Boris. With Stu's supposed approval, Boris made his decision. He scooped up Stu, placed him into his traveling case, and headed out the door.

Boris drove thirty minutes north, taking the I-75 to get to Alachua, Florida. He remembered hearing stories of the overrun population of iguanas and thought Stu would enjoy living out his last days with his cousins. He could make friends, join a gang, or find a lover.

Boris pulled over to a clearing and placed the carrier on the ground under a bush along with a baggie of Stu's favorite food: cockroaches. It took a couple of moments for Stu to waltz out, but when he did, he stared up directly at Boris.

"I'll miss you, Stu. Thank you for doing this."

Stu lifted the flaps of his neck and flared his frills at Boris before scurrying off into the distance. On the entire drive home, Boris cried. When sleep came, he dreamed of cracking open his newest batch of beer and sharing it with Stu.

§

A week after the tenth anniversary of his mother's death and a week after Boris and Stu had parted ways, Boris was ready to re-enter his beer den and taste his newest batch of beer. The idea of not sharing this moment with Stu pained Boris, but he knew it would all be worth it once he tried sipping his beer.

Boris could feel nothing but anticipation until a photograph on the news caught his attention. The news anchor spoke as pictures of a teenager and videos of the outside of a home were shown.

"Police are on the lookout for the suspect who goes by the name of Victor. He is presumed to be armed and dangerous, and traveling with pregnant sixteen-year-old Alexandra after shooting her parents, leaving them in critical condition. If you have any news, call the number below, and stay tuned for more information."

Boris' hands quickly found the TV remote and turned off the screen. That was none of his business. He had beer to taste.

Boris lifted himself from his mustard-stained couch and strolled to his beer den. Before entering his den, he stopped by Stu's room. Just as Boris opened the door, the timed mist began, and Boris started to weep. He missed his best friend.

He had decided this week to honor Stu and name the perfected brew after him—Stu's Brew. Boris knew that Stu would have approved. He made his way to the Beer Den, slowly turning the handle and letting the smell of his delicious beer fill his senses, but it smelled slightly of burnt sulfur.

Boris' eyes widened as he realized the source of the smell. His precious jug of beer sat under the fold-out table, mocking Boris. He had forgotten to bottle the beer. It had fermented in the tank for too long. This was the work of autolysis—the yeast had started to break down.

Boris opened the valve and tried some of his beloved beer, desperate for a hint of quality. It tasted of burnt rubber and smelled of eggs left out to boil. He would have to start all over again at square one.

Warning

Kayleigh Woltal

I feel I should warn you, my friend. What you are doing is treacherous.

If you date a writer, she will confuse you. She will spend her money on books she'll never read, a typewriter she'll never use, and notebooks she'll tear apart.

Your room will be consumed by black and white and filled with stories she will hold closer to her heart than you.

You must get used to the fact that she will always be cheating on you with the characters in her stories. She will fall in love with them as she sleeps with you at night.

Sometimes she will break, and she will not want your help. She will push you away and find comfort in the personalities of fiction.

She will never be the girl you first met because that was the broken girl from the poem hanging in your living room, while today she is the fierce narrator in the incomplete manuscript laying on your desk.

If you date a writer, she will use you. She will make a metaphor out of every part of your body.

But I swear, they will be the most beautiful words you will ever know.

An Act of Translation is Always an Act of Betrayal

Oriana Galvis Marín

To translate,
is to share the secrets of your past,
las historias preservadas por tus ancestros,
and the traditions that were protected
from foreign visitors.

A second chance for languages,
that had an expiry date
to re-emerge, to re-surface, *de re-vivir,*
de volver a endulzar oídos ajenos,
and enchant new minds with the words of a region.

To translate,
is also to demolish the restrictions of *el idioma.*
The barrier that protects *las heridas del pasado*
and that prevents them from reopening,
from *repetirse.*

To let *las lenguas nativas y adoptivas* collide.
Let the past, present, and future
be represented on the same page,
be written using the same ink
and read by the same voice.

An act of translation is an act of betrayal,
of letting parts of *historia*, *cultura*, and *humanidad*
get erased, disappearing from the page.

But also an act of connection.
Opening an old book to new readers.
Intrusos in a new world.

Es un acto de compartir los encantos
y los misterios que unen a la humanidad.

Excerpt from *PERENELLE*: A Novel

Shea Dunlop

Chapter One: The Summons

The news of the queen's death nearly cost Perenelle a finger.

Feet pounded the boardwalk overhead, a young messenger's shrill cries breaking her concentration on a calculated slice. Her familiar paring knife slipped under a barnacle with unintended force, grazing the pad of her right thumb. No curses escaped her lips, only a slow stream of air as she squeezed her eyes shut for a moment. She used the sting of pain to sharpen her wits, to solve the problem.

She had been here before and made this same error the first week of university. Her professor had poured spirit from a flask on his handkerchief and wrapped it tightly around the wound. It stung, but not as badly as the shame of incompetence.

"I only made that mistake once," he'd chuckled, twirling the wide iron ring on his right thumb. "Flips up into a sort of guard, see? Had it custom-made." His tone had dropped to something confidential, like he had all the world's secrets to share with her. "Barnacles have never been worth a blood sacrifice."

Perenelle's precious few coins had never been worth a custom ring. So she harvested carefully in the calm of the evening's low tide, usually uninterrupted by heralds of chaos.

With precise movements, she repeated the professor's actions, disinfecting the wound with the medicinal flask of alcohol at her hip. Already she was mapping out the shortest route home to avoid the unrest surely sweeping through the streets of the new land. Loyalists would be preparing to sail to the mainland to meddle in the royal appointments, while revolutionaries would be climbing on soapboxes to reiterate their cases for freedom.

Perenelle didn't much care who collected the taxes so long as no one stopped her from brewing. The alchemical arts took discipline, patience, and ingenuity. She found these traits lacking in most royal and political figures and, therefore, lost interest rather quickly.

Above the pier and through the alleyways, elbows and baskets jostled her from all sides, people calling to one another and bustling to and fro. Perenelle kept her own basket tucked close, the barnacles inside rattling as she sought the path of least resistance toward her parents' garden apartment.

In all the commotion, she nearly missed the ruby-red banners and rich mahogany of the Delancey's coach parked at the end of the street, impressive white stallions snickering. One of their henchmen—someone fairly green, by the skittish air about him—stood at attention, blocking her front door. Another watched her from the back of the coach, beady eyes tracking her every move.

Perenelle stopped before the first grunt, setting her feet in a mirror of his stance.

"What's this, then?"

"Miss... Verne?" The burly man squinted at her, then back at the parchment in his hands.

"Obviously. May I help you?"

"Perenelle, is that you?" her mother's voice leapt through the entryway, their front door ajar.

Pedestrians scurried by in the narrow lane, forcing Perenelle to move closer than comfort to Delancey's man.

She swept around him without missing a step, as if she'd meant to invade his space. "Coming, Mum!"

"Miss—" The henchman caught her elbow as she passed. Perenelle glared at his touch and he managed to look apologetic, releasing his grip. "Mind you, don't take long. Lord Delancey is expecting you at half-past."

Keeping her expression blank, Perenelle dipped her chin in acknowledgment and slipped inside.

Ducking through the low arched frame, she pulled the door shut behind her with a soft click. Dried herbs and woodsmoke tickled her nose, electric lamps flickering in their brackets along the hall. Her father cleared his throat as he shifted pots and pans about in the kitchen.

Experiencing a disjointed sense of calm, Perenelle recognized this moment; it was the one before everything was about to change.

Materializing from the master bedroom to her right, her mother gripped Perenelle's shoulders in her weathered hands. Anyone else might not have noticed anything amiss, but Perenelle knew her mother never let the wispy flyaways of her graying hair fall from her bun. The summons to the Delancey's was rattling her.

Perenelle swallowed, nerves finally materializing.

"What is it?" she asked, trusting her mother not to mince words.

"Lord Delancey is moving his household to court. We're to accompany them."

"To the mainland?" Perenelle felt her chest constrict. "Now?"

"Don't waste your breath on questions you know the answer to," her mother chided, squeezing her shoulders once, then her upper arms. "Hop to it. Only pack your rucksack, they won't take kindly to unnecessary luggage on the ship." Mrs. Verne turned Perenelle toward the second bedroom, giving her a gentle push inside before bustling down the hall toward the kitchen.

Perenelle's heart thudded dully in her ears. She'd logically known this summons was a possibility, but for the past hour, she had managed to keep the implications of it pushed to the outskirts of her mind.

Now, her feet were glued to the woven rug she'd played on as a child, entertaining herself as her parents brewed. Her gaze was drawn to the dog-eared stack of journals on her nightstand overflowing with notes from each year of school, the upholstered desk chair she'd salvaged from the street and repaired on her own, and the shelves of glass bottles all meticulously labeled with ingredients she'd gathered and prepared herself. The high strip of window was cracked open, ushering in the scent of the fresh lavender she'd planted in the small side yard leading to the garden. Under the window hung her rucksack on a hook, empty and limp.

Perenelle's jaw clenched. Her life couldn't just be packed away into something so small. She'd worked far too hard to build it for herself.

"No," she said, mostly to herself, to test it out. She set down the basket of barnacles on her work station.

"No," she repeated, louder, throwing her voice over her shoulder. "I'm not going."

Perenelle paused, not really expecting a response, but listening anyway. None came. Striding down the hall, she clattered through the curtain of seashells marking the entrance to the kitchen.

Mr. Verne moved about in his usual breezy yet efficient manner, wrapping his specialized brewing equipment in kitchen towels and nestling them in the crate at his feet. Knowing the vanity of the elite, Perenelle wouldn't be surprised if the Delanceys demanded face paints and tonics of youth even on the arduous two-month seafaring journey to the mainland.

Perenelle's mother worked by his side, packing her jars and sachets of prepared ingredients into a padded crate of her own. Between Mrs. Verne's encyclopedic knowledge of natural resources and her husband's talents in the kitchen, the pair rarely failed to produce a cure to any ailment. However, the Delanceys primarily kept them on staff for their particular gift with cosmetics. An absolute waste of talent, in Perenelle's opinion.

"Did you hear me?" Perenelle tried again, doing her best to keep any petulance out of her tone. "I said I'm not going."

"Don't be silly, Perenelle." Mrs. Verne smiled, jars clinking softly in her hands. They were shaking slightly, and her smile didn't reach her eyes. "It will be a delightful adventure." She hefted her crate onto her hip and shuffled past Perenelle toward the front door. "The mainland! We haven't been since before you were born."

"Exactly," Perenelle dug in, turning to her father. "I was born here. I'm not leaving at the whim of some Lord. I'm *so* close to graduating, and I need—"

"Don't be disrespectful," her father cut her off. "You wouldn't have gotten so far in that education without Lord Delancey's generosity."

"But it's all paid off now, right? I could stay this last month, just to—"

"I can't let you do that, Perenelle," Mr. Verne pinned her with a look, staring her down over the spectacles perched on the edge of his nose.

She held her tongue.

"Lord Delancey expects his assets to travel with his household to the mainland. Having invested in your education, you are one such asset, poised to join us on his staff. And as your father, he expects me to ensure you are on his ship by dawn, as the tide goes out."

Perenelle knit her brows, mentally reviewing his words. She didn't find anything new.

"I know, Father. But wouldn't I be a more valuable asset if I could finish my education and complete an apprenticeship?"

Mr. Verne gave her a soft smile. "Yes, I believe you would. But Lord Delancey made his orders clear; I am to put my entire family in that coach with only the necessary supplies. Those guards will hardly let you stay behind."

The apothecary set one last bundle in the crate with an air of finality that didn't quite match his words. He shifted the box to the side with a gentle nudge of his knee and took a step closer to her.

"Perenelle. Do you hear me? I cannot just let you stay here, they will simply muscle you away."

Perenelle met his gaze, beginning to understand. "So then, I'll... Go."

"To your room, I'm sure. To pack." Her father raised an eyebrow. "And do make sure your window is closed tight before we leave."

"Right," Perenelle muttered, slowly backing away. "Will do."

She turned to leave, but rotated around again to offer a grateful nod to the man who'd raised her.

"Good luck, Father. With... Packing."

He may not have played with her much, not the way other fathers might toss a ball with their child or dig in the sand, but his steady hand over hers as she stirred a boiling cauldron or balanced delicate scales was worth more to her in the end.

Swallowing back her distracting emotion, Perenelle passed Mrs. Verne on her way back to her room. She opened her mouth to say something, though she wasn't sure what. Mr. Verne called his wife back to the kitchen before she could get a word in. Perenelle shook her head and forged on, trusting her father to explain.

She spread her possessions out on her quilt, eyeing her rucksack to judge what might fit. An extra skirt, blouse, and underthings. One knit sweater. A few pencils. And only this year's journal—she would just have to trust she had her prior school years' memorized by now. Her money pouch, now nearly full with the emergency savings from under her mattress. A handful of barnacles. And a small pot of muddled hobblebush berries from her desk for a group project due the day after next.

One by one, they disappeared into the worn leather rucksack until Perenelle found she was out of space. And out of time.

She turned to find her mother framed in the doorway. The forager surveyed the room, pulling out her hairpin and twisting her frizzing curls back into a tight bun. Her fingers weren't shaking anymore.

"Perenelle." Mrs. Verne said her name like it was a complete thought.

Perenelle drew herself up to her full height. "Mum."

Eye to eye with her mother, she was again struck by the permanence of her decision. There was no telling when, or if, Delancey would move his household back to the new land. The rising monarch and the politics of court may keep him occupied overseas indefinitely.

Her mother took a deep breath, looking her up and down. "You're as ready as you'll ever be, I suppose."

Untying the loop of keys at her hip, Mrs. Verne removed a simple iron key unlike any of its fellows. It was about the length of her thumb, slightly blackened with age and grime. She folded the key into Perenelle's palm, cupping her closed fist with both hands.

"We know you don't approve of our employment in cosmetics. We've always known you'd be chasing a higher purpose than fanning the vanity of 'some lords.'"

Perenelle huffed a laugh, her earlier words turned back on her.

"It was my hope that we'd be able to find you a way out of the Delanceys' household after you were educated, somewhere you could pursue your own ideas and projects. I thought you'd have more choice, perhaps if you married well…"

"Married into a family like the Delanceys? Who would no doubt expect me to fulfill the very same role you do?"

"In any case," Mrs. Verne brushed past Perenelle's indignation, "we started saving a dowry for you with the Office of Officiants when you were very young. It's separate from our other accounts. Lord Delancey doesn't know about it and won't find it when he sends for our funds from the bank."

Perenelle laughed hopelessly. "Mum, this is very kind, but—"

"You don't believe in the institution of marriage and plan to die a spinster, I know." She patted Perenelle's hand and released her. "Just keep the key. The money's not going anywhere, and it may be a bargaining chip you need someday."

"I can't just withdraw the funds?"

"What did I say about questions you know the answer to?"

Perenelle sighed. She'd need wedding papers and a husband to access that money. Relenting, she pressed her fist to her heart.

"Thank you, Mum."

Her mother smiled. It reached her eyes this time.

Breaking the sanctity of the moment with a dip of her chin, Perenelle turned to her desk. Digging around in the top drawer, she located a spool of leather cord. Propping her foot up on the chair, she drew her paring knife from its sheath in her boot and sliced a length away. Threading it through the key's bow, it quickly became a necklace she could tuck away for safekeeping.

As Perenelle worked, Mrs. Verne rifled through her daughter's closet. "It's a bit late in the season for this one—you'll be warm—but you'll want the cover." She held out Perenelle's darkest cloak. "You'll go straight to The Gruit, I presume?"

Perenelle nodded, slipping her arms into the cloak sleeves. "Mary and Rose will put me up for a bit, I'm sure. I can pitch in behind the bar most nights."

"And then you'll be joining the Flamel household for your apprenticeship?"

"Mum, he hasn't taken an apprentice in all ten years that he's taught at the university." She drew the desk chair up under her window, grabbing her rucksack as she went.

"Well, you'll be the first, then."

Despite herself, Perenelle blushed. "We'll see about that." Laughing, she bounced on the balls of her feet, nerves crawling under her skin at the leap she was about to take. "I might have to blackmail him for it!"

"You'll do what you have to." Her mother nodded as if this was a done deal before dropping her tone. "I can only give you a few moments of a head start before I raise the alarm."

"Make it believable, Mum," Perenelle half-joked, half-pleaded, growing serious. "I don't want them to blame you. Or hurt you."

"They wouldn't dare." Her mother winked, making a shooing motion. "Off you pop."

Perenelle stepped up onto the chair, once again filing away the emotions stirring in her chest. She cranked her window open as far as it would go, feeding her rucksack though and pushing it to the side to make room for herself. Taking one last look around her room, she forced herself to meet her mother's gaze.

"Be careful, Perenelle," her mother whispered, a rare mist clouding her eyes.

Perenelle swallowed. "I will, Mum. You too."

Without hesitating another moment, she hoisted herself up and through the window, leveraging against the brick wall outside to shimmy out into the garden on her stomach like a snake. She brushed herself off as she stood, scooping up her pack and looping both arms through the straps. Hoisting up her skirts to leap over the low garden wall, she took off running toward the main avenue with its teeming crowd of travelers dressed just like her.

Perenelle grinned into the night, her mother's dramatic screams echoing to the beat of her pounding footsteps.

List of Contributors

Elizabeth (Liz) Abrams graduated with a Bachelor of Arts in Creative Writing and French Language & Culture from SUNY Purchase in 2021. She is an avid reader and writer of fantasy and fiction. In her spare time, she can be found pursuing fiber arts.

Brandie Black (writing as S.B. Black) is a Houston, Texas native. Her interest in writing fantasy began in 2002 when her father saw her work on a school creative piece and gave rare praise for it. Since then, she has given it her all to complete works. She earned her bachelor's in English: Creative Writing from the University of Houston in 2018. What she tends to focus on in her fantasy pieces are the autistic woman's experience, being plus-sized, and Ancient Egypt, with a smattering of social hope. This is her first credit. Her superhero fiction blog can be found at https://siwyenbast.wordpress.com.

Shea Dunlop is two-thirds of the way through the MS in Publishing program, taking classes part-time while working full-time at ABRAMS on the Special Sales team. She currently lives in South Slope, Brooklyn with her sister and her cat, but she's originally from Vermont and won't let anyone forget about her bachelor's degree in ski resorts. In her free time, she tends to oscillate between overbooking her social calendar and spending too much time in the gym or out on a run. You might also catch her playing D&D, line dancing, or reading and writing romance, fantasy, and fanfiction.

Oriana Galvis Marín is an MS in Publishing student at Pace University. Her dreams and passion for books made her move from Medellin, Colombia, to the United States to finish her undergraduate degree in English at The College of Wooster and pursue publishing. She attended the NYU Summer Publishing Institute in 2023. Her main interests range from writing, diversity in literature, books in translation, literary fiction, accessibility, highlighting underrepresented voices, and the Latin American publishing industry.

Amber Grell currently works in the Art Rights department of Penguin Random House Audio. Originally from Wyoming, Minnesota, she earned a bachelor's degree in both English (Creative Writing) and Communications (Journalism) from Adelphi University, graduating *magna cum laude* with honors. She is a proud member of the New York Public Library and the New York Book Forum, considers herself a YA junkie, and aims to read 120 books annually. Amber finds happiness at home with her cat, Riley Matthews Grell, surrounded by dessert and new books.

Jillian Hinz holds a bachelor's degree in Writing and Rhetoric from Pace University and is currently pursuing a master's degree in Publishing. Born and raised in Brooklyn, Jillian draws inspiration from the pulse of the city to craft thriller narratives through her novels and award-winning plays.

Hailey Hovey began the Pace MS in Publishing program in Spring 2024 after half a gap year from school, when she graduated from the University of Southern California in May 2023. Currently, she works as a Communications Specialist for human resources at USC and lives just outside of Los Angeles. She is a life-long lover of all things books, and it is her dream to publish her own young adult novel someday.

Mia Ilie has recently received her bachelor's degree in Writing and Rhetoric at Pace University at the Pleasantville campus and is now pursuing her Master of Science in Publishing on the New York City campus. She writes whenever inspiration strikes, and most of her works consist of fiction in horror, queer short stories, and fantasy. Mia's main goal is to write and publish LGBTQ+ stories she always wished to have when she grew up.

Emily Jones, though often lost in her own head, managed to graduate *magna cum laude* with a Bachelor of Arts from Drew University. Her *Cinematic Women as Warriors Against Capitalism* was submitted into Drew University Library and Archives to earn her specialization in English Literature. She manages full time at Barnes & Noble but truly enjoys ranting about classic literature and film to anyone who will listen.

James La Barbera is an avid reader of young adult and queer literature. He is a first-year student in the MS Publishing program at Pace University and is currently studying Children's Marketing and Publishing. His love for reading comes from his struggle as a child to read well or at all. He strives to see more queer representation in books across all categories. When he isn't studying, he is reading, listening to live music, walking around his neighborhood on Staten Island, and exploring new bookstores in the city.

Jana Lewis lives and works just outside of Cincinnati, Ohio. With over fifteen years experience in educational publishing as a production editor, she decided to add new skills and potentially branch into other areas of publishing through the Master of Science in Publishing degree from Pace. Her passions include reading, writing, and studying history. She also enjoys traveling with family and boating at Lake Cumberland.

Kate Nahvi is a second-year graduate student in Pace University's Master of Science in Publishing program. She studied film as an undergraduate student at the University of Michigan, earning a Bachelor of Arts in Screen Arts and Cultures in 2014. After a career in the film industry, specializing in the Camera Department, Kate began her publishing MS to pursue a new direction of storytelling. She loves reading fantasy, science fiction, and nonfiction exploring mythology and gender politics. She also loves live music and exploring New York City with friends.

Jack Niemczyk is a writer and comedian living in the East Village of New York. He refers to himself as a champagne socialite and often uses his experiences in the city's nightlife scene in his writing. As a proud homosexual, Jack embraces the intersectionality and queerness of life and love in a city as eccentric as New York. He is in his final year as a student at Pace University, finishing his Master of Science in Publishing.

Madhuri Pawar is a graduate student pursuing an MS in Publishing at Pace University, blending her love for storytelling with a focus on editorial and marketing. Outside of academics, she has dabbled in event management and taught English. When she's not editing or brainstorming novel ideas, you'll find her indulged in her favorite hobbies: dancing, exploring new restaurants, reading new books, experimenting with creative writing, and organizing events that bring people together. She is passionate about crafting stories both on and off the page!

Misha Puello Brasil is a current Marymount Manhattan College senior majoring in English, Creative Writing, and Psychology and a first year in Pace University's MS in Publishing program. She has previously been published in *The Carson Review* and is the 2024 winner of the Joesph P. Clancey Award in Poetry. A first-generation Brazilian-Dominican-Peruvian, Misha PB is a lover, a dreamer, and an aspiring writer looking to work in the publishing industry. She spends her free time reading, writing, and taking photographs, hoping to one day become an old and seasoned traveling professor.

Chardonnae Simpson is a passionate writer from The Bronx pursuing her MS in Publishing at Pace University where she also serves as a Graduate Assistant in the program. She also earned an English degree with a concentration in Creative Writing from SUNY New Paltz. With a deep love for storytelling and the power of words, she is dedicated to shaping the future of publishing by fostering creativity, heartfelt connections, and inclusivity. Outside of academics, Chardonnae enjoys writing, exploring new food and adventures from her growing bucket list, shopping, cooking, baking, and music. She takes pride in achieving her goals and continuously seeks growth and meaningful experiences.

Kianna Swingle is a first-year graduate student at Pace. She graduated from Hawaii Pacific University where she won a writing contest with "Detangling."

Brittney Terrian is an educator who works with high school students to achieve academic excellence. In her own time, she focuses on immersing herself in the publishing world by attending and volunteering at book fairs throughout the city and attending poetry slams. She has a love for short story memoirs. Her goal is to become an editor in the industry and help other writers find their unique voice.

Alena Williams is a writer and media enthusiast pursuing her Master of Science in Publishing. With a passion for storytelling and the arts, her work explores themes of creativity, connection, and community. She currently works in higher education, blending her love of literature with her role as an associate editor of a magazine that celebrates diverse voices in academia. Alena is inspired by literature's ability to bring people together and enjoys contributing to projects that amplify underrepresented narratives. When not immersed in books or making music, she enjoys exploring creative outlets and spending time with her Havapoo puppy.

Zetta Whiting is a first-year MS in Publishing student from Las Vegas who currently works as a graduate assistant for Pace University Press. She earned her BA in English with an emphasis in journalism from Chapman University and minored in dance. Several of her news stories have been published in the *Voice of OC*, a local newspaper in Orange, California. She has also written over sixty articles for *Her Campus* magazine, covering topics that ranged from election season updates to makeup trends. Upon graduating, Zetta is determined to work in children's book publishing and possibly write her own young adult novel one day.

Kayleigh Woltal is a second-year MS in Publishing student pursuing a career in design. She hopes to work on middle grade and young adult book covers some day. She is especially passionate about books with disability and mental health representation, and she hopes to be on a team that brings stories like those to life for other readers. In her free time, Kayleigh is usually scouring the city for the best mocha latte, reading a romance novel, or working on a new crochet project. She is honored to be The Publishing Lab Volume 2's Editor-in-Chief.

The Publishing Lab Team

Liz Abrams..Editorial

Alicia Benett..Editorial

Shea Dunlop .... Managing Editorial

Oriana Galvis Marín..Editorial

Rachel Geller .... Marketing and Social Media

Sydney Heidenberg... Managing Editorial

Hailey Hovey ....Editorial

Heaven Jenkins .... Marketing and Social Media

Brittany Kitchen .... Marketing and Social Media

Professor Eileen Kreit .... Faculty Advisor

James La Barbera ....Editorial

Jana Lewis..Editorial

Valentina López-Pérez..Editorial

William McKeever..Editorial

Abby Mutton..Editorial

Misha Puello Brasil ....Editorial

Isha Repal ....Editorial

Chardonnae Simpson ....Editorial

Professor Manuela Soares... Faculty Advisor

Alena Williams .... Marketing, Social Media, and Design

Kayleigh Woltal .... Editor-in-Chief and Design

PACE
UNIVERSITY

MS IN PUBLISHING PROGRAM

Get Ahead in Publishing

We prepare tomorrow's publishing leaders with internships, scholarships, and mentoring.

Cutting-Edge

Current industry trends move at a fast clip. Our forward-thinking graduate degree allows students to learn hands-on and explore topics such as:

- Acquisition and sub-rights
- Content creation and editing
- Marketing and publicity
- Sales and distribution
- Finance and legal
- Production and design
- E-books and digital media
- Comics and graphic novels
- Artficial Intelligence
- Social Media

Comprehensive

From manuscript to finished product, in both print and digital media, you'll be equipped with in-depth knowledge needed to build a successful career.

- Pace offers scholarship opportunities to finance your education
- We offer in-person and online classes that set students on track to graduate in two years
- We send two students to the London Book Fair, Bologna Book Fair, and/or the Frankfurt Book Fair each year

Connected

Our top-notch faculty are industry professionals who bring their expertise to the classroom.

- Students cultivate professional connections with industry leaders through one-to-one mentorships, internships, guest lectures, and industry-sponsored events
- Our alumni have gone on to work at literary agencies, digital media, advertising companies, and publishing houses large and small

Creating Community

We offer unique opportunities for students to come together and collaborate, including:

- *The Publishing Lab*, an annual student-run anthology of student creative work
- Dedicated publishing student space with a computer lab and lounge area
- In-person and online student events
- Our one-to-one mentorship program pairs student-protégés with industry professionals for one semester
- Build your network of publishing professionals

Contact the Office of Graduate Admissions:
graduateadmissions@pace.edu or call (212) 346-1531

Apply today or attend an information session:
www.pace.edu/grad

WORDS WE USE

A Glossary and Reference Guide for Publishing and Media

This glossary of publishing terms is for anyone who is interested in a career in publishing and digital media or those already working in the field. The words used in publishing and media are a distinct and essential part of our ability to communicate with each other. Language is not static and the language in publishing has grown, changed, and continues to evolve in our digital world. Compiled by industry experts, this book provides a wide-ranging and inclusive compilation of terms that will assist anyone interested in learning more about publishing and media.

For more information or to order *Words We Use* and other titles published by Pace University Press, please visit www.press.pace.edu.

Pace University Press
41 Park Row
New York, New York 10038
212 346 1405

The second volume of *The Publishing Lab*
was published in Spring 2025 by Pace University Press

Cover and interior layout by Kayleigh Woltal
The anthology was typeset in PT Serif, Century Gothic, and
Garamond Premier Pro and printed by Lightning Source

Pace University Press

Director: Manuela Soares
Faculty Advisor: Eileen Kreit
Design Consultant: Joseph Caserto

Graduate Assistants: Zetta Whiting and Vidhi Sampat
Graduate Student Aide: Kianna Swingle

www.ingramcontent.com/pod-product-compliance
Lightning Source LLC
Chambersburg PA
CBHW070504030726
47503CB00004B/1160